C0-DKP-002

"Why are you being so stubborn?"

"Why are you being so stubborn? If you want to research Scotland, you could do that in another highland village, or lowland for that matter."

"Let's just say that someone has told me this village needs me."

He grunted. "Needs you I would say like a hole in the head."

"How very civilized of you," she muttered. Shivering again, she reached inside of her purse for her digital camera. Positioning it correctly, she was about to snap a picture of the man in front of her when he disappeared.

"Shit!" She muttered, tossing her camera back into her purse. She'd had him just where she wanted him, and he'd played the part of mouse to her cat. "I know you're still here," she called out, hoping to bring him back into the open. Moving forward, she nearly slid in the sticky mud that was on the ground. Two sets of footprints were on the wood floor. One set was hers, and the other was his.

A cool breeze buffeted past her, causing her to shiver. "I know you are here. Stop hiding from me!" She thumped her foot against the floor, and then was rewarded when he emerged from the shadows.

Twilight's Kiss

by

Marly Mathews

This is a work of fiction. Names, characters, places, and incidents are either the product of the author's imagination or are used fictitiously, and any resemblance to actual persons living or dead, business establishments, events, or locales, is entirely coincidental.

Twilight's Kiss

COPYRIGHT © 2006 by Marly Mathews

All rights reserved. No part of this book may be used or reproduced in any manner whatsoever without written permission of the author or The Wild Rose Press except in the case of brief quotations embodied in critical articles or reviews.
Contact Information: info@thewildrosepress.com

Cover Art by *R.J.Morris*

The Wild Rose Press
PO Box 706
Adams Basin, NY 14410-0706
Visit us at www.thewildrosepress.com

Publishing History
First Faery Rose Edition, January 2007
Print ISBN 1-60154-007-8

Published in the United States of America

Dedication

To my mother, for always believing in me and supporting me, and introducing me to the world of magic.

To my editor, Amy Herald, for her passion for my writing.

Chapter One

Sean Sutherland pulled his hood up to cover his head. Slouching his shoulders, he stepped out of the shop into the pelting rain. Twilight crept across the rugged landscape. The village was restless tonight. Tomorrow they would be graced with the company of a minor celebrity. He sighed. His heart was far too heavy. Nothing could save him. He would be doomed for all of eternity. Halting in mid-stride, he turned to stare at the Village Church. Gravestones loomed before him. He pushed the latched gate open and stepped onto the damp ground.

He headed for one gravestone sectioned off from the rest. Reaching inside of his cloak, he pulled out the bouquet of flowers that he had brought for his mother. He heaved out a heavy and sad sigh. Bending down, he caressed his bare hand across the rough surface.

"How are you tonight, my son?" He nearly jumped at the sound of the priest's voice. Whirling about, he plunged his hands inside of his cloak and grimaced.

"I feel lost." It was not an unusual feeling for him. The restless sensations he experienced would only intensify over the next few days.

"Ah, that is unfortunate." The priest's friendly blue eyes glittered at him. "It is too damp out here for my old bones. Why do you not come inside with me? Perhaps, I could ease your worries."

"Thank you, Father." Glancing up at the grey stormy clouds that enveloped the landscape he was reminded of the many wild storms that he had weathered. He mustered a slight smile for Father Clancy and followed

1

him into the church. Candles were lit up at the altar, and he moved to the front of the church.

"I was just preparing my sermon for the service on Sunday. But now that you have come, I shall finish in the morning."

"I wouldn't want to keep you from your duties," he said, starting to stand up.

"Sit! You are a member of my flock. I cannot run the risk of having you go astray, now can I?"

Sean grunted. Indeed, that would be a sin. He looked up at the Madonna and child, and felt his heart sink. His mother had been very religious. If she had not fallen so in love with his father, he felt sure that she would have become a Bride of Christ.

"Are you nervous because we are expecting an outsider?"

At Father Clancy's softly spoken question, his thoughts were wrenched back to the present.

"I don't know. I think that I will stay indoors as much as possible." Sean had an aversion to strangers and it was one that the townsfolk completely understood.

"I have read a few of her books. She's quite talented."

Had Sean been drinking something, he would've choked. "Father, you can't be serious!"

"I'm a priest, Sean. Not a saint." Father Clancy smirked, and then as quickly as it had appeared his grin faded, only to be replaced by his serious visage.

"Tell me what weighs on your mind, Sean."

"I feel the stirring again."

"Ah. That is troublesome." Father Clancy's eyes flickered with worry, and then grew pensive.

"I shouldn't have told you." He rushed out, feeling the need to flee the church.

"Have my forebears not always assisted you and your family?"

"Aye," Sean mumbled.

"Then I shall carry the burning torch, and do so with great relish. It was an honor to be selected for this parish. Why, the parochial house alone was a great incentive." He chuckled and then sobered once more. "Now then, what shall we do? In all of my years here, I don't think you've ever been this concerned about a stirring."

"That's because it's never been this intense. I can feel myself being sucked into that dark hole...it's like a deep vacuum. I need you and the others to keep me in the light, but if they can't..." He cleared his throat and leveled his gaze at Father Clancy. "On second thought, instead of helping me weather the storm, perhaps someone should lock me in a secured room."

"I think that might be a wee bit drastic don't you? Tell me, who do you think would do that? The people of the village adore you."

"There is always the council."

"We only call upon the council when all hope is lost. I still have faith, don't you?"

"My faith is the only thing that has carried me through these desperate years."

"From what I've heard your mother would have been proud of you."

Sean nearly choked up at the mention of his mother. "She was a wonderful woman," he said gruffly. They rarely spoke of his mother, as Father Clancy realized it was a sensitive subject for Sean. But right now, as the stirring crept toward him, he needed to be reminded of his mother. She had been an angel. She had to have been from the Fey or Elvin born. He had to remember the light she'd brought to every life she touched.

"Aye, I imagine she was. If only I had known her." Father Clancy smiled, and then rubbed his hands together briskly. "We could go down to the pub. Perhaps the merriment there would take your mind off of the stirring."

"I'm afraid, Father."

"Afraid of what? You are in God's house. There is nothing for you to fear." Father Clancy touched his hand briefly, before Sean could draw it away.

"Ah, but you're mistaken, Father. There is something for me to fear." He clenched his eyes shut, feeling the anxiety rolling like an untamed animal in his gut.

"And what would that be, my son?" Father Clancy asked, furrowing his snow-white brow.

"I fear myself!" He confessed in a hoarse voice. He dropped his head into his hands. "I can't go on like this forever. I will break! I know I will. And if I do...I couldn't

3

bear the consequences. I just want to be whole again, Father."

"Sean, you will survive this. It will pass, and then you'll be back to your old self. I fear you tend to sell yourself short, lad. You come from a line of strong and noble warriors. Face the stirring like any other battle...one to be faced and conquered."

"I haven't been back to my old self in years. I don't even know who I am sometimes."

"You are Sean Sutherland. You are a good, kind and just man. Never forget that!"

"I won't, Father." He believed in Father Clancy. Fortunately, there were plenty of people to remind him of his past and his present, if ever he became uncertain.

"Now, then. Are you certain there is nothing more I can do for you?"

"I must struggle through this on my own. If you will not agree to lock me away, then I'll have to keep control of myself. I will fight the raging beast within. I have to. There is no other way, unless..." He gritted his teeth together.

"Don't even think those wicked thoughts, Sean. No one in this village would survive your loss. Remember, you're not a monster."

He locked gazes with Father Clancy. For being such a relatively new priest to the parish, Father Clancy had settled in remarkably well, despite the extraordinary situations that surrounded his new placement.

"How can you be certain of that?" His voice was desperate and in a weak moment, he reached out to circle his fingers around Father Clancy's wrist. He knew that his grip was strong and tight, but Father Clancy didn't seem concerned in the slightest.

"I know because I believe in you. I have spent many nights praying for you. God is good. He will listen, and he will help you. You must believe that."

Sean coughed. "You sound just like my mother."

"From your lips to God's ears." Father Clancy smiled.

"I pray to God several times daily, but I don't know if I am worthy of his Grace."

"You are his son. You are worthy. Every good man and woman is worthy of God's love and protection."

4

"Then I pray that he will protect me from myself."

"He will endow you with the greatest strength known to human kind. Do not fret, my son. You have persevered through much worse, of this I am certain."

Sean wanted to listen to Father Clancy. Everything he said was spot on. Through the years, Sean had been forced to call upon strength that he'd never thought was there. Somehow, he had endured. And he would fight the stirring. He had no other choice. For if he gave in, he would revile himself, his life would be worthless. Based upon what it was worth right now, that was saying something.

"When she comes, I will watch her closely, you may rest easy."

He smiled up at Father Clancy.

"Thank you Father. I don't want her near me, if she seems different. I can't risk her discovering who I am...what I am."

"I understand. Now, the hour grows late, and the pub is calling my name." Father Clancy chuckled. "I could do with a pint of Stout." He winked at him, and stood up.

But Sean still clutched his wrist.

"If I ever lose my way, I mean really lose my way, you must promise me something."

"Son, I will not hear it. I can't do what you are going to ask me to do."

"You said that you would help me no matter what, and you said that you had taken up the torch of your forebears. If you agree to this promise, then you'll be doing what the rest of them have always agreed upon. I must have your word."

"Aye," Father Clancy said, sighing heavily. "But they never had to fulfill that promise did they?"

"I have always maintained my composure in the past."

"Then why would you lose it now?"

"You don't understand. I am losing my grips on my sanity. The stirring pulses inside of me, like a beating drum. I can't stop it. It is always there. There is only one thing that could decrease its intensity." He looked at him pointedly until recognition dawned in Father Clancy's eyes.

"So the only thing that shall appease it is the real thing." Father Clancy groaned. "Oh, my son, now I do sympathize."

"I won't give in to it, Father. I would rather die first. That's why you must promise me."

"I know what you want me to do. We shall not speak of it further. If it comes to that desperate hour, than I will do what you've asked. But I will pray for you, after I fulfill the promise."

"Thank you, Father." He said, releasing his hold on Father Clancy's wrist. "Unfortunately, I think that all of the prayers in the world can't save me."

"The power of prayer is great. We still haven't grasped its full power."

"I know." His eyes were hooded, and he hoped that Father Clancy could not see what was shining inside of them.

"My father always told me that a good stiff drink and the company of good friends could ease all of a man's worries. Why don't we go and have that drink I proposed earlier?"

Biting his lip thoughtfully, Sean nodded his head. "It might take my mind off of other matters." He stood up, and stretched.

Father Clancy walked to the Church door, and patiently waited for Sean. Sean went up to the altar dropped down to one knee and bowed his head. "Give me strength to endure," he murmured. He hoped that his fervent plea would not go unanswered. Touching his fingers to his lips, he then crossed himself. Closing his eyes, he envisioned his mother and family in his mind's eye. He would survive. For them, he would walk through the fires of Hell, and if he wasn't careful, it might just come down to that.

It didn't take them long to walk to the pub. Every time he was in the village, he was reminded of his childhood. His father had spent a great deal of time down here, tending to his people's concerns.

Sutherland Castle was situated just outside of the village. Sean had been born to a title, wealth and privilege but his parents had instilled certain values in him that many of his contemporaries lacked.

Father Clancy opened the door to the pub, and Sean smiled as its bell jingled. Wincing against the loud thumping noise of several books closing at once, he pursed his lips into a thin line.

"Your Lordship!" Several voices rang out in an excited chorus.

"Mary and I were just talking about you," Rupert MacKay murmured, rubbing his hands on his apron, as he rushed toward them. Sean smiled at the pub owner. It had been in the MacKay family since it had been built. "The usual, sir?" Rupert asked, leading them over to Sean's favorite seat.

"Aye," Sean muttered, stealing a glance at the closed book that sat on the next table.

"And what shall I pour for you, Father?" Rupert asked, turning his attention to the parish priest.

"A frothing pint of Stout." Father Clancy followed Sean's gaze. "Ah, I see that everyone is brushing up on the works of..."

"Don't say it," Sean growled. He reached for the book, and stared at the wild passionate scene on the cover. Actually, to his surprise, the cliffs on the front of it bore a striking resemblance to the cliffs in the area. Someone had definitely taken great lengths to portray highland life accurately.

"Honestly, Sean. She'll be here come the morning." Father Clancy's voice actually sounded impatient.

"Aye, well, no one invited her."

"It's a free country, lad," Father Clancy pointed out, while Rupert hurried away to fetch their drinks.

"Be that as it may, I hope she decides to go to another blasted village!" He slammed his fist down on the table, as his reign on his control slipped.

Father Clancy jumped and clutched his hand over his heart. "In the future, would you mind warning me when you're about to take a fit? My heart can't take many sudden surprises." Father Clancy eyed him warily. "She is just coming here to visit."

"To poke around you mean."

"I don't think that she'll be poking her nose into private matters. She may be a rather passionate young woman, but I don't think you'll have to worry about her

7

nosing into your private affairs."

Sean looked across the table at the Dublin born man. "Father, you do not know my history. There have been people..." He cleared his throat. "Women like her have come before. They have caught my scent and they don't want to let go, until I am forced to do something that greatly distresses me."

"Don't worry. Everyone knows that you're a confirmed bachelor," Mary MacKay said, sitting their drinks down in front of them. She sat down on the bench beside him, and sighed. Shivering, she scooted toward him.

"Don't look for me to keep you warm," he warned.

She smiled at him, and laughed. "I'd be more apt to get warm from rubbing a bloody rock up against myself. I just wanted to sit near you that's all."

He shifted uncomfortably. Mary had once had eyes for him. But that was before she had married and settled down with Rupert.

He yearned for a mate. Someone that could take away part of the burden that rested on his shoulders. He was sick and tired of his cold bed. Desire began to build inside of him, at the thoughts of taking a mate. Rubbing his body up against the lush, full curves of his mate would at least sate some of the hunger that continually battled for domination. He swallowed thickly, and quickly took a drink of his whisky. But still, there it was clenching and unclenching in his gut. He grasped his glass so tightly, that Mary stared at him in concern.

"Would you like something to eat? I could whip you up a nice rare steak," she offered.

He nodded his head. Perhaps that would do something to ease his growing agitation.

"Brilliant. I'll be right back." With that, she was off to the kitchen. The village people helped him to the best of their abilities, but sometimes he had to help himself.

"Sean, you must cease your brooding. It does not become you."

"What would you have me do, Father?"

"I would have you try to find the good in the situation that we will find ourselves in tomorrow. This woman that you seem to dread meeting, could in fact turn out to be absolutely lovely."

"Aye, she could at that," he grudgingly admitted. Tipping his glass up, he emptied it of its last precious drop.

"Here you are, then," Mary murmured, sashaying her hips as she lowered the plate in front of him.

"Gracious, Mary, did you even put that on the grill?" Sean could hear Father Clancy, though he really wished that he didn't have an audience. He wanted to shove the steak into his mouth as quickly as possible, and then lick every last drop of juice off of his plate.

"Aye," Mary said hotly.

Sean shakily began to civilly cut his meat. He placed the first oversized bite into his mouth and sighed. Yes, this had been what he had craved. Or at least the next best thing.

"See, Father, Sean appreciates my cooking skills." Mary planted her hands on her hips, and eyed their priest.

"Aye, I can see that, lass."

Sean grimaced. His cheeks bulged with the red meat. He knew that he looked like a gluttonous pig, but he was so desperate that he didn't even care. He picked up the saltshaker and covered the meat in it. For appearances sake, he began to eat his baked potato. Before he knew it, he had finished the mouthwatering steak.

He fought the strong temptation to lick the juices off of the plate. Grimacing, he was about to give into the sinful thought, when someone barged into the pub.

"Come quick." Ridley Montgomery's eyes filled with relief when he spotted Sean. "Your Lordship, you must come. It's one of them. I've assembled the crew into action, but we might still need you."

Anger boiled through Sean.

How dare they come into his territory? He wiped his mouth and hands with his napkin, and stood up.

"Where is he?" He demanded.

"She's on the outskirts of the village. We were caught by surprise. She nearly got to Donald before I could repulse her."

"Fine. Bring me my necessary supplies."

Horrified gasps had by now ricocheted through the

pub.

"Will you be able to handle her on your own, Sean?" Mary asked, pulling at his sleeve.

"I think we're evenly matched don't you, Mary?"

Her green eyes widened dolefully. "Aye. But nevertheless you must be cautious. You don't think the way that she does."

"That may be so. But I know how they think, and I don't do what they do. This shifts the balance of power."

"But I still worry about you."

"Mary, why?" His eyes softened.

"If the village lost you, we would be lost ourselves."

Sean smiled. "What am I, Mary?"

"You are the best and bravest man I've ever known."

Rupert grunted his agreement. "My Mary's right. You take care."

"Bolt this door behind me. Ridley, spread the word throughout the village. Make sure that everyone knows not to invite any strange women into their homes, until I've given the all clear."

"Right away." Ridley saluted him, threw a bag of supplies at him, and bolted toward the door.

Sean hadn't really wanted to spend his night hunting. But if that was what he had to do to make sure that his villagers could rest easy, then he was more than up to the task. He slung the knapsack over his shoulder, and stepped out of the pub. He waited while Mary shut it securely, and bolted it. Then, with a smile twitching at the corners of his mouth, he went to hunt the bitch that was in their midst. Before the night was through, he would have looked pure evil right in the eye, and escaped unscathed.

"God give me strength," he muttered, as he trudged out into the wildly windswept night.

Chapter Two

Bridget Sinclair dragged her carry on piece of luggage behind her, as she traipsed through the muddy wet ground. Her wet straggly blond hair kept falling into her eyes. She was tired, hungry, and miserable. The night she'd just been through had been absolute hell. At the last minute, she had decided to take an earlier flight into Heathrow Airport. Then, she had taken a connecting flight into Wick Airport. It was the first and last time that she would take a commercial flight. They definitely weren't the fun that her friend Nora said they were. Now all she wanted to do was plunge into a soft bed, and pull the covers up over her head. But first, she would have a nice long steamy shower. Shivering, she pulled her raincoat closer around her body. Her teeth chattered. The weather had taken a wild turn. She had never experienced such raw power. Mother Earth was certainly showing off. Grimacing, she jumped when a shadow brushed past the corner of her eye. Squinting, she tried to make out the dark form.

"Who goes there?" She called out.

But her voice was lost on the howling wind. She didn't know where she was. The cab driver had dropped her off and told her that he wouldn't go any further. When she had inquired about his hesitation, he'd refused to answer her questions. So, not wanting a problem on her hands, she'd paid him. Then, with a skittish look in his eye, the man had driven off. All that she had was her small carry on, because the airport had mistakenly misplaced her luggage.

Damn, commercial flights!

"Well, Bridget, that's what you get for traveling to a place that's out in Hell's half acre," she mumbled to herself.

Water dribbled into her eyes momentarily blinding

11

her. A loud howling noise ripped out across the landscape, making the hairs on the back of her neck stand on end. Breathing deeply, she continued to make her way toward what she supposed would be the local village. She glanced up at the stars and gasped. They seemed so close to her, almost as if she could snatch one out of the sky.

An owl hooted from somewhere in the trees, momentarily startling her out of her reverie. She hit a rut in the wet ground, and tripped. She fell against something solid, and her heart raced.

"Who's there?" Suddenly, the force she'd fallen against moved. As hard as she tried, her keen hearing could not pick up anything, save for what she believed had been a sigh. But then, the wind sighed all of the time, so she couldn't be sure. Groaning, she slapped her hand against her forehead, and pushed her wet hair out of her eyes for what seemed to be the umpteenth time. She was nearing what seemed to be a signpost. The moonlight grew scarce, as it had fallen behind a canopy of clouds. And for some reason, she was sick of being in the dark. She was a city girl. She'd never imagined that the Scottish highlands could be so pitch black. In fact, she knew that it shouldn't be pitch black. Something was amiss. It was still a fairly early hour, especially considering the fact that it was a Friday night. So why in God's good name, were all of the lights in the village out?

The question puzzled and unnerved her. Her eyes lit up, when she remembered something that she'd shoved into the bottom of her large leather purse. She opened the zipper, and began rummaging inside. Finally, her hands slid over the smooth surface of her miniature flashlight. Hooting triumphantly, she enclosed her fingers around it, lifted it out of her purse, and flipped the switch. She sighed. At long last, she could see. *Stupid girl, you should have thought of that sooner.*

She directed the beam of light toward the village, and began walking toward it. By the time she reached the inner sanctum of the village, she'd be right at her wits end. The jet lag was catching up to her, and if she didn't get to the little B&B soon, she'd collapse from sheer exhaustion. Yawning widely, she turned at the sound of another loud sigh.

"Now that was not the wind," she said to herself, instinctively quickening her pace. She didn't think that there was anything to get alarmed at. But in her weakened state, she had to be cautious. The night had been very hard on her. She'd run into a roadblock that she certainly hadn't been expecting. She turned onto what seemed to be the village's main road. "Praise the lord," she murmured.

Her eyes caught one lone light, flickering behind a half closed drape. She read the sign and found out that it was the village pub. Smiling, she walked toward it. She didn't know where her B&B was, but she felt fairly confident that the people inside of the pub would be able to give her directions.

She knocked on the door, and turned her flashlight toward the window. Unless she was losing it, she could've sworn she heard a half muffled scream. Fearing that someone was being hurt, she knocked again and then tried the doorknob.

"Let me in!" She shouted. But again, the loud wind cut off the sound of her voice. "Damn!" She was sincerely worried about the woman inside. But she sensed no imminent danger. If she'd not been so tired, she would've done something that certainly would've raised a few eyebrows. Instead, she banged her fist against the door again, and listened for any other sound of distress. Either way, she had to find help, for the woman and for herself.

Standing up to her full height, she reached for the handle to her carry on. Then, with it rolling behind her over the old cobblestones, she headed for the building adjoined to the pub. Again, she knocked. Again, she received no answer. She did the same thing with four more shops, and what seemed to be three houses. No answer, at either one.

"This is bloody ridiculous!" She muttered, wrinkling her brow. She'd heard that Scottish hospitality was unparalleled, but this, this was disgusting! Unless, the village had suddenly experienced a mass exodus, she was being shunned, for some reason.

Then, as if being guided by an invisible hand, she craned her neck to the side, and saw the small stalwart church off in the distance.

Marly Mathews

"Thank you!" she whispered, rolling her eyes to the heavens.

Ask and you shall receive.

Smiling, she headed toward the church with a new skip in her step. At least the church could not turn her away. The gate was open, so she stepped through it with no problems. The church was old. She figured that it was probably around during the crusades, but then she could be wrong. Something caught her attention out of the corner of her eye, and she jumped when she discovered that it was a large headstone.

Leaning down, she stared at the wet and almost wilted bunch of Lily of the Valley. Gradually, her eyes were drawn to the epitaph.

It read *Beloved mother and wife. Lady of our hearts. Lady Janet Sutherland. Born, 1620, Died, 1714.*

Smiling, she brushed her hand over the gravestone. Obviously, she had been well loved, for someone still bothered to put flowers on her grave. She pulled herself away from it, and made a mental note to ask the villagers about the famous noblewoman. Turning, she rested her eyes on the church door.

The door to the church opened with little difficulty. As it swung open, the wind rippled through and blew out some of the lit candles. Shrugging her shoulders, she stood her carry on up beside the door, and then carefully shut the door.

"Hello?" She called out. She looked at the religious icons and decided fairly quickly that she stood inside of a Catholic Church. Warmth permeated the atmosphere, and she instantly felt at ease. She walked up to the altar, genuflected and then lit a candle. She stared up at the heavens and began praying. Now more than ever, she needed a sign.

Her gold Celtic jeweled cross felt heavy around her neck. Sighing, she enclosed her hand around it. She didn't suppose that her cell phone would be able to get a signal. Besides, fat lot of good it would do her, as it was probably almost out of power.

She was just about to call out again, when she heard a loud bang. Whirling around, her eyes rested on a cloaked figure standing in front of the door. Tightening her hand on her cross, she leveled her gaze.

"Who are you?" It could be the priest, so she had to be careful of what kind of a reaction she gave off.

"You are a stranger to this village."

It was a statement not a question, and quite frankly it irked the crap out of her. Narrowing her eyes, she stepped forward, and raised her eyebrow when he stepped back and hit the door.

"I am expected here." She kept her voice steady. She had to show the man that she would not be easily intimidated.

"Are you now?" The voice said snidely.

She'd liked the sound of the man's voice before, but now it was cold and empty.

"You still have not answered my question. Who are you?"

"I am a man of many names and talents." This time his husky voice held a hint of arrogance that she found unbecoming.

"Really?" she scoffed, folding her arms across her chest. "Why don't you start by giving me one of your names? Or should I just call you what's his name? Or better yet..." He cut her off before she could zing him with her jibe.

"Clever. I had not expected you to be intelligent. I had thought that you would be a brainless twit. The others I've met that were like you had sandpaper for brains." A taunting edge trickled into his voice.

"You have me at a disadvantage, sir. If you know who I am, then you should introduce yourself to me, and do so quickly." She slanted her mouth into a small smile.

"I don't want you to know who I am. You're better off being in the dark."

"And what if I already know who you are?" This time her question startled him, and he bounded toward her. She stepped back. He was larger than she had anticipated. She swallowed thickly. He was reaching out for her, when the door opened again. He stopped short, and stared back. Yet oddly enough there was no one there. She smiled.

"Damn blasted sea wind."

"Yes, blast the wind," she remarked, shaking her fist

15

high up in the air. It was then, that she saw him catch sight of her large cross.

"That's a beautiful piece of jewelry," he mumbled.

"Would you like to touch it?"

He jumped back. "No, I think not!" She followed his gaze, as he briefly glanced at the crucifix above the altar. "What do you intend to use that torch for?"

"Torch? I...ah. My flashlight, that's right. I forgot that some things were different over here."

"Where are you from?" Obviously, he hadn't picked up any of her books.

"Well, to be honest, that's a hard question to answer. I was born in the States, and raised in Canada. So, I'm a citizen of both countries. My parents used to move around a lot."

"Ah," he whispered.

She raised her hand to her wet hair. For the life of her, she couldn't understand why he seemed so fascinated with it. She watched as he licked his lips.

"Your hair is like spun gold."

"Thank you...I think," she muttered self-consciously. Then, she made sure that there was still a wide distance between them.

"You'd be well served if you left this village immediately."

"I'm not going anywhere, please and thank you!" As if to accentuate her meaning, she plunked her butt down into one of the wooden pews, and reached for a bible. "You can't tell me to leave without getting to know me first!"

"This is my village. I make a point of finding out who the strangers are that shall soon be in my midst. You, girl, came early."

"Is that a sin?"

"By the looks of you, you wouldn't know what a sin was," he snorted.

"What do you mean by that?"

"Nothing." His eyes glittered.

She leaned forward. In the dim light, she couldn't tell if his eyes were grey, green, blue, or brown. But whatever they were, they were dark in shade and nature. Tumultuous, didn't even begin to express the look he had in his eyes.

"My first experience with this village has told me that the people here are hostile anyway. You may rest easy in knowing that I won't enjoy my stay here, but stay I will. You can't say anything to change my decision."

"Why are you being so stubborn? If you want to research Scotland, you could do that in another highland village, or lowland for that matter."

"Let's just say that someone has told me this village needs me."

He grunted. "Needs you I would say like a hole in the head."

"How very civilized of you," she muttered. Shivering again, she reached inside of her purse for her digital camera. Positioning it correctly, she was about to snap a picture of the man in front of her when he disappeared.

"Shit!" She muttered, tossing her camera back into her purse. She'd had him just where she wanted him, and he'd played the part of mouse to her cat. "I know you're still here," she called out, hoping to bring him back into the open. Moving forward, she nearly slid in the sticky mud that was on the ground. Two sets of footprints were on the wood floor. One set was hers, and the other was his.

A cool breeze buffeted past her, causing her to shiver. "I know you are here. Stop hiding from me!" She thumped her foot against the floor, and then was rewarded when he emerged from the shadows.

"Why do you persist in torturing me?" His voice held a dangerous edge.

She shivered. "I've done nothing," She murmured innocently, moving toward him. She could see a muscle twitching in his cleanly shaven cheek.

"You did everything when you came to this village. Must I ask you again to leave?"

"I've told you already that I won't leave." Her voice held conviction, and she tilted her head as he let out a hollow sigh. "Even though almost every door in the village has turned me away, I will not be turned off. I flew across the Atlantic for this, and a pleading, sniveling man like you, isn't going to stop me."

"What did you say?" He raged. He jumped over the short distance to her, and grabbed her by the shoulders.

17

Marly Mathews

His eyes filled with a reckless abandon. His hood fell back, and she saw for the first time that he was young. Startled, her head whipped back.

"Let me go." She stared bravely at him, waiting for something that even she couldn't explain. His grip softened, as something changed within him. It was almost as if another force had entered his body for a few seconds.

"Get out," he growled.

"Get out, yourself," she retorted hotly. "In case you haven't noticed this is a church. You don't own it." He took his hands off of her, and wiped them on his cloak. "Since you seem to know so much, why did a woman scream when I knocked on the pub door?"

"She did what?" His voice was hoarse, and his breath was shallow. He clenched his hands tightly at his sides.

"She screamed. Howled like a banshee, actually."

She was unprepared for his stoic visage to break into a smile. Smiling, he was actually handsome, but when he looked the other way, he almost seemed gruesome and threatening.

"That's Mary for you," he murmured. "What do you expect? It's nearly midnight, or the witching hour, as it's thought of around here. The people here are quite a superstitious lot."

"To the point of being loony," she muttered, dropping her eyes to the floor. "So since you've already had your hands on me, are you going to tell me who you are?"

He stiffened. "The thought of having my hands all over you is not repulsive. But until then, you will not learn of my name. Not from me anyway." He lifted his hands off of her shoulders, and dropped them to his side. It was then that she saw something slung across his shoulder. It was a backpack.

"What do you have that for?" Her question caught him off guard. He perused her intently, and then shrugged.

"None of your damn business." He strode away from her toward the door.

"You are the most impossible man I've ever met."

"And you are the most idiotic woman I've ever met." With that, he left the church, and closed the door quietly behind him.

In hindsight, she might have handled their social exchange a bit differently. She yawned loudly. Sinking down into the nearest pew, she stretched out, and closed her eyes. In a few minutes, she would get up and try to find her B&B. But right now, she needed to rest her eyes. She'd just rest them for five minutes and then she would be up and about. She closed her hand around her cross, and sighed, as exhaustion crept over her body, winning the battle she'd been fighting. As she slipped into dreamland, she heard his voice calling her name, and she wrinkled her brow. Now, he would get an earful. She'd let him have it, and then he would see that he just couldn't order her around. Smiling, she walked toward the voice. She'd get him someday, and when that day came, he certainly wouldn't be laughing.

Chapter Three

Sean knocked on the door. He saw the drapes twitch, and then the door opened.

"Thank the lord!" Mary cried, moving forward, she was about to throw her arms around him, when he moved out of her reach. "Ah, sorry," she mumbled, redness blooming across her cheeks.

"She was here, Sean," Father Clancy said, moving forward. "I expect you found her and vanquished her in the village square?"

"No," Sean muttered, tossing his bag of hunting supplies aside, he sat down in the nearest chair. Raking his hands through his black hair, he groaned.

"So, where did you kill her, then?" Rupert asked, eagerness in his voice.

"I found her, but I didn't kill her."

Everyone gasped and raised their eyebrows.

"Saints preserve us. You didn't set her free did you, my son?"

"No."

"Well, what happened to her, then?" Mary asked.

"When I found her, there wasn't anything left but a pile of ashes."

"Impossible!" They all breathed in unison.

"Did she just combust on her own?" Ridley asked.

"I think not. When have they ever done that?" Sean asked, cringing.

"Well, stranger things have happened. Perhaps the hand of God struck her down," Ridley suggested. He grunted when Rupert nudged him in the ribs.

Sean closed his eyes.

"Here, Sean, drink this. You definitely look like you need it...why you've lost all of your color," Mary murmured, pressing a glass of brandy into his hands.

"Well, then. She must have left the village, and met

her doom out in the open. Maybe she fell on a jagged twig and then went poof!" Father Clancy suggested.

Sean sighed. "That's just it. I don't think she even came into the village, or else I would have intercepted her. When I found her ashes, they were cool to the touch."

"Ah, a mystery," Father Clancy surmised. "I'm always up for a challenge."

"Wait a minute, Sean. If that wasn't you know who at our door, then who was the woman that was here?" Mary turned to stare at him.

He swallowed his brandy, and grimaced. He could do with something else, but he'd have to wait until he had some privacy.

"I was getting to that." He stared into his brandy.

"Well?" Father Clancy asked, sitting down in front of him.

"The woman at the door was that blasted romance writer."

Shocked gasps rang throughout the pub.

"Oh, goodness me," Mary muttered, sinking into a chair, and dropping her head morosely into her hands. "We turned her away because we thought she was..."

"A vampire," Sean finished. He placed his glass on the table and smiled. Actually, now that he thought about it, it was quite funny. But something still gnawed at him. Over the next few days, he had to find out who had killed the female vampire.

"Where is she now? Do you know, Sean?" Father Clancy asked.

"Aye," he murmured.

"Sean, you are becoming quite annoying with your short answers."

"I agree with Father Clancy, this isn't like you. You are normally much more talkative," Mary mused.

"Tonight just isn't my night. And I didn't want her here."

"Is she safe?" Father Clancy asked, anxiously.

"Of course. She's safe as houses."

"Where is she, my son?"

"In the church," he mumbled, sipping at his brandy again.

He winced as everyone stampeded toward the door.

Groaning, he rested his hands on the table, and let it support his weight as he stood up. Now he had to go and make sure that she didn't receive that warm of a welcome. Rolling his eyes, he glanced up at the clock. It was nearing one o'clock. His boots clanged against the floor as he walked through the open pub door. All of this fuss and bother over one woman. Why it was too much!

He tramped into the church and stopped at the strange scene in front of him. Mary turned back to him with her finger over her lips. He recognized her sign of caution, and deliberately coughed. He was met with a bunch of shushes.

"She looks like an angel," Father Clancy murmured in awe.

Sean shoved his way past a few of the villagers, and stared down at the woman's sleeping form. She was sprawled out in the pew, with her hand up to lie across her one cheek. Her golden hair streamed out around her, creating quite the sight. A lump lodged in his throat. He didn't dispute that she created a beautiful sight.

"Why is everyone gawking at her? Just wake her up, and tell her to shove off," Sean muttered, moving toward her.

"Don't you dare!" Father Clancy snapped out. "You will frighten the lass half to death. Look at those dark shadows beneath her eyes, she's shattered."

"Well, that's not my problem," Sean grumbled. "If she'd stayed in the States, or Canada, or wherever the bloody hell she is from, I wouldn't have her sitting in front of me now."

"She's laying down, Sean," Mary mumbled. Sean groaned. If he didn't encourage the villagers to have such a friendly rapport with him, they might just heed his orders when he gave them. As it was, they revered and adored him, and unfortunately thought of him as one of their own. "And don't be so snippety," Mary snapped.

"Besides, it isn't her, is it?" Rupert asked, leaning toward the woman.

"What?" Sean muttered. "Of course it's her."

"She doesn't match the picture in the back flap of her book."

"The lad's right, she doesn't. That woman has red

22

hair, and looks different," Father Clancy murmured thoughtfully.

"Well, no matter who she is, the lass needs our help," Mary murmured, pushing past the men. "We could look for her passport. That would tell us who she is, and we wouldn't have to rifle into any of her personal belongings."

"Mary!" Rupert chastised. "How could you think of such a thing?"

"Do it," Sean ordered.

Mary was just about to reach for her purse, when the woman brought her hands up, and pulled it away from her.

"My God. She's awake!" Mary gasped, pulling her hands back.

Sean smiled when the girl let out a loud snore. "I don't think so. But why don't I just take her to the pub anyway?" Now that the seed of doubt had been planted, he felt guilty for treating her so badly.

"Do you think she'll have a reservation at me mum's?" Rupert asked.

"I asked your mother. The only woman that had rung to make reservations was Bridie Sullivan," Mary said, nodding her head. "So we'll just let this wee one have one of our guests rooms above the pub."

"Someone will have to carry her, with my bad back, I don't know if..." Rupert trailed off as Ridley eagerly raised his hand.

"I'll carry her," Ridley offered.

"Look at him. New blood, and already he's jumping up and down," Mary muttered, shaking her head.

At the mention of blood, Sean swallowed thickly. "I'll carry her." Everyone turned to rivet his or her, bewildered gazes on him. "I'm the biggest and the strongest. I'll be sure not to drop her."

"Aye, now that you know she isn't that romance woman," Father Clancy pointed out.

Sean smiled. He loved to shock people. Bending down, he gently gathered the small slip of a woman into his arms. She'd stood so proud before that he hadn't noticed her fragile size. Smiling, he brought her up to cradle her against his chest. He sniffed at the air. She wore some sort of beguiling perfume. She murmured something inaudible in her sleep. Her purse was still crossed over her shoulder, and she gripped it tightly. He dropped his eyes down to her cross, and made note of where it was snuggled between her breasts. Beautiful.

Suddenly, a realization struck him like a lightening bolt. She was the exact same size of his long lost love. His mouth went dry. He needed to get her to Mary's guestroom, and then he had to go back to his home and partake of some sustenance.

"Be careful with her, she will break you know," Mary quipped, falling into step beside him.

"Do I look like I was born yesterday?"

"You don't want me to answer that question," Mary returned, giving him a cheeky wink.

Ridley opened the church door, and the wind began howling around them. Except for the sound of the howling wind, the night had become calm and still.

"Follow me," Mary said, leading the way back to the pub.

Sean really wished that he hadn't found himself in this awkward situation. Here he was, holding a woman that he hardly knew. And from their heated exchange earlier, he knew that she wasn't really fond of him either.

Mary held open the door to the pub for him, and he followed her up the back staircase.

"I'm so happy I redid the guestrooms." She opened up the first door on the right, and cheery wallpaper and a homemade quilt filled the room with hominess.

"You've done a bang up job on redecorating," he mumbled.

Mary beamed. It wasn't often that he dolled out compliments.

"Do you think I should change her clothes?" Mary asked.

Rupert emerged into the bedroom at that moment, with the woman's carry on suitcase. He stood it up by the desk chair, and sighed.

"I don't think that she would appreciate being undressed by a strange woman, my dear," Rupert stated.

Mary reluctantly nodded her head. "I suppose you're right. Your lordship, just hang on to her while I go fetch an old blanket to drape over the duvet." She ran from the room, and then returned scant seconds later.

Sean wished that he could say his arms were getting tired, but they weren't. He felt as if he were holding onto a cloud. Could she be the woman that could save his soul? He put the foolish notion out of his head. This woman didn't seem strong enough. In fact, by the way she looked now; she'd probably blow over in a great gale of wind.

"Prophetic," she mumbled in her sleep, just as he was laying her down on the blanket that Mary had spread across the surface of the bed.

Mary jumped at her mumbled word. "Do you think she knows?" Her voice was anxious.

"How could she?" Rupert's sensibility reared its ugly head.

"Well, we'll keep an eye on her just in case." Mary nodded her head, and then took the other blanket that was in her arms and draped it across her.

"First, we have to find out what her name is. Tomorrow, I expect everyone to move into the first phase of the operation."

"Of course we will. Now, shouldn't you be getting back to the castle? You look a wee bit peaked." Mary's eyes shone with concern.

"Actually, I do need to recharge. I'll see you both tomorrow."

"We'll be waiting." Rupert saluted him, and grinned.

Sean dragged his feet along the carpet. For some unexplainable reason, he was hesitant to leave.

But Sutherland Castle called out to him, as did a certain drink. He raced out of the pub before anyone else could intercept him. Glancing up at the full moon, he pulled his hood up, and started up the long path toward his castle.

If this woman were the one that he'd been waiting all of these years for, then he would get down on his knees and pay homage to her. She would give him a new lease on life. He groaned, and walked into the great hall of his castle. Everyone must have retired to bed. He peeked into some of the rooms and frowned. He had so wanted to chat with someone that could make some rational sense of what had occurred that night.

He flew up to his suite of rooms, and sat down in

front of his television. Moving to the small fridge that he had in his room, he opened it. "Ah, this is exactly what I needed." He poured the crimson substance into a wineglass and happily sat down to watch his favorite program. Raising the life essence to his lips, he took a long satisfying drink. The tide of his fate was changing. He could feel it in the air. If this angelic woman were the one to save his soul then it would be fitting.

For what else but an angel and a saint, could save a monster like him?

He sipped at his drink again, and swallowed the blood that was in his mouth. The curse was beginning to eat away at him. But if he knew there was a light for him at the end of the tunnel, then he would fight with all of the strength that he had.

And as Father Clancy had said earlier, he'd become the man that he had once been.

"Please God, help me to endure, help me to survive this curse that plagues my existence." He shut the television off, and groaned when he was yet again met with no reflection.

Chapter Four

Bridget stretched and let out a big yawn. Scrunching her pillow beneath her head, she buried her face in it. She sighed. She felt refreshed, and yet strangely icky all at the same time. Then, she groaned as memories of the night before kicked into effect. The last thing she could recall was falling asleep on the church bench and then dreaming about a strange group of people clustered around her. And, he had been there. Though she didn't know his name, she knew that he was very different from the rest of the people in the village.

Reluctantly, she fluttered her eyelids open and carefully studied her surroundings. She was still in her traveling clothes, and she seemed to be lying on top of a double bed. There was a large window off to her right, and a cherry wood wardrobe stood next to the bed. Over on the other side of the room was a writing desk, and in front of it stood her carry on.

Sighing, she sat up, and flung her legs over the side of the bed. She was as stiff as a board. Standing up, she did a few stretches to limber up her tight muscles. As soon as she figured out whose house she was in, she wanted to take a shower and start questioning the villagers. Too many things didn't add up. She wanted to know why everyone had locked her out last night. By all appearances, it seemed to be a quaint and sleepy village. Her purse sat on the night table. Someone had taken it off of her. She moved toward it. Luckily, no one had been nosy enough to open it up and pry. If they had, they would have discovered her secret.

Brushing her hair back from her forehead, she stared into the full-length mirror, and grimaced. She looked like she had been to Hell and back.

Her mouth felt as if it needed a good scrubbing. Slipping her feet into her shoes, she walked toward the

27

door, and almost had it open, when she heard hushed voices.

"His Lordship shouldn't expect us to do his dirty work for him!"

"Rupert, you just be quiet. Why, with all of the good deeds that he does on our behalf, you should take it on as an honor to do this one thing for him."

Bridget narrowed her eyes. She needed to find out whom the man was that they were calling *lordship*.

The female voice continued. "Anyway, she could be the one we've been waiting for. The one that he's been waiting for."

"I know, my love," Rupert said grumpily. "I just wish that the man would come out of hiding once and a while when these women are around."

"He doesn't want to become involved, unless he knows for sure that she's the one."

"Aye. So he gets us involved instead. How many women have we gone through in the last fifteen years?"

"Only five. You should see how many they went through in my grandmother's time. If you read my grandmother's diary, you'd be counting your blessings!"

"Mary, if this is the one, then I shall happily prance around the village square in naught but my underwear."

"Rupert, you are quite fortunate that only I heard you make that vow. Why, wouldn't you look ludicrous, if she did turn out to be the one?"

"How do we explain locking her out last night?" Rupert demanded.

Bridget leaned toward the door, so she wouldn't miss Mary's answer, when from somewhere within the house a phone began ringing.

"We shall think of something," Mary murmured. "Now, Rupert, go and answer that telephone. I'm going to see if the wee woman is awake yet."

"You go and do that, my dear. And while you're at it, make certain that you find out what her name is!"

Bridget heard his retreating footsteps, mingled with Mary's advancing ones. She stepped away from the door, just as Mary knocked on it. Mustering a cheery smile, she pulled the door open.

"Ah, it's so good to see you awake and looking well."

28

Mary smiled.

Bridget did a quick appraisal of the woman in front of her. Mary was big. She resembled a Nordic Goddess.

"I take it that this is Maureen's Bed and Breakfast?"

"Ach, no," Mary murmured. "You're in the MacKay Pub."

"But why not the B&B? I made reservations there."

"You did?" Mary frowned. "Under what name?"

"Well, my own name of course. What other name would I use?" She laughed airily.

Mary nodded her head, though her eyes were still filled with doubt. "Unfortunately, Mrs. MacKay, the owner of the B&B, has only had one reservation made for this week. And that was made by the romance novelist, Bridie Sullivan."

"Yes, I know. Because Bridie Sullivan and I are one and the same."

Mary shook her head. "How can you be Bridie Sullivan? Why, you don't even look like her."

"Ah, well, I can explain that."

"You can?"

"Yes. That was my sister in the photo. I had my own personal reasons for not using my own likeness."

"You did?"

Mary obviously wanted her to elaborate, but at the moment Bridget didn't have a believable explanation. If she told Mary the real reason, the woman wouldn't believe her, so just keeping quiet was the best policy for now.

"And, I believe you should know that I just write as Bridie Sullivan. My birth name is Bridget Sinclair."

"Truly?" Mary gasped.

"Yes," Bridget answered. Mary dropped the stack of towels she held, and simply gaped at her. "Would you like me to help you gather those?"

"They were just going to the wash anyway," Mary muttered.

But Bridget stepped into the brightly lit hallway, and bent down to pick them up for the stunned woman. When she handed them over to her, Mary and she locked gazes. Mary screamed. Wondering what had spooked the woman, Bridget looked over her shoulder expecting to see some sort of ghost or something. Instead, she saw only an empty room. When she looked back, Mary and the towels were gone.

She'd wanted to ask Mary where the showers were. Deciding that she would have to find Mary and ask her, she clicked the door shut behind her and started down the hall. She was just about to turn toward the staircase, when a man came barreling up the steps toward her.

"I take it that you're Rupert," she murmured.

He stopped at the top step. "Do you have the second sight?" he muttered. He stared deeply into her eyes. He had an odd glint in his eyes.

"Do I have something on my face?" she asked, deliberately avoiding his question.

"No," Rupert answered, with a perplexed look on his face.

"Could you tell me where the bathroom is? Or should I go down to the B&B?"

"No. You can stay here. For as long as you like. You are most welcome. The bathroom is the door that's right across from your bedroom. We don't have anyone else in the house at the moment, so the bath is private...Mary and I have our own." Rupert grinned at her. He reminded her of a little boy on Christmas morning, for he looked as if he'd been given the greatest gift of all. "You can go and freshen up, and then come down for a bite to eat. Mary and I are just about to start making lunch."

She groaned. She hadn't thought to check the time. Pulling her sleeve up, she looked at her watch. "That's strange."

"What is?"

"My watch has stopped. And I just put in a new battery the other day."

"Ah, well, perhaps it was faulty." But an odd look had again taken control of his features.

Her stomach chose that moment to let out a loud growl.

Rupert smiled indulgently. "I'll let you get to your bath. But we'll be waiting for you, Ms. Sinclair."

"Please, call me Bridget."

"Thank you, Bridget." He turned to walk back down the steps, and stopped midway. Turning back to her with a thoughtful expression he said, "Do you know that you're named for a saint?"

"Yes. And Bridget was also a Celtic Goddess. But my mother named me after the saint. My mother's faith is very important to her." She forced out a smile.

"Isn't it important to you as well?"

"Oh, yes. My mom raised me well."

"Aye that she did. Very well indeed." Rupert pivoted around on his heel again. "Right then, I'll let you get to it. I'll see you in a few minutes."

"More like a half-hour," she muttered, turning back toward the bathroom.

Exactly thirty-five minutes later, she emerged from the still steamy bathroom. She had felt filthy. She was glad to be rid of the grime from yesterday's adventure. Walking into her bedroom, she shut the door, and locked it. Then she moved over to her carry on, and pulled out a pair of jeans, tank top and sweater. She pulled on the jeans first, and then, since she was already wearing her bra and panties, she pulled the purple tank top over her head. Lastly, she put on her black sweater.

It didn't take her long to comb out her hair and slide it back into a high ponytail. She pinched her pale cheeks and sighed. She reached for her purse and pulled out a tube of lipstick. If her luggage was not delivered today, she'd have to buy some clothes...or she'd have to resort to her own other devices. She blotted her lipstick, tucked her purse under her arm, and slipped her feet into her running shoes.

Now, she had to go down and face the music. No doubt they would all have loads of questions for her. She was just about to reach for the doorknob, when something occurred to her. Unzipping her purse, she rummaged inside of it. Somewhere along the line, she'd misplaced her camera and flashlight. She would have to ask the villagers and the priest if they had seen them. They were both very special to her, and if they fell into the wrong hands, the consequences could be severe.

The villagers seemed nice enough, but she'd remain on her guard. In her line of business, it was wise to keep a safe distance, until you knew the people around you. Emotional detachment sometimes could come in handy...especially if she was forced to take action.

Tossing her head, she called upon the entertaining side of her personality. She had to put on a good show. They needed to think that she was wonderful. Something funny was going on in the village and she was going to find out what it was. But first, she had to win some people over to her side. And she had to carefully guard her secret. If someone did have her camera and flashlight, they would find out what she was. And if they did, she'd have to silence them.

She shut the door behind her, and put on a bright smile. *It's show time*. She headed toward the staircase.

She emerged into the pub after walking down two flights of steps. By the looks of it, every one from the village had conglomerated in the room.

"Bridget!" Mary cried, rushing toward her. "What would you like for your lunch?"

Bridget didn't know what she felt like. After the previous evening, she really didn't crave anything. "How about a sandwich?"

"What kind?"

"Chicken," she decided.

"Brilliant. I'll have it ready for you in no time at all." Mary bustled away from her, and then as if on cue, Rupert came toward her.

"Where would you like to sit?"

She scanned the dining area. "How about in that booth?"

Rupert followed her gaze and gasped. Then, he recovered spectacularly. "Of course. That's a good seat you've chosen." He began walking toward it, and Bridget had no other choice but to follow. Every one watched her as if she were some sort of entertaining television show. Obviously, they didn't get too many tourists in their neck of the woods.

A bell tinkled and a man in a priest's frock, walked into Bridget's line of sight. He had snow-white hair and an affable smile. He rubbed his hands together briskly, which meant that it had to be quite damp and cold outside.

"Is she awake, yet?"

Bridget didn't know how he'd missed her, but he had.

Suddenly, his eyes fell on her. He squinted, and reached for his glasses that hung around his neck on a cord. "Ach. That is better." His eyes widened, as he moved closer. "Good heavens! God almighty!" he recoiled.

She grimaced. If everyone had this reaction to her she was going to get sick and tired of it.

"Father Clancy, this here is Bridget Sinclair," Rupert murmured, gesturing to Bridget.

"Very pleased to meet you, Father Clancy," Bridget murmured, extending her left hand. Her shirtsleeve rode up, revealing her wrist.

Father Clancy's eyes dropped to her wrist and he gasped.

"Good Lord in Heaven!"

"Is there something wrong, Father?" She asked, quite alarmed by his reaction.

"I just noticed those moles on your wrist. They seem to have been put there by the hand of God."

"Oh, that." She rolled her eyes. "I've had these since the day I was born, and no doubt before that."

"No doubt," Father Clancy repeated, his blue eyes glittering.

Goosebumps raged across her skin. Suddenly, she felt as if she'd walked into an alternate universe.

Mary came bobbing toward her, and then gently plunked her sandwich down in front of her. She leaned down toward her with a moony smile on her face.

"You have such lovely eyes. They are yours, right?"

"Well, who else's would they be?" she asked laughingly.

"No, what I meant to say, you aren't wearing those new fangled color contacts are you?"

"Color contacts? Of course not, I have perfect vision." In fact her vision was more than perfect but that was another story entirely, and not one that she wanted to share with people that she had just met.

"They are very unique. One eye is the color of the greenest emerald, and the other, why it's the color of the darkest sapphire."

"I know. I've seen them before," she joked. She smiled, shrugged her shoulders, and picked up one half of her sandwich. Biting into it, she sighed. "Father, I think I might have left my camera and my flashlight, behind in the church last night. I must have been so tired that I didn't put them back into my purse."

"Flashlight?" Father Clancy looked puzzled.

"My torch," she murmured, suddenly realizing her mistake.

"Well, I haven't seen any signs of those, but I'll keep an eye out."

"Thank you. I don't suppose my luggage has come yet, has it?"

"No. Not yet, but I'll be looking for it. You might have to call about its whereabouts," Mary suggested.

"Yes, that might be a good idea. I met the strangest man in the church last night. At first, I didn't think that he was human." She smiled.

Mary dropped the plate and glass she held. "Gracious me. Look at that, I'm all thumbs today."

Bridget tilted her head to the side, and pursed her lips. She would have some of her questions answered and soon. "He was dressed all in black, much like you, Father, except he was wearing a long cloak, which concealed most of his face. Come to think of it, he was very tall, and quite handsome. You all must know who he would be, in a village this size."

Mary gulped. "Well, he's..."

"He'll be along later this evening, and the two of you can have a proper introduction. He's quite a lovely lad," Father Clancy said, jumping in and interrupting Mary.

Bridget narrowed her eyes. They were being quite cryptic. Why couldn't they just tell her who he was? She also wanted to know the identity of the *lordship* Mary and Rupert had been discussing earlier.

"Well, I might not be here. I intend to explore the area. In fact, I feel like I'm due for a walk right now." She swallowed the last bite of her sandwich and stood up. Something outside called to her; she had to get out of the smoky pub so that she could find out what it was.

"I could do with a little jaunt myself," Father Clancy said, standing up.

Bridget groaned. She really didn't want to have any company.

"I wouldn't want you to change your plans on my

account," she murmured, hoping that he would get the drift.

"Ah, no. I haven't walked with a lovely lady like you in many a long year." He smiled at her, and made her heart sink. Now, she couldn't turn him away. Then, with her keen hearing tuned in, she picked up on what two men were saying. They sat up at the bar, but she still heard them.

"Now all we have to do is see if she has a birthmark on her shoulder."

She narrowed her eyes to thin slits. How did they know about her birthmark? These villagers were stranger than she thought. It would seem they knew more about her than they should.

From out of nowhere, another young solidly built man emerged. He went over to Mary and leaned down to whisper in her ear.

"The council has been summoned. There is a crisis we need to attend to. More are coming."

"What?" Mary muttered.

"I can't say anything else." The man darted a furtive glance toward her.

But Bridget didn't want to stay and eavesdrop.

"Father, I think I could do with that walk now."

Father Clancy seemed to be distracted, but he hid it rather well.

"Aye, well, come on my dear." He held his arm out for her to take, and she accepted it.

She walked toward the door in thoughtful contemplation. She could sympathize with the villagers. They were concealing secrets much as she was hiding one whopper of a secret. But she'd find out what they were hiding, and they would never discover hers, not as long as there was breath in her body. But she knew one thing. She had twenty-four hours to find the person she hunted. And when she did, he'd get the shock of a lifetime, and the last face he would see would be hers.

Chapter Five

Sean kicked the covers off of his body and bolted upright. His breathing came in ragged gasps, and he raked his hands through his tousled hair, as he tried to burn her image out of his mind. Taking a shattering breath, he jumped out of bed, and stared toward his drapes. It was still daylight, and he would not be able to emerge for another few hours. He went through his daily routine, and drank down the vile liquid that he was forced to consume on a daily basis. Shuddering, he wiped his mouth with a napkin. Now for some food he could actually stomach. Though he didn't need it, he still liked to eat real food. In a way, it made him feel more human. He grunted. He wouldn't begin to feel human again until this bloody curse was broken.

He was just about to bite into his scone topped with clotted cream and jam, when his door flew back on its hinges.

"This had better be good," he muttered, dropping the scone. He was just about to tear into the person that had dared to invade his inner sanctum, when he saw who it was.

"You have to come quickly."

"I don't have to do anything." He gave his niece a lazy grin, and leaned back in his chair.

"You don't understand. It's her. She's the one, we've been waiting for."

Well that got his attention.

"What do you mean?" He sat up straighter, and leaned forward as Grace sat down in the chair beside him.

"The woman from the church. She's named for a saint, and her eyes are two different colors. One is green and the other is blue. She matches the prophecy, right down to the three moles on her left wrist. It's a miracle to be sure!"

"Then what are we waiting for? I have to get to her, and make sure that she becomes my love."

"Hey, wait a minute stallion. You don't know anything about her. Mary, Father Clancy and the others, are still trying to see if she has that birthmark on her left shoulder. You could make a bloody fool of yourself for no reason. If she doesn't have the birthmark…"

"She's come closer to the prophecy than any of the other women that have ever come to the village. Leave it to me, I'll find out if she has that blessed birth mark."

He was filled with enthusiasm. He could see it now. All that he had to do was woo and win her heart. He had been quite the rake in his day. Winning her heart would be as easy as pie.

"Wait a minute." Grace caught his wrist, and pulled him back. "She's out walking. You couldn't get near her if you wanted. You will just have to wait until twilight, I'm afraid. We've come this far…I don't want to carry you around in an urn, thanks very much."

He grunted, and scowled. "Why is she walking?"

"She told Father Clancy that she wanted to explore the village. I suppose she needs to start her research…I mean that's why she came isn't it?"

"There isn't much to see or explore. Her research trip won't take that long. It won't be too long before she's back at the pub."

"You don't understand. You might have your hands full with this one."

"Oh, I sincerely hope so."

"Don't be smart, Uncle Sean. You know what I'm talking about. The prophecy said that she'd be strong willed and strong spirited. According to the sorceress that put the curse on you, she'll be more than a suitable match for you."

"She's a female. I have no difficulty when it comes to winning over the fairer sex. You forget; I was quite the Casanova in my day." He gave her a playful wink.

"In your day…key words. You had your youth in another time and place, Uncle. Casanova, my arse!" She snorted. "If I didn't care for you so much, I'd have to hit you for that galling remark," Grace muttered. "Either way, you're stuck here until twilight. You will just have to be patient. I know that it will be a challenge for you...but you could always play a roaring game of solitaire." She laughed.

"Smart mouth." He sighed. "I could use the tunnels." He stood up and walked over to the sink. Just as he finished wrapping his scone up, another person came running into the room. "Has everyone lost their manners? What ever happened to knocking?"

"Sorry." Ridley was nearly breathless, and he was doubled over as he tried to catch his breath. "It's...just...that...we are going to be in trouble when the sun goes down."

Sean raised one eyebrow. "What are you trying to say, Ridley?"

Grace stood at the younger man's elbow, trying to press a glass of water into Ridley's trembling hand.

"Deep breaths," she murmured.

"We have had word that more vampires are coming. It would seem that the one we killed last night had some pretty loyal followers."

"We did not kill her."

"Oh, my apologies, your lordship. I mean the one that you staked."

"I didn't kill the bitch. I already told you that." He groaned. Explaining himself was becoming a bit annoying.

Ridley stared up at him in befuddlement. "I suppose it doesn't matter who killed her, because it won't really be all that important once her subjects descend upon us."

"Have you gone and warned everyone?" Sean demanded.

"Aye, we will even ring the siren at sunset."

"Excellent," Sean murmured. "What about the girl? What's her name anyway?"

"Bridget," Grace whispered.

He started at the name, and then quickly regained his composure.

"Have her locked in tight. She won't be able to do anything to help us. We'll have to make sure she's kept safe."

"I'll make sure she's under guard," Ridley promised. "I think we should have everyone gather in the Church. Considering the circumstances, I think it will be the safest place. I know they aren't supposed to come into your house uninvited, but I don't think we should take any chances. Most of the people in the village wouldn't know what to do if they came face to face with a real vampire."

"Tell me, Ridley, what is your definition of a real vampire?"

"Sorry, sir?" Ridley stared at him with perplexed eyes.

"Ridley, look at who you are talking to," Grace chastised.

"No, I didn't mean anything against you, your lordship. I just meant that you aren't a human bloodsucker, so we don't have to fear you. It's not like you're going to take a bite out of us anytime soon."

"Aye. But you might have to fear me kicking your arse out of here. Stop dilly-dallying. There is work to be done. Is someone posted at the watchtower?"

"It's all been taken care of. Have faith, Sean. I do know how to do my job." Ridley put on a brave smile.

"Then, I will leave it in your able hands. I have to get out of my pajamas and into something that I can fight in."

"Might I suggest those black leather trousers of yours?" Grace murmured, staring up at him with her bright eyes.

"Why?"

"I thought you said that you were able to win the heart of a woman easily. Well, take my word on it, if you wear those trousers, they'll help to increase your odds dramatically." She gave him a cheeky grin, and ducked out of his reach.

"You and your mother should get down to the church as well."

"I don't think any of those undesirables would want to come up here," she scoffed.

But he gave her a dead serious look, which sobered her up.

"Fine. But I thought I'd be out in the fray with you."

"Over my dead body," he muttered. She stared at him pointedly, and he sighed. "I'm going to regret agreeing to this, but if you want to go out with us, you'll have to have a fighting partner."

"Agreed," she said eagerly. "I'll go and get that new stake I've been sharpening. I'm rather good at it you know. I think I've inherited the talent from Uncle Gideon."

"Just get a move on." He laughed.

She scooted out of his quarters, and he walked into the adjoining room that served as his dressing room. He looked around at all of his clothes. Heaving a great sigh, he reached for his tight black leather trousers. He hadn't won the heart of a woman for three hundred years, so he felt fairly certain that Grace's advice was far more accurate than his was. He would have to travel through the tunnels. He had to get to the pub so they could strategize.

It didn't take him long to dress. He shook out his cloak, and slung it around his shoulders. Pulling the hood over his head, he reached for his knapsack and slung it onto his back. By the sounds of Ridley's report, they were in for one bloody good battle. But he wouldn't let his village fall prey to the horrid creatures that encroached on his private domain.

As soon as he took care of all of the vampires that were descending on them, he'd have to start courting this Bridget. She was very comely. He would be most pleased to take her as his mate, and then as his wife.

Once she uttered the three blessed words that would release him from the curse upon his life, then he'd put his human life into her hands. In essence, he would be hers forever, until his heart ceased to beat.

He neared the tunnels. Another few feet and he would be there, then from there, it wouldn't take him long to reach the village.

"You know, Father, I never dreamt in my wildest dreams that Sutherland Castle would be so welcoming."

He stopped dead in his tracks.

How on God's green Earth, did they let her get inside of his castle?

"Bridget, we should be heading back toward the village. The hour grows late, and I fear that many people shall require my guiding hand this night."

"Of course, Father. As soon as I see the upstairs, I'll be sure to walk back with you. This has been on my list of places to visit, and since you said they give tours here, I had to jump on the opportunity. You see, I want to put this kind of a castle in my next book."

That was it! He'd heard enough. Rounding the bend to confront them, his mouth fell open when his eyes fell on the woman standing in front of him.

"You!" He hissed.

"You!" She gasped, pointing furiously at him. Her eyes dropped to his bag, and he tried to shove it behind his back but he was too late. She pursed her lips into a severe line. "You wouldn't happen to have my flashlight and my camera in there, would you?"

She moved forward, and he stepped back. "That is none of your concern. If I did have it, I'd have already given them back to you."

Her eyes narrowed suspiciously. "I don't believe you," she said, still moving in on him.

Suddenly, she stopped, and a faraway expression covered her face. He passed his hand in front of her face, and to his chagrin she didn't blink once. He gestured to Father Clancy, and the older man merely shrugged his shoulders in disbelief.

Her behavior was odd. Then a jolt ran through her body, and her eyes lit up with fire.

Those eyes.

They both disturbed him, and exhilarated him. He wanted to drown in them, if they didn't hold such animosity toward him.

"I must go," she murmured, backing away from them. "It's been tons of fun, Father Clancy, but I think I'll be able to find my way back. You two have a lovely night, and perhaps you should stay inside. I noticed that it's frightfully damp. Well, got to go. People to see, places to go, don't you know," she babbled.

Then, at a full clip run, she bolted toward the castle exit.

"I wonder what got into her," he mused, rubbing his chin.

"I know what it was. You scared her away," Father Clancy remarked, falling into step beside him.

"Me? I scared her away? I think not. We met last night, and the woman didn't seem intimidated in the least bit. She's as stubborn as a mule. Take it from me, I ran into her determined side. No, I think that something else set her off. I don't know what it was, but I intend to find out."

"You're in a bit of a rush yourself," Father Clancy pointed out.

"Haven't you heard?" he asked, staring down at the priest.

"No. What's going on?"

"The vampire bitch that I found dead last night seems to have her own loyal following, and they have taken offense to her absence." His voice grew dry, cool and collected, but inwardly something waged a war in his gut.

"Oh, Heaven forbid!" Father Clancy shuddered.

"Aye, well, we're moving into defensive mode."

"And knowing this, you sent that wee girl out into the encroaching darkness?"

Sean shrugged his shoulders. "I'll have you remember that I didn't send her anywhere. She tore off on her own accord. Don't worry. She'll make it back to the village in time. At the speed she was going, I'd be hard pressed to catch up with her. Besides, there is something strange with that woman, and come hell or high water, I intend to find out what it is."

"Well, I wish you luck, my son. She's tighter than a clam when it comes to revealing personal information. I did everything to try and urge her out of her shell, and I found out nothing. All I know is that she has a sister."

"A sister?" He stopped and stared down at Father Clancy. "But that can't be. The prophecy said she'd be the only girl child in her family."

At his revelation, Father Clancy halted as well. Biting on his lip, he stared up at Sean. "I distinctly recall her mentioning a sister, when I asked her about her family. I was so excited about the prophecy that I mustn't have paid it any mind. Oh, dear, this does create a problem, doesn't it?

"Aye. A very big problem. Since Bridget isn't the one, we'll have to get rid of her as soon as possible. She can't find out what I am." He was determined. He was going to be rid of Bridget and he knew just what to do to get her to run screaming from the village. As soon as he was done with the vampire loyalists, he was going to scare the living daylights out of Bridget, and enjoy every single minute of it.

Chapter Six

Only one shaft of sunlight still streaked across the horizon. This meant that she still had time before they would arrive.

Bridget circled around and bent to pick up a rock on the ground. Tucking it into her purse, she turned about when she heard a scratching sound in the thicket of trees nearby. Clutching her purse tightly, she stalked toward it. She nearly let out a startled scream when a bright cherubic like face appeared. Pressing her hand to her heart, she tried to calm her nearly shattered nerves.

"Uh, hello," the young woman said. She was younger than herself. The girl looked to be about nineteen, to Bridget's twenty-six years.

"You should be more careful, you nearly gave me the fright of my life!"

"Sorry," the girl mumbled.

Bridget cocked her head to the side. "Do I know you from somewhere?"

The girl wiped her hand on the front of her jacket, and extended it for Bridget to shake. "I'm part of the Sutherland family. My name is Grace Sutherland."

"Why in the name of God, are you out here at such a strange hour?"

Grace seemed amused. Stepping over the thick branches and leaves that were strewn across the ground, she giggled.

"Are you not aware that you're out here at a strange hour as well?"

"Yes, well there's a reason..." Clamping her hand over her mouth, she scowled at Grace. "I'm older than you," she mumbled.

"Aye, about five years I'd warrant. Not that much of a difference when it comes right down to it. We're both adults, you know."

Now that Grace had stepped out into the waning sunlight Bridget noticed for the first time that she carried a bag slung over her shoulder that was much similar to the bag that the jerk of a man carried.

"Why are you out here, anyway?" Grace asked. She tilted her head to the sky and began to watch it.

"I was trying to find my way back to the village."

"Oh, well, you're a little off track, then. It's that way," Grace said, pointing in the opposite direction.

"You don't say. Well, I'll be going." Bridget reluctantly began trudging toward the village. Then, after a few forced steps, she stopped and looked back at Grace. "Aren't you coming with me?"

"Och, no." Grace mumbled, redness flushing her cheeks. "But when you do get to the village, you should know they are having a town meeting in the church."

Bridget arched her eyebrows. "Really?" She rolled her eyes heavenward. "Why?"

She bit her lip. Why wouldn't Grace just go and leave her to take care of the business at hand? She couldn't risk putting Grace in the line of fire. If they arrived while Grace was with her...she didn't know if she'd be able to protect her.

"Huh?" Grace muttered. Obviously, the girl hadn't been paying the slightest attention to her.

"I said why are they having a village meeting?" She kicked a few branches out of her way with the tip of her shoe.

"They need to decide what the official village drink is going to be," Grace mumbled.

Bridget planted her hands on her hips. That was it. Grace was inventing this nonsense. And, she wasn't doing such a bang up job on her stories. Just as she turned around, the last ray of sunlight slipped beneath the horizon. "Bugger it!" She cursed, staring at the barren path ahead and behind them.

They were out in the middle of nowhere, and the daylight had just abandoned them. Even though it was twilight right now, they wouldn't have much time before it was pitch black. With black sorcery at work...the pitch black was inevitable.

Her ears perked as a shattering wail, reminding her

of a banshee's cry ripped through the clearing toward them. It was obviously a lookout siren. Though she didn't know why they would have need of it in this time and day. Unless...could they be expecting the same attack she was preparing for?

"Oh, look!" Grace said, feigning a bright smile. "They're ringing for the people of the village. If you scoot along, you just might make it time." She still seemed hopeful.

Bridget wasn't appeased. Then, she heard it. She made a mad dash toward Grace and pulled her into the small grouping of trees. Grace hit the ground, with Bridget not too far behind. She was crouched in front of Grace, in a defensive stance.

"Sean isn't going to like this." Grace coughed.

"Who is Sean?" Bridget asked, suddenly interested.

"He's uh...my uncle," Grace said, glowing with her quick explanation.

"He wouldn't happen to be tall dark and handsome would he?"

"That's uncle." Grace sat up and shook her head. "You know, you should be more careful, why I think you're rougher than Uncle Sean when he's training..." Grace trailed off.

"Training you for what?" Bridget muttered.

Tossing Grace a confused look, she began rearranging the leaves and branches. She reached for one long twig, and bent down, as she began dragging it in the dirt around Grace. Her breath came out in long huffs, though Grace didn't seem to notice anything, because she was too busy watching the sky again.

"Well, he trained me in the ways of self-defense."

"Oh," Bridget muttered. Finally she was finished.

Throwing the twig away, she reached inside of her purse for a round object and pointed it at the outlined circle. Smiling triumphantly, she backed away from Grace.

She turned toward the noise that quickly approached them. Darting a furtive glance toward Grace, she whirled back around and stood her ground. Grace, on the other hand, seemed quite agitated. She tried to walk toward her, and hit the invisible shield that Bridget had erected.

Bouncing backward, she hit the ground.

"Wow that stung! I think I've been gobsmacked!" She shook her head, rubbing at the back of her neck.

But Bridget didn't have time to pay any attention to her. Unfortunately for her, Grace was still conscious. She snapped her fingers, and light lit up the area.

"Damn," Grace muttered. "That is bloody bright...who put the lights out?"

Bridget winced. She had probably just inadvertently blinded Sean's niece. And though he was one big bear to get along with, his niece was actually quite charming and personable. It was a shame really, but it couldn't be helped. No one could discover her secret. Grace's eyesight would return but it would take at least fifteen minutes, and the way that Bridget worked she wouldn't need that long.

Dark figures dropped from the sky, and began hissing. She shot up in the sky, and pounced down on the first three. One of them got caught up in her handy mini little circle of light. They combusted as soon as they fell into it.

"Stake!" she screamed. A long wooden stake appeared in her hand. She brought it straight for the first one's heart. Whirling around, she knocked the other two off balance. The last two were moving toward Grace. As she made short work of the two that had their fangs bared at her, she watched the other two howl in pain when they tried to breach the protective circle. She grinned. Shooting up in the sky again, she twisted around, yelling, "Stakes!"

Both of her hands filled with stakes. She flipped in mid-air and barreled toward them as if a cannonball had spewed her forth. Stabbing them into the vampires, she grinned as they exploded. She dropped to her feet, and brushed the dust off of her herself.

"That was bloody brilliant!" Grace muttered.

Wonderful, she had seen the whole thing.

Bridget frowned.

"How did you see that whole thing?" Bridget sighed impatiently. She wiped sweat from her brow, and scratched her nose.

"I wasn't blinded for long, and I could hear the screams, grunts, and shouts," Grace muttered. "So where

47

did you learn how to fight vampires?"

Bridget groaned. This wasn't going to be easy.

"I didn't do anything," she tried, hoping that Grace would let it be.

"Oh, don't be modest. And this circle of light, how did you manage that one?"

Bridget groaned again. She couldn't let Grace figure out her secret. Raising her hand, she deactivated the protective circle. Smiling, she stepped toward Grace, with her hand outstretched. She waved it across Grace's face, smiling knowingly.

"So when are you going to answer my question?" Grace asked, tapping her foot on the ground. "You know, we really should go down to the village there might be more of them."

"How can you still have your memory?" Her stomach fell.

Obviously, the Sutherland's had some secrets that they carefully harbored as well. She should've been briefed on their magical family history. When she got back to Headquarters, she'd definitely have to rip someone a new one.

"What? Oh, that. My uncle says I have the memory of an elephant. I can remember everything in the most miniscule detail."

"Can you, really?"

"Aye. But what I can't understand is why you changed your appearance. Though, I have to say, you look good with blond or red hair. Wow. You have to show me some of those stellar moves."

Bridget grimaced. This was going to be hard to cover. If as Grace said, she had a terrific memory, then that obviously meant quite possibly that her memory was immune to her powers. There was definitely something more then met the eye about the Sutherland family. Abruptly, she turned around, and grabbed Grace by the shoulders. She stared at her quizzically.

"You can't tell anyone about me, or I swear I'll take care of your uncle." She stared at Grace pointedly, and watched the girl's face dawn with recognition.

"We could use someone with your talents though. I mean…you'd make a grand addition to our team."

"I'm sure that I would. I am one of the best in my trade. That's why I'll be staying here in the village for quite some time."

"Oh, excellent. But you do realize there is one person I can tell and you can't stop me."

"Yes." Bridget dropped her eyes to the ground. If only they didn't have a friendly neighborhood priest, 24/7.

A house being lit on fire down in the village caught both of their attention.

"Oh, screw it!" Bridget muttered. She couldn't leave Grace, but she had to get to the village. "So, how do you feel about flying?" she asked, pulling Grace high up in the air.

Chapter Seven

Things weren't going as Sean had planned. But then, when had they ever? He lunged out of the burning building. Playing with fire was just as dangerous to him as it was to the evil vampires. From within the building, he could hear the agonized screams of four cornered vampires. Jolly good for them, and for him. At least he had been able to escape still in one piece. But he wasn't looking forward to putting out the flames. Fortunately, the building had been built in 1950 and had been separated from the rest of the village's older buildings.

He hit the ground with a painful thud. Stars swam in front of his eyes.

He jumped to his feet, and quickly brushed the dirt off of himself. Something glittery caught his attention, and he stared up at the sky, expecting it to be another incoming vampire. Instead, it was a sight that nearly made his blood curdle. There was a strange woman holding Grace as she flew over them, and for all that he knew, she could have been one of the cursed vampires he currently fought.

The hairs on the nape of his neck prickled, and without darting a glance behind him, he pulled his fist up and punched the approaching vampire. He was just about to whirl about and finish off the loathsome creature when Ridley shot off his armed crossbow.

The red-haired beauty carrying Grace floated down and landed right near the village square. She talked to Grace and pointed her arm toward the church. Grace emphatically shook her head.

Groaning, he crossed the short distance in three easy strides. The vampires had been put off for now, but they would return soon. For now, they swooped high in the sky, preparing for a counter attack.

"Grace!" He shouted, over the racket. He reached out,

and pulled Grace behind him. The red-haired beauty fell silent, and wrinkled her nose.

"You should really tell Grace to get inside of the Church. This is no place for a girl of her tender age."

He glanced at the red-haired warrior. There was something about her that made electric tingles ricochet through his body.

"I'm almost the same age as you..." Grace stopped in mid-sentence, when the woman glared at her.

"Who are you and why are you here?" He demanded, taking a step toward her. He sniffed the air. She reminded him of someone he'd met before.

She smiled. "First off, you may call me Claire. Secondly, I'm here to save this village. It was calling for a protector."

"I'm its protector."

"Well, you're doing a bang up job of it, aren't you?" She gestured toward the burning inferno that had once been the village's bookstore. She turned around with her amazing hair billowing out in the wind. Raising her hands, she recited a small incantation. A few clouds appeared above the burning building, and then began to shower buckets of rain down upon it. In a few moments, the flames sputtered out.

"Well, I'll be damned."

"I thought you already were," she murmured, turning to face him. She arched one eyebrow, and her eyes glittered.

Those eyes.

They were blue and green. He swallowed. This had to be her. It wasn't Bridget that his heart was meant for. It was Claire.

All three of them looked up at the dark sky as the vampires howled. Their wails were worse than that of a banshee.

"Grace, run and get your bum into the Church. You'll be safe there. Your mother must be going mad."

"Actually, how can she be going mad, when she's over there, Uncle Sean?" Grace murmured, pointing toward the village's tearoom.

"Doesn't anyone in my family listen to me?"

"Oh, we listen. We just don't always follow your

orders. You're rather like an army Commander, obstinate and stubborn." She laughed.

"Only my family could joke around during a vampire blitzkrieg." He rolled his eyes, and then riveted them on Claire.

"I could just get rid of them all right now, but then you would be taken out with them," Claire murmured.

She didn't sound at all remorseful.

Grace gasped horrifically, and valiantly threw herself in front of him. "You can't be serious! He is good. He wouldn't suck on human blood, if his life depended upon it!"

Sean groaned. Grace had her arms flailed out. Then, Orla came rushing from her position, in the tearoom.

"Grace, you're coming with me. It's too dangerous out here in the open." She grabbed a hold of her daughter and dragged her toward the shelter that Ridley and she had erected.

"I have to stay here. Br...I mean Claire, is about to kill Sean."

"Oh, of course she isn't. Wait a minute, who's Claire?"

"That's Claire," Grace said, pointing.

"I won't kill Sean until I've gotten rid of those ones up there. As much as I hate to let him live, I'll give him this one pardon. But he's only being granted one. I'll be taking your ashes home in my bag when I finally leave this village."

"Oh, now don't make promises, you can't keep," Sean scoffed.

"Oh, I keep every single one of my promises," Claire argued. She darted a gaze up at the sky. "You two strain my patience." She pointed at Grace and her mother, and they disappeared.

"What did you do with them?" He demanded.

"Nothing at all. They're safe and sound in the Church."

"You don't know what you're doing," Sean seethed.

"Oh, I don't, do I? Let's see, I was the one that saved your village from their queen last night."

"Pardon me?" Now he was royally pissed off!

"Their Queen. Didn't you know that she had you marked as her next paramour?" Claire turned away from him without a further word, and took to the sky.

"Next paramour my three hundred year old ass," he muttered, stalking toward Ridley. Several other members of the council were staked out around the village.

"They're coming back down for a second go."

"Who was that wonderful woman?" Ridley murmured, sighing happily.

"Wonderful? She could've been a vampire and you thought she was wonderful?"

"She isn't a vampire. She glows. Vampires don't glow; they really are an unhappy lot."

"Thanks," he muttered, blowing steam out of his nostrils.

"No offense, your lordship."

"None taken, this time," Sean muttered.

"Well, the rest of the villagers will be very excited when they see her. She looks like one of the Sidhe."

"Nonsense. The Sidhe don't exist. It's all mythological folklore."

"Some people think that vampires don't exist," Ridley said, looking at him pointedly.

"Point taken," he murmured.

"Whoa," Ridley said, in awe. "Look at her! She's magnificent."

Sean whirled around. "I should go and help her."

"But you hate to fly. You say that it makes you sick."

"Well, that's a chance I'm willing to take. I can't let the answer to all of my prayers be taken down by vampires. She's just a woman. She won't be able to muster the stamina necessary to take down that many blood suckers."

"Just a woman, my foot. She's magical and you know it. She made Orla and Grace disappear into thin air. What sort of an ordinary woman could do that?"

"Ridley, do me a favor."

"Anything, your lordship."

"Shut your gob!"

He flew up into the sky, and grimaced. He fought the overwhelming urge to retch. He had never liked this part of his curse. Flying just wasn't in his blood. He much preferred to have his feet firmly on the ground. Ridley's philosophy that Claire was of the ancient race known as the Sidhe was pure nonsense. She couldn't be of The Gentry. She was quite tall, aye. And she looked like a princess, but that meant nothing to him. She was his key to salvation. That's all that he needed to know. That was all that he needed to believe in.

He watched as she drew what seemed to be a sword.

"What do you intend to do with that?"

"This!" She speared one of the howling vampires with it. He burned up so quickly that he didn't even have time to scream.

Sean swallowed thickly. *Note to self, stay away from that blade.*

He watched as she used it to finish off two more vampires.

"You are quite the swordswoman."

"Thank you; I had the best teachers in the world."

Sean grimaced.

Aye, she probably had had the best teachers but if they were from his world, then he would eat his socks.

The tide of the battle was turning in their favor. He smiled. Whether or not he wanted to willingly admit it, Claire's helping hand had done wonders. Though he was able to take down quite a few vampires at a time, she seemed to wield super-human powers. She could move much faster than him, and for a moment, it seemed as if she'd become a blur. He grunted when one vampire rammed into his back. He spiraled with great momentum toward the ground.

He hit the ground so hard that it felt as if an earthquake had shaken the village. Cries of concern rang out from the Church. Before he knew what had happened, he saw Grace rush toward him.

"No!" he gasped, but he couldn't seem to make his protest much more than a grumble. Though he was a vampire, he could still be taken down. He recovered quickly, but he feared this time would not be fast enough. The same vampire that had collided with him, now barreled toward him. To Sean's despair, the vampire caught sight of Grace. He tried to call out to her in warning, but again he was unable to speak. At that moment, he noticed the wayward stake that stuck through his left shoulder. Blood gushed from the wound.

Miraculously, it had missed his heart by mere inches. He gritted his teeth together and pulled out the stake. Staggering to his feet, he could only watch in horror as Grace was whipped off of her feet. He tried to run toward her, but only fell to his knees. Though the stake hadn't killed him, it had weakened him considerably. He looked toward the heavens and silently implored Claire to help Grace. As if she had heard his mental plea, Claire turned in mid-air and spotted Grace.

Then, in fast forward motion, she turned her body around so quickly that she created a whirlwind effect. The remaining vampires got caught up in the furious wind. Howling with pain, they went arcing off into the distance.

As if she were an avenging angel, she headed toward Grace, only to be waylaid by a vampire that she had missed.

Time slowed to a standstill. Agony speared his heart.

As soon as the vampire that carried Grace reached a high enough altitude, he dropped her.

He had to give his niece some credit for her courage under fire. She was free falling and yet he couldn't even hear her scream. He scrambled toward her, and heard the rest of the villagers emerge from the church. If he could reach her in time, he would be able to catch her. But he moved too sluggishly. And unfortunately Claire was distracted. He wondered why she just didn't blink Grace to another location. He couldn't watch another loved one die because of him.

"No!"

Everyone screamed out in horror when Grace hit the ground. Unlike him, she would not live through the ordeal. He finally reached her side.

Orla already cried over her daughter's body.

A bright flash of light lit up the sky.

In a heartbeat, Claire was at their side.

"Move out of my way," she ordered, pushing people aside. "Please, I have to help her, while there's still a window of opportunity!"

Mary moved forward and gently pulled Orla away from Grace.

"What can you do for her?" Sean asked.

"I can save her. She still lives. I am able to heal. But

you must give me my space. If I don't heal her right now...she will drift away on us...and even I can't bring people back from the dead." Fierce determination lit her eyes...for one brief moment they flashed with lavender like fire.

"Lad, allow her to do her work. Perhaps she is an angel sent to us for this very reason," Father Clancy murmured, pulling him away from Grace.

Claire knelt beside Grace, and held her hands over her chest. Her eyes rolled back and her hair began to stream around her. For a moment, Sean could have sworn that her entire appearance shifted again. Instead of seeing a red-haired warrior, he saw a lavender haired beauty. She was tall, almost six feet. Her hands shimmered and long angelic like wings fluttered out behind her. The blinding light enveloped Grace and he had to step out of its glare, because his skin had grown hot.

Stepping behind Father Clancy, he peered out at the miraculous scene. Grace's body levitated off of the ground, and light sparks shot out. Within a few moments, she gasped for air, and opened her eyes. Then, her body was gently lowered to the ground.

"Bridget," she murmured happily.

Claire's appearance changed back to the red-haired warrior. Her shoulders slumped, and she seemed quite drained.

"I must diminish," She murmured. She gave them all a weak smile, and then in another bright burst of light, she vanished.

"Damn!" He moved forward.

Everyone was still speechless.

Orla held Grace so tightly that Sean feared she would break all of her bones...again.

They all fell into silence only to jump at the sound of Ridley's shocked exclamation.

"Look!" he said, pointing toward the Church door.

Bridget limped toward it. Her hair was matted with blood, and her eyes were wide-eyed with fear.

Sean's heart leapt as she collapsed to the ground. Wearily, she stared up at all of them. He could tell that she held on with but a hope and a prayer. He waited to make sure that Grace was all right. But when Grace jumped up and started toward Bridget all of his worries were put to rest.

"Bridget!" Grace cried, running to envelop her in a tight hug.

Sean narrowed his eyes to mere slits, when he heard their anxious verbal exchange. Without any explanation, Grace smiled.

"Oh, you poor lass. What happened to you?" Father Clancy asked, moving toward her.

"Vampires, they came at me. Didn't think they existed." She gulped, and then heaved a shaky breath. "Then, this red-haired warrior-woman descended from the sky and took them all out. Bloody fantastic job she did. But I was already beaten black and blue, so I couldn't muster up enough strength to get back to the village."

"Oh, lass, I should have worked harder to convince you against setting back to the village all on your own. You will never get away with that again, I assure you."

"Thank you, Father."

She stared up at Sean. And in that gaze he saw something that unsettled him. There was still more to learn about Bridget. And when he found out everything there was to know, he didn't know if he'd still be standing.

Chapter Eight

Bridget felt like death warmed over. She swallowed thickly, feeling a shiver pass up her spine. Sean's penetrating gaze unnerved her to her very core. No mortal man had ever affected her so deeply. She could drown in his eyes, though at the moment they were filled with suspicion. Not suspicion about the vampires they'd just fought, oh no. The suspicion was meant solely for her. She knew that he had questions for her. Though he couldn't have already deduced that Claire and she were one and the same, she still knew that he'd be watching her very carefully now. Her lot in life was a hard one to bear, but she bore it willingly. Being a literal Huntress of Hell sometimes made it difficult for her to forge personal relationships aside from the ones she had with her own kind. She tried to wrench her eyes away from him. But it was as if she was hypnotized. She shut her eyelids and dragged in a long heavy breath. Why had they not prepared her for a vampire like Sean? How could she kill him, when he seemed so human? Pain tore at her heart.

"Bridget, we really should get you inside where it's warm." Grace's eyes filled with concern.

She smiled. She was grateful to have a found such a friendly ally in Grace. The girl was as loyal as they came, and she knew deep in her heart that Grace would never betray her secret. Especially now, since she had brought her back from the land of the dead. Grace's spirit had been about ready to cross over.

The light had opened up streaming down from the heavens. Bridget knew that she had to save Grace, and keep her from ascending. Grace was needed. She could feel it in her bones. The girl was a piece to the puzzle. And though Bridget knew the village was in need of her, she still didn't know everything. The future was unpredictable that way.

"I'm fine," she mumbled.

She hated it when people fretted over her welfare. She was supposed to be the one that protected and helped others. When the roles were reversed, it always made her uneasy.

In saving Grace, she had weakened her own body. She was not a full-blooded faerie. Her grandfather had been human. Thus, healing Grace had taken away some of her glamour. She would regain it, but it would take time. She coughed, and earned another alarmed glance from Grace.

"Mother, help me get her up. She's as stubborn as a mule, but look at her; she looks about ready to drop."

"Ah, my dear lass. You are a sight to be sure. Here, allow us to assist you."

"Let her go!"

Bridget jumped, as did Orla and Grace.

"Well, you don't have to be so ornery," Grace snapped, her eyes blazing.

Sean forced his sternly set lips into something that resembled a smile.

"I'm sorry." His words were forced, and his eyes were still filled with curiosity. "I'll try to behave more like a gentleman."

Bridget laughed. For some reason, she couldn't control herself. The absurdity of her situation had just begun to sink in.

"You? Behave like a gentleman. Oh, please. You slay me."

Deathly silence resonated around her. She pursed her lips into a sour line. Oh, no. She'd done it again. She had let her guard down and allowed her mouth to run away from her.

Sean cleared his throat. "You two are still in no condition to be supporting Bridget's weight. I'll carry her."

She stiffened. Right now, the last thing she wanted was to have his hands all over her body.

"I can walk on my own, thank you," she snapped.

Pushing Grace away, she forced herself to stand up. Blood rushed in her ears, and a queasy sensation overwhelmed her. She'd never brought someone back from the brink of death before, and she was beginning to understand that she had given up some of her life force for Grace. She'd recover, but obviously not as quickly as she had expected.

Blackness seeped into her vision. She shook her head, and reached her arm out for something to steady herself with. She felt a solid arm, and she gripped onto it. She was still momentarily blind, but she felt quite certain that it too would pass with time.

"Allow me to help."

That voice.

Sean.

Had she been able to see, the expression he wore probably would have tickled her pink. She would not fall unconscious. She bit her lip and tasted blood.

"Sean, she looks deathly pale. I'm quite worried about her," Orla murmured. "Perhaps you should take her to my surgery, and I'll look her over."

"No," she moaned. She couldn't run the risk of having a physical. Her physicality though similar to mortals was different in some aspects. Orla would be tipped off and then the cat would be let out of the proverbial bag. "I'll be fine. I just need to sleep. I need a bed."

"Fine. You can have mine."

As his intimation registered, her head jolted. Stars now swam in front of her eyes. Hopefully, her vision would return and she'd be set to go.

Her stubbornness yet again reared its ugly head.

"No. I don't want to be anywhere near you."

Through her hazy vision, she briefly caught sight of the hardened gleam that passed through his tumultuous eyes.

"Well, it won't be a walk in the park for me either, girl. But like it or not, Orla will be near enough in case you need her, and well...my bed's the most comfortable up at Sutherland Castle."

"Cease your nonsense, Sean Sutherland. Why, you'll scare the wits out of her," Orla chastised. "When you get to know, Sean, you'll find that he has a heart of pure gold."

She snorted and nearly choked.

"She's a romance novelist. I thought she loved the dark and brooding hero," he teased. If she had the strength she would have hauled off and belted him one. As it was, she was barely managing to stay on her feet with his support, let alone stay awake.

"You needn't insult my career," she said brokenly. Her eyelids drooped. As much as she tried to fight it, the lethargy was beginning to take its toll. The wasting feelings were overtaking her and making her feel as if she were floating away.

Grace reached over and pressed her cool hand against her forehead. "You're really red, and yet you feel cool to the touch. Isn't that strange..." Grace trailed off, as Bridget locked gazes with her. She tried to activate her telepathy, but for some reason, she couldn't even do that.

Telepathy was a second nature to her. She was weaker than she thought. She let out a small moan. And then rocked on her feet.

"At this rate, you're going to fall down and crack your head open." Before she knew what had happened, Sean had her swooped up into his arms. "You know something; I'm beginning to think that you're more trouble than you're worth."

She grimaced. If he only knew. She was worth a lot to her mother and father, and if they ever heard that she was in the arms of a vampire, they would flip in their throne chairs.

"If I did crack my head open, I have the feeling that you would do a bloody jig."

He moved her in his arms and snorted.

"Has anyone told you that you weigh like a load of bricks?"

She rolled her eyes, and then began wheezing. It was too much! She knew for a fact that for him, it would be like picking up a child. "Has anyone told you that you seem to have a load of bricks in lieu of a brain?"

He stopped short at that remark. "I should drop you. But regardless of what you may think of me, I do have a kind heart."

"And a good and untarnished soul too, no doubt?"

That quip stung him to the core, by the heated gaze in his eyes. He pursed his lips. A muscle danced in his cheek. She was grating on him. And by Jove, she was delighting in every little barb. If nothing else, he was

61

definitely entertaining.

His long strides began to jostle her.

"Would you mind being a bit more careful? You are carrying a precious load, you know."

He remained silent. Ever since her little slaying remark, the rest of the villagers had begun to disperse. Even Father Clancy had seemed horrified by what she had said. She didn't know why they had taken such offense. They didn't know that she knew of Sean's rather gruesome secret. Why in all of the wonders of the world, were they treating her like a bloody leper? Were they so devoted to Sean that they couldn't see past the tips of their own noses? She harrumphed.

"Why are you so shaken?" He murmured. For some reason, they were now alone. She tried to look around for Grace and Orla but to her despair, she couldn't find them anywhere.

"Never you mind."

"Why are you bobbing your head about? You look painfully tired, and battered up. Conserve your strength. I assure you, I will not ravish you on the way to my castle. I am not as beastly as you think."

"And what are you, then? A saint? I'd wager not! And to my way of thinking, you seem almost too wild to be a normal man."

He tightened his grip. She swallowed. Maybe it hadn't been the best idea to rile him further. Especially when she was now alone, and weakened to a worrisome point. Fire danced in his eyes.

"Wild can be good. Without a mean streak, wild men are unparalleled when it comes to the arts of seduction."

She widened her eyes, and swallowed. What in the world was he getting to? He was a vampire.

A vampire.

His only lust should be bloodlust. She found it awfully disconcerting to have him raking her body with those passion filled eyes. Perhaps she had found more than she had initially bargained for in Sean Sutherland. He wasn't just your ordinary run of the mill vampire. There was something strangely special about him, and by the Grace of God, she would discover just what that quality was.

"On the other hand, if I were a lesser sort of man, I'd jump at the opportunity that is in my arms."

She made a loud noise in the back of her throat. "I've been beaten nearly black and blue. If you did take advantage of me, you would be no better than a...."

"Than a what?" He tossed back at her. His eyes sparkled mischievously. He was garnering a good deal of satisfaction from her discomfort.

"Than a monster."

Her words made his face transform. Mottled color, streamed through his cheeks. His stormy eyes darkened further. A prickling jolt of fear arced up her spine. He looked about ready to lose the last vestiges of his control.

"I...am...not...a...monster." He finally managed to bark out.

The night became eerily still. It was almost as if the creatures of nature waited for what he would do next. She bristled with anxiety. With her powers weakened, she didn't know what would become of her, if he gave into the stirring.

"You, girl, are beginning to grate on my nerves."

She could tell by the jumping muscle in his cheek and the tight set of his jaw that he was trying to regain control.

"I have a name, you know."

"I know. And no matter what your name is, I'll refer to you as 'girl' whenever the fancy strikes me."

She shut her eyes. She could no longer bear looking at him. He was as handsome as they came. It was a shame really that he had such an annoying personality, and that he was a vampire. If he were human, well...she could actually consider giving into the feelings that overcame her, whenever she was in his presence.

His pace quickened. She looked toward the hill where the majestic castle towered. Twilight had begun to creep across the rugged landscape. She smiled. Now, she knew why he quickened his step.

"Why don't we stay out here and watch the sun rise?"

"Because my dear, I like to ravish my victims at twilight."

Her right eyebrow twitched. She couldn't tell if he was joking or if he was serious. Obviously, he still enjoyed poking fun at their situation. Before she knew it, they were inside of the castle and he was pounding up the steps. With every move he made, her head was jostled.

By the time he got her to her bed, she'd have one splitting headache. He kicked open a door at the far end of the hall. Then, he lunged over the threshold. She didn't like the butterfly sensations that fluttered in her lower abdomen.

Her danger sense finally seemed to be kicking back into high gear. Seeking to stall him, she lifted her hand and slapped him soundly across the cheek. He halted in mid-stride. Then, he simply stared down at her. Something simmered in his eyes. He looked near to the breaking point. She wetted her lips. And then chomped her teeth down on her lower lip, when his eyes sparkled with intent.

Uh, oh. She'd done it again. She had given him what he seemed to be taking as a wordless invitation.

He lowered his head toward hers. She tried to move out of his reach. But in doing so, she only caused him to move forward, toward the rumpled bed.

Her eyes widened. This bed had been slept in. Of all the gall! He had taken her to his bedroom as originally threatened. Her breathing came in ragged gasps. She couldn't seem to delay him. He was bent upon having his sweet revenge upon her.

Just as he captured her mouth with his torturously hot one, she heard him murmur the words, "A kiss at twilight is the sweetest kiss of all."

Chapter Nine

Her lips molded beneath his, and he heard her let out a delightfully arousing moan. He bristled, and then with the fire burning in his ears, he gently lowered her onto the bed. Her eyes were as wide, as he had ever seen them. He could certainly lose himself in their depths. They haunted him with their intensity. She was a woman that was full of soul. And he was a man that had been cursed to lose his.

He halted. What in God's name was he doing? He couldn't do this. Well, there wasn't anything that physically limited him from making mad love to her. But, he still held himself back. He could offer her nothing. And really, when it came right down to it, was he feeling lust or love? He couldn't be sure. It had been a very, very long time since a woman had warmed his bed.

Her eyes darkened. Though he had found their varying shade of color to be disconcerting at first, he now discovered that they were what gave her such alluring character. He watched as she blinked. She waited for him to make the next move. By the way she looked; his searing kiss had rocked her to her very core. Her eyelids became hooded, and a small yawn escaped her mouth.

He should leave.

A saner man would've already fled the bedroom.

But under the current circumstances, he was far from being sane. The blood rushed in his ears, pounding in his chest, and making every muscle in his body twitch with the primal need to make his own. If only...

Her breathy sigh caught him off guard. He moved toward her, and watched her try to shrink away from him.

"Do you actually think I would hurt you?" His voice was soft, yet it sounded as if it came from far away.

Her eyes held his gaze. In that one brief second, he almost felt as if they connected on a higher level. He moved his hands on her body, and felt a rippling shiver dance through her.

"Your kiss surprised me. But with that current glint in your eye, I'm not sure if you want to make love to me, or if you want to eat me."

Her words stung him.

Why was she torturing him so?

He let out a groan that resembled something of a growl. He released her. Then, with sure-footed steps, he backed away from her. The sun was rising, and soon the bedchamber would be filled with light. He had to close the drapes, before it became toasty hot. His thoughts wandered, as he pulled the blackout curtains across.

"I could gobble you up with my eyes, but I assure you I am ever a considerate lover."

The snort she let out made him want to throttle her. Why did he desire her? Why were images of her invading his mind? This was insanity. Reaching his hand out, he picked up the Caithness Glass paperweight that sat on his desk. Without a further thought, he hurled it across the room.

His emotions were about to get the better of him. He was like a caged animal that had just been released. Coming so near to finding a release for the frustration he felt, and then losing it had put him on edge.

She was right. Her experiences that night had taken a toll on her. He could sense her exhaustion. And in that he could also sense a disturbing change in her. Bridget needed to be watched. He would not be dissuaded in having her remain at Sutherland Castle. Come what may, she was a permanent guest, until he found out what she so carefully guarded.

Perhaps, she had done something terribly gruesome in her past. But alas, he couldn't imagine the angel that sat in front of him doing anything beyond muttering a hurtful word. And even then, he'd stake his salvation on the fact that she only said hurtful things to truly spiteful people.

His salvation.

The possibility of it hung over him like a cloud filled with rain. Who exactly was the answer to his prayers? Bridget fulfilled all of the terms of the prophecy, though she had let it slip about her sister. If Bridget truly did have a sister, then she couldn't be the one.

"You must be shattered. You really should go and leave me in peace."

He turned around.

Peace? What right did she have to ask for such a thing? He stalked toward her.

"I'm not leaving you. Call me an ignoramus if you will, but I'd feel much more comfortable staying here and watching you."

Her eyes filled with animosity. But he had become accustomed to such a reaction from her. Instead of giving out a heated rebuttal, she relied upon the age-old silent treatment.

He paced back and forth. Raking his hands through his hair, he began to mutter to himself. Temptation the likes of which he experienced at the moment had to be a mortal sin. Images of his body entangled with hers, made him bite down on his lip. The pulsing in his head began to fall into a steady beat.

Control.

He had to exercise his control. What if Claire was the answer to his prayers? He couldn't grow attached to Bridget only to find out that Claire was his only hope.

No, he wasn't that sort of a man. Balling his hands up into to tight fists, he slammed them down to his side. His eyes drifted to the full-length mirror that he still had present in his bedroom. Swallowing thickly, he traipsed toward it. It was cracked hideously, from where he had punched it all of those years before. Then, his heart stood still. He backed away from the mirror, and slammed into the bed. He was a jumble of quaking nerves.

The hot fire that thrummed through him had nearly been his undoing. If he had wandered any closer to the mirror, Bridget would have discovered his secret.

Almost afraid to turn around, he had to force his feet to do the dirty work. His eyes roved over the length of her body, and rested on her cherubic face. Oh, how he wanted to rain kisses across her brow, her cheeks... he shook his head. His wicked thoughts had to be discarded. Now wasn't the right time to mate.

His body said otherwise, but his mind told him to cool

it. If she was his savior then he couldn't risk inciting her rage. Her eyelids were shut, and her eyeballs moved beneath the almost translucent lids. Her thick dark eyelashes fringed her face and created the most earth shattering vision. His throat grew dry.

He needed sustenance. Yet, he also needed something to ease the clenching in his gut. One more kiss.

It would do no harm.

No invisible boundaries would be disturbed. Everything would be fine. He gradually eased himself toward the bed. Within a few scant moments, he was stretched out beside her. Tenderly, he reached out his index finger and trailed a line from her forehead down to the tip of her nose. In her sleep, she raised her left arm up, and gently rubbed her nose with her hand.

He smiled.

God forgive him.

This woman made him almost forget what sort of a monster he had become. As the word monster ebbed into his psyche he felt his body muscles clench. She had called him a monster. She had made him almost lose control.

He wetted his lips. It had been nothing but a misplaced insult. Bridget had no way of knowing what he was.

Unless...unless she had the second sight. It was rumored that seers could see through his façade, past his thick skin and into his soulless body. That thought made him want to punch his fist into the wall. If she were second sighted, she would have known that danger was coming. And if she knew that danger was coming, the vampires wouldn't have attacked her. He crinkled his brow.

Appearances could always be deceiving. He knew that well enough. But he still craved the feeling of her soft lips pressed against his own. He wanted her. He lowered himself down, and reached for her pliant body. Then, ever so gently, he brought her toward him.

One stolen kiss, after that he'd take his leave and go for his supper. She let out a soft mewing sound. In the next moment, he had claimed her lips. She came alive beneath him and responded in kind. Encircling her arms around him, she began to meet the urgency present in his kiss.

He was in Heaven. He was past the point of no return. If this were to be his only pleasure in three hundred years then he would take it. By all intents and purposes, she now seemed completely willing. They began the mating dance. He was about to start undressing her, when her eyes suddenly snapped open.

In that instant, he felt the blood drain away from his face. Her eyes filled with voracious anger. She seemed about ready to kill him. Even in that short time that she had been asleep, she seemed as if she had regained some of her strength. His arms fell away from her.

Silence nearly sucked him into its unrelenting terror. As if the strength of two hundred mortal men had suddenly surged into her body, she pushed him from the bed. He went hurtling through the air, and actually flipped a few times. With a loud crash he slammed into the wall, and fell to the floor. Pain riddled his body. He tried to push himself up from the floor only to collapse once more.

Now he knew there was more than met the eye to Bridget. She seemed to be filled with superhuman strength. He shook his head, and rubbed the back of his neck. Pain still ebbed through his body. He had to get control of himself. He couldn't let her see the effect she'd had on him. Forcing himself to his knees, he leaned against the wall.

"I told you to stay away from me." Her voice was deadly cold.

He could feel her anger rake down his back, almost as if she had scraped him with her fingernails. He grimaced. One definitely didn't steal a kiss from Bridget and get out in one piece.

"What are you?" he hissed. Pushing himself to his feet, he turned to stare down at her.

"If you ever try to do that again, I can promise you one thing."

The scorching heat that exuded from her eyes transfixed him. He brushed his hand against his forehead.

"And what will you promise me?"

"I'll promise to make the nightmares that haunt you, come true."

Chapter Ten

Bridget was shaken to her very core. She wanted to lunge at him, and stake him through his heart. How dare he presume to take advantage of her? She wanted to turn him into a little toad. But if she did any of that, she would give away her secret. Fixing her eyes on him, she set to calming her laboring breaths.

"What do you know of the nightmares that haunt me?" His voice turned gruff, and his eyes darted all over the room. It was almost as if he didn't want to meet her gaze.

She couldn't blame him really. Sean was a conundrum that she would never be able to figure out. Why would he desire her? For that matter why didn't he just try to bite her? Was he in fact a vampire that was trying to redeem himself? None of it made any sense and she was beginning to give herself a headache the size of Canada. She felt like packing it all in...and going back to Headquarters for another assignment.

"I know a good deal more about you than you probably even know about yourself. We writers tend to be a very intuitive lot."

He grimaced. "How many other things do you hide, Bridie?"

His grimace turned to a sneer. She watched as he began to brush the dirt off of his black leather pants. He turned around, and put his back to her. Licking her lips, she felt her heart skip a beat.

For a vampire, he had one hot ass. She could really...wrenching her thoughts back to the present she resisted the urge to slap her own face.

Shame on her!

Having such sinful thoughts about a creature of the night wasn't something that she'd ever consider. He was working a strange sort of magic on her. It had begun as soon as she'd seen him in the church. However much she tried to deny it, she couldn't shake the feelings that she had for him. It had to happen soon.

The sooner she staked him, and turned him to dust, the better off they'd both be. A faerie could not fall in love with a vampire. It was not to be heard of.

Ludicrous.

But he was awfully good looking. And his eyes. They were so tormented, that she almost found herself wondering about his past. How old was he? And why did he try so damn hard to deny the stirring?

Any of the vampires she had ever had the displeasure of meeting, had always fully embraced their darker side. What drove Sean to try to be a good man? She wanted answers. Before she killed him, she wanted to know his story. No mercy could be had for him, but...perhaps she could at least understand his situation.

He whirled around on her, and locked those intense eyes on her again. She swallowed, and shifted uneasily on the bed. When she'd reacted by throwing him across the room, it had drained what little strength she had. If he tried anything now, she'd have one hell of a struggle on her hands. Soon, she found herself drowning in his eyes. Were they dark cobalt or were they brown?

Dare she inspect them further?

"You never answered my question."

His voice was like velvet. It caressed her skin, and made delightful little tingly sensations run through her.

Stop!

She had to quit fantasizing about him. She had never found a life mate. She wasn't about to get all moony eyed now. When the right time came, she would fall in love with someone of her own kind, or at least someone that possessed a soul.

"I'm very good at alluding men like you."

Something indescribable flickered in his eyes. He bunched his hands into tight fists. He took a step forward. Then, he threw his hands up in the air.

"You lie! And beneath those lies, there is the truth that just might set me free."

She didn't know what he meant. Now he was speaking complete and utter nonsense. He slinked toward

71

her again.

"I'd advise you to keep your distance. You might not want to bite me, but I assure you, I will do whatever it takes to defend myself against you."

He cocked his head to the side. The thing he did next surprised her more then anything else that night. He laughed. His throaty laugh made her shiver from the tip of her head to the tip of her toes.

He surely didn't have a sinister laugh. It almost reminded her of...no. He was a vampire.

He was her enemy.

"Despite what you are, I will not harm you. You are but a defenseless woman. Say what you may, but I do not prey upon the weak."

"What do you prey upon, then?"

Her question caused his eyes to fill with suspicion. "What are you?" Her breathing quickened. In one quick stride, he had made it around the bed, to stand by her side. "I asked you a question and I want an answer!"

"I am a romance novelist." Her short response made the lines in his forehead crinkle.

"I know that. Or at least I did, as of yesterday. What I want to know is who you truly are. What is your true nature?"

This merry go round had gone on long enough. She was sick and tired of his line of questioning. He had no right to demand such things from her. Exhaustion ripped at her being, and here he was still intent upon interrogating her.

"I am merely a woman."

"No woman is just a woman. Even I know that. You're special. And I intend to find out what makes you special."

"Maybe what makes me special should be your clue to leave me alone."

He extended one hand toward her cheek. She was so tired that she couldn't even seem to move her head on the pillow.

"You intrigue me, Bridget Sinclair."

"And here I thought I pissed you off."

His eyes softened, and a hitch formed in her throat. She plastered her lips together. The feeling of his kiss still lingered on her lips. He was a man full of passion.

"How did you find the strength to toss me across the room? You handled me as well as any highland warrior would throw a caber."

"I was filled with a sudden surge of adrenaline."

A smile crinkled the corners of his mouth. "Adrenaline, eh?" She could tell by the tone of his voice that he did not believe her.

"When adrenaline pumps through your veins it fills you with the most unimaginable strength."

"Does it really?" He had dropped to his knees, and he rested his elbows on the bed. Of all the frigging nerve! Why wouldn't he just decide that she was annoying and leave the room? If she were able she would have already fled the room. She wondered where Grace and Orla were. Didn't they live with Sean? Couldn't someone come to her rescue?

The pad of his index finger touched her cheek.

"Your skin is so soft." His eyes bore right into her soul.

She flinched. He caught sight of it and stiffened. His jaw hardened. She watched as a cloudy tempest filled his dark eyes. Jerking away from her, he stood up.

"Hunger gnaws at me. I must eat." With that, he began to walk toward a door that obviously led out not into the hall, but into the next part of his quarters.

Her stomach lurched. At the mention of his hunger, she now felt nauseous. She rolled over, and flattened her head into the pillow. She was dirty, and yet, she didn't have the strength to undress or shower. Yet again, she'd be sleeping in her clothes. Closing her eyes, she heard him begin to mutter. As he left the room, she could've sworn she heard him mutter a few words that would damn him for eternity.

"As long as you're around, my hunger will never be sated."

Chapter Eleven

Sean was in quite the temper. He bashed around in his kitchen as he rifled through his cupboards. He slammed a saucepan down on the stove, and then moved to the fridge. He did need to recharge, aye that was true, but for the moment he couldn't seem to bring himself to even look at the other fridge that held his blood. He stared aimlessly into the fridge and then smiled when his eyes rested on the package of shaven chocolate and the bottles of milk.

Hot chocolate.

Aye, he could do with some of that precious brew. He shut the fridge door, and then moved back over to the stove.

"Is she awake?"

Grace's softly spoken question startled him and as a result, he sloshed some milk onto the hot burner. The scent of burnt milk wafted up to him making his eyes water.

"I don't know." He set his mouth in a grim line, and purposefully averted his niece's gaze. He was still a bit sore at her, and he wasn't really in the mood for another row.

"That's the chocolate I brought back for you from Belgium." Her voice was still soft, and he could feel his insides melting.

He had to give her credit. She still knew how to wrap him around her baby finger. All of the women in his family had been blessed with that annoying talent. How many nieces had he buried over the years? Would he have to endure outliving Orla and Grace as well? The thoughts terrified him.

"Aye. I know."

His curse kept him confined to the area surrounding his village. He had never tried venturing farther, and he didn't know what kind of consequences would await him if he did take on the risk.

He could hear the sound of a chair scraping along the floor as Grace settled herself at his table.

"Mum is still attending to the injured. She looked me over from tip to stern, but it seems like I don't have any marks on me at all. Even those few scars that I had from the Chicken pox are gone. It's the strangest thing she's ever seen...at least that's what she told me. I told her to come up to the castle soon...I'm afraid she's going to run herself ragged. Everyone tried telling her that they're none the worse for wear, but you know mum. Stubborn to a fault when it comes to the health and welfare of this village."

He frowned. A fleeting memory of Grace covered in the blasted pox came to his mind. The milk was almost hot. He reached for the bowl that he had poured the chocolate into.

"I could do with a large cup of that, you know."

He pretended that he didn't hear her, though he knew she'd know better.

"Have you asked Bridget about tonight at all?"

He avoided Grace's question. At the moment, the last person he wanted to dwell on was Bridget.

"Why don't you ask her yourself?" His question came out gruffer than he had expected.

"Oh, I don't think that's necessary."

He raised his left eyebrow. Something didn't sound right in Grace's tone. He reached for the large mugs for the hot chocolate.

"You speak in riddles, Grace." He turned to her after he shut the stove off.

"You really need to have a good long, civilized chat with Bridget." Grace's eyes twinkled.

The little scamp was hiding something, and he'd have it out of her by the time they drank the last drop of the hot chocolate.

"And why is that?" Sean narrowed his gaze.

Grace's eyes widened and she clamped her mouth shut.

"No reason. No reason at all. Why do you think I have a reason? Can't I just play matchmaker for once? I mean...she isn't that bad to look at," Grace mumbled, sipping at the hot chocolate. She winced, and then stuck her tongue out. "Whoa, that's hot!" She dabbed at her mouth.

"Grace I've known you for your whole life. If there's something you need to say then spit it out."

"I can't." She clenched her napkin until her knuckles turned white with the exertion. "I really can't...and nothing you can say will twist it out of me. I just can't!"

"Why not? You know that everything you say to me won't go past these walls."

"I gave my word to someone. You know how much that means to us Sutherlands."

He didn't like the sound of that. "Is this something that I need to know Grace?"

"Well, that depends. Maybe. It depends on how you define the depth of your need." She clenched her eyes shut. "I can't. If I do, that person will know, and let me tell you, I'd rather risk your wrath, that's for sure."

"Grace, if this is something that is going to affect the safety of the village than I need to know. You have to see that's the only right way. Grace, come on...you know it will make you feel better. Whenever you hide something from me or your mother it plays on you...and makes you crazy."

Grace looked up at him. Tears gathered in her eyes, and suddenly he felt like the biggest monster on Earth.

"I want to tell you. I do. I really do. But I can't. She'll never trust me with anything if I betray her in this." So, she'd made a promise to a woman. Well, that certainly eliminated a lot of his suspects. "Uncle Sean, I've never kept anything from you. And this...well, let's just say it's big!"

Sean was beginning to get a throbbing pain behind his eyes. No matter what people might think, vampires were not immune to physical pain. Rather, he wasn't immune to physical pain.

"Grace." His voice came out as the barest of whispers. He loved Grace as if she were his own. He hated to see her in such turmoil. "If you can't tell me then I'll understand."

"So you won't hate me when you finally see the truth?"

76

His heart nearly broke at the plaintive plea in her voice. "I could never hate you. You're one of the brightest lights in my life. My family and the inhabitants of this village are the main factors that keep me sane. You all keep me on the right path. Without your love, I truly would be lost."

"Uncle Sean, why don't you just tell Bridget about the curse?" Grace's inquiry made him nearly spew a mouthful of chocolate out through his nostrils.

"Whatever brought that question on? Bridget can't know about what I am. You know that as well as I do."

"But if she's your salvation, then she needs to know, doesn't she?"

"Grace, we aren't even sure if the answer to the prophecy is Bridget or Claire."

He snapped his head around at the sound of soft footsteps padding across the floor.

"What prophecy?"

He swallowed the last mouthful of his hot chocolate, and met Bridget's gaze.

Chapter Twelve

Bridget met Sean's gaze head on. She would not be dissuaded, this time she would get some answers. There was a prophecy that had been in this village...and she didn't know about it?

The Research Department at Headquarters really wasn't doing their duty.

Of all the nerve!

"Bridget! You look...well you look quite tired. Why don't you come over here and I'll get you a cup of hot chocolate."

Grace's entire face lit up and Bridget couldn't help but smile. She unconsciously licked her lips, at the mention of hot chocolate. It wouldn't be Elvin hot chocolate but it would satisfy her nonetheless. Her bare feet padded across the floor and she sat down in the chair that Grace had pulled out for her.

Sean still stared at her. He closed his eyes. She had the feeling that he was wishing she'd be gone when he opened them back up. He opened his eyes...she stuck her tongue out at him. "What prophecy were you referring to?" She tried to keep her voice at a civil tone, but with him in the room being civil wasn't on her to do list.

"Ever heard the phrase, none of your damn business?"

She flinched. So, they weren't exactly on the best of terms. In the past, she had faced down worse, and she wouldn't allow his asshole attitude to get to her. The little kitchen that he had in his suite actually exuded warmth, which surprised her to no end. It reminded her of one of those homey country kitchens that one found in magazines. It was also impeccably clean. The fridge and stove nearly sparkled. She raised her eyebrow when Grace plunked the steaming cup of hot chocolate down in front of her.

"I hope you like it." Grace's eyes still shone, and her infectious grin spread from ear to ear. She fidgeted in her chair. The tension was so thick between them that it could've been sliced with a knife.

"Uncle Sean, why haven't you ever told her about the prophecy? Why she might be able to use it in one of her books," Grace suggested.

Bridget watched as Sean turned a searing gaze on Grace.

"Bridget is still an outlander. She needn't bother herself with any of our ways."

Grace groaned and rolled her eyes. "Really, Uncle Sean, you have to learn to loosen up a wee bit." Her eyes sparkled, as she leaned her elbows on the table, and rested her chin on her hands.

"Long ago, one of the Sutherland Lords was cursed, by an evil Vampire Sorceress."

This revelation caused Bridget to sit up straighter. She pulled the blanket that she had found in Sean's room tighter around her shoulders. She also wore one of his flannel shirts, since she had grown tired of trying to lie on the bed in her stiff jeans.

"What happened to him?" She pinned her eyes on him.

Sean cleared his throat. "Drink your hot chocolate, and then you should think about going back to bed. You still look as if you're half dead."

Bridget pretended that she hadn't heard him. She didn't know much about this part of Scotland, and in truth she was rather single-minded. When it came to the hunt, she had her mind fixed on one agenda and that usually ate up most of her time.

"I'll decide what's best for me please, and thank you." She gave him a serene smile, which only served to annoy him further.

"Grace, you should go to bed as well. You've had quite a harrowing ordeal tonight. You need to recuperate."

"Oh, uncle. I feel as if I could jump off the walls." Bridget was raising her cup to her lips to take a sip when Grace spoke. Her hands shook and she nearly spilt the hot chocolate all down the front of herself.

"Well, in that case, I wouldn't advise that you try

that." Bridget gave Grace a pointed look. Had she inadvertently passed on some elements of her power to Grace when she'd healed her? The thoughts terrified her. If that were the case, than she'd have to have a good long talk with the younger girl.

Sean was now interested. He looked between the two of them, obviously trying to figure out what was going on.

"Why ever would Grace have to be concerned about bouncing off the walls?"

Grace, on the other hand, actually seemed giddy with anticipation.

"Do you think I'd be able to do what Claire was doing?"

"Okay, hang on. What's going on here?" Sean shook his head and pressed his hands to his temples.

"What is going on is that Grace was telling me about the Sutherland prophecy." She wanted to tell Grace to shut it, but that would only gain Sean's interest. If she did that, he'd definitely know something was up.

"Oh, well, I forgot where I left off." Grace shook her head.

"The lord was cursed by an evil vampire sorceress."

"Oh, now I remember." Grace's eyes gleamed, and she was about to open her mouth when Sean cleared his throat.

"It doesn't matter. That particular Lord is quite dead."

"Aye, but she should know the rest of the prophecy. You know the thing about the woman with the strange eyes." Grace let out a cry of pain. "You didn't have to do that!"

Bridget smothered a smile. By the looks of things, Sean had just kicked Grace beneath the table. This could only mean one thing. Sean wanted Grace to shut up. This in turn, meant that she had to get Grace to tell her everything. It wouldn't be too hard to get her to open up...Grace looked like the sort that loved to chat.

Sean widened his eyes innocently. "Why don't you run along and go and see your mum. Better yet, I'd advise that you retire to your bed."

Grace's mouth was still stretched into that surprised 'o'. She was glaring daggers at Sean, and Bridget was beginning to become uneasy. She didn't exactly want to get stuck in the middle of a family spat.

"I can see that I'm not wanted. Come on, Bridget. I'll get you some night clothes, and you can take a shower in my bathroom."

"Grace, Bridget stays with me."

Grace jerked her body around when she stood up. "You can't be serious? Come on, Uncle Sean. Get with it, would you? Stop joking...okay...you don't look like you're joking. But you can't be serious."

"I am." His eyes glinted stonily.

Bridget laughed. "If you think that for one minute that I'm going to stay here like a good little girl, then you can guess again! I'm out of here." She stood up and put her half finished cup of hot chocolate down on the table.

"You stay with me."

She inhaled the pungent scent of the hot chocolate and sighed. Bridget wanted to punch him. But for now, she didn't seem to possess the strength.

"You don't own me, your lordship! I think I'll be going." She moved toward Grace, and then stopped as something occurred to her. She could hear Grace saying *cursed Sutherland Lord*. Her eyebrows rose, and she leaned onto the table for support.

"You're the cursed lord, aren't you?"

His eyes blazed.

"Bridget. How could you think that? I told you he was cursed a long time ago."

Grace clamped her mouth shut when Sean glared at her. For all intents and purposes, he seemed quite livid. He was paler than usual, and his hold on the hot chocolate mug was beginning to alarm her. If he didn't ease up a bit, his vampire strength would snap it in two. She swallowed past the large lump in her throat, and inhaled deeply. She could sense his trepidation. For some reason, he didn't want her to discover his past. At least she now knew that he had been a vampire for a long time. Furrowing her brows, she sat back down at the table.

"Grace, please leave us alone," Bridget asked in a calm voice.

Grace looked torn. Bridget could instantly tell that Grace hadn't wanted to cause her uncle the pain that currently rolled through him.

So, he was a tortured vampire. Why should she care? It wasn't her job to counsel the creatures that she was sent to vanquish. She closed her hands around her lukewarm hot chocolate cup, and drank down the rest of it in one large swig.

His eyes were riveted on her. She could feel the electricity that crackled between them. In another life, and in another world, maybe they would have been compatible. But as it was, Sean was definitely off limits.

She could see Grace dashing toward her out of the corner of her eye.

"You don't want to stay with him in this foul temper. He can be unpredictable."

"I don't think your uncle's going to try and eat me."

Grace let out a horrific gasp, and pressed her hand over her mouth.

The dangerous look in Sean's eyes intensified.

"I'd warrant you'd give me indigestion anyway." He had no way of knowing that she knew his secret, and yet he rose to the challenge.

She admired that. "Besides, Sean is much older than you. And knowing him, he no doubt believes that he knows much more than you do. So you go and take yourself to bed. I'd be delighted to hear Sean regale me with tales of the Sutherland legacy."

"The only tales you'll be hearing will be the ones where the enigmatic stranger mysteriously disappeared." A shiver ran up and down her spine. "And I can't keep you up. You need your rest." He snaked his hand around her fingers, and squeezed tightly.

She winced. She didn't like him touching her. It made her feel open and vulnerable. Inwardly, she knew that he couldn't sense or read her thoughts as he could with other people, but his dark eyes still made her leery. His eyes seemed to bore straight into her soul. The taste of chocolate lingered in her mouth, and she thought fleetingly of a toothbrush and some toothpaste.

"You can freshen up in my bathroom. I'll go and put some fresh sheets on the bed, and then you can be my guest for as long as you stay here at Sutherland Castle."

"That won't be long."

"Oh, are you leaving tomorrow, then?"

She snorted. The man was impossible. She'd be better off talking to her ass than trying to reason with him.

"Something tells me this village of yours will have need of me in the not so distant future. So, never fear, I'll stick around until that need is resolved."

"I'll just be going," Grace murmured, backing toward the door. She was wringing her hands, and she looked about ready to start pleading with Sean.

"That's good. You go."

At Sean's softly spoken words, Bridget tilted her head to the side, and gave Grace a reassuring smile.

"Are you sure you'll be okay with Uncle Sean?"

She bit her lip. Perhaps Sean's idea of her staying under his nose was a good one. If she did stay near him, she'd be able to keep an eye on him and to make certain that he didn't get up to any of his bad habits.

"Oh, certainly. Something tells me that your Uncle Sean is just as curious about me as I am about him."

Grace still seemed unsure. She was about to speak when Sean gave her look that not only made her shut up, but also made her run to the door. "I'll see you in a few hours." With that, she opened the door and shut it soundly behind her.

"Alone at last." She caught his gaze and held it. He still had his hand resting on hers. "Tell me about this curse and the prophecy, Sean."

"You don't need to know any of it."

She knew that it involved him. He was trying to avoid the subject because it pertained directly to him.

"I need to know what you're hiding."

"I could say the same thing about you. I've already asked you who you really are Bridget, and you avoided me like the Black Death. So I don't think that I owe you anything. If and when you're willing to open up for me, I might be willing to reciprocate."

An uneasy silence fell between them. He pulled his hand away from hers and stood up.

"Fine. Be that way. But know this, Sean Sutherland. I'm going to get right under your skin. Within a few days, you'll be begging me to leave Sutherland Castle. I have no

Marly Mathews

doubt that I'll even have you down on your knees."

"I don't go down on my knees for anyone!" His voice was harsh.

Her gaze dropped to his hands. The stirring called to him once again. He obviously was in need of some sustenance.

"Why do you have two separate fridges?" He turned to look down at her.

"I don't think you need to know that."

Again he was hedging. But she already knew. She grinned, and bit back a reply. She wouldn't give him the satisfaction. She pushed herself to her feet, and wobbled slightly.

"On second thought, perhaps you shouldn't shower."

"No, I'll be fine. That short rest seems to have given me some energy."

"You'll need those wounds attended to."

"What?" She raised her hand to her forehead, and felt the dried and caked blood. Grimacing, she tried to think of a way to get out of the kitchen before he inspected them more closely. It was all for show. They weren't really cuts at all. Without answering, she walked toward the door that led back into the sleeping quarters. She was almost there, when the world in front of her and around her suddenly went black. She instinctively stopped, and swayed slightly. "Damn." She was having yet another blackout. Proving to her that she still was not up to snuff.

"Take my hand."

For a vampire, he certainly was attentive. He must have been watching her like a hawk. As she touched him, she felt that now familiar current that hummed between them. She couldn't see his hand, but she could sense him raising it toward her forehead.

She tried to dodge his hand. His fingers brushed against her skin. Then she heard him intake his breathe when he realized that her skin was not broken, or marred in any way.

"What are you?"

His voice seemed so far away. She looked up into his eyes as her vision began clearing.

"I am the one that has been sent to save this village."

His eyes filled with dawning recognition. In the next

moment, he had swept her up into his arms and covered her mouth with his.

She pushed her hands against his chest, and tried to get out her protestation. He ended the kiss abruptly, and looked into her eyes with confusion shining in his own dark depths.

"Whatever is the matter? You just admitted that you were the savior of this village."

"Aye. I did. But I obviously didn't mean it in the way that you think."

"And what way would that be?"

She bit her lip. Hedging around this question was going to be quite difficult. "Never you mind. The blood on my forehead wasn't from a cut, you idiot. It was from my hands. I must have nicked them when I fell, and when I wiped my brow...well you see where I'm going, don't you?"

His eyes had narrowed to mere slits. Who was she kidding? He wouldn't be able to believe her fabrication any more, than she believed it. She'd never been a good liar. All the more reason to avoid answering questions if at all possible.

"I don't know what sort of games you're up to, but the inhabitants of this village do not take kindly to deception."

She cringed.

"Would you please put me down?"

"I don't know why you are being so close mouthed. What do you think I'll do? Murder you in your sleep?"

If he knew what she was, he'd probably be bloody tempted. How could she admit to a vampire that she was the huntress that had been sent to slay him? Furthermore, how could she explain that his village would soon become a hot bed of vampire activity?

The Faerie Intelligence Task Force had reported that the vampire clans were beginning to fight with each other. Soon, they'd descend upon Sean's village in all of their hellish glory. She had already slain the Queen of a rather large vampire clan. It was only a matter of time before news spread of her death. Last night they'd battled the few members of her clan that had been in the area. Once the news traveled, they'd have a full out war on their hands. She had no way of knowing if her kind knew what sort of a war she faced.

No doubt the other hunters and huntresses were still busy rounding up vampires and other various dark creatures.

She shuddered. If he only knew. She suspected that Sean was small potatoes, when it came to the vampire clan thing. Maybe he didn't even realize that creatures like him banded together to wreak havoc around the world. But whatever he knew needn't concern her. She was sent her for one reason, and that was to kill Sean before he could join a vampire clan and tip the scales of power in their favor.

"You know, if I didn't know better I'd think by that dreamy look you're wearing that you're moony eyed over me."

"Get over yourself, Sean."

The scoff in her voice really didn't cover up her true emotions. God forgive her, but she actually was attracted to Sean. Being near him made goose bumps emerge across her flesh. Not to mention the fact that it was quite the turn on to have someone almost as strong as she was at her beckon call.

"Have it your way then. Be a tight-lipped shrew. I don't give a care what you decide to tell me."

Sighing, she rolled her eyes. She couldn't tell him her real identity. He'd flip.

"You care for Grace, don't you?"

He blinked. "Of course I do. She is my niece after all."

"Yes, but you seem to love her deeply."

"I've watched her grow up. If I didn't care for her, I'd be a heartless wretch, wouldn't I?"

She couldn't seem to figure him out.

"Do you miss your mother and father?"

This question made his eyes fill with fury.

"My parents died a long time ago. Besides, my past isn't any of your business."

"How long ago did they die?" She had a hunch that they'd died a long, long time ago. She wanted to find out how old he was. His age would have a bearing on his strength, and his appeal to the other vampire clans.

"Didn't I just tell you to shut it? My personal life is just that, and I would appreciate it if you kept your nose out of my business."

"Well. Perhaps, somewhere along the line I got the wrong end of the stick. Here I was thinking that I'd be entitled to know a bit more about you, since you've taken me to your bed and all."

"You are more trouble than you're worth, I'll definitely grant you that. I haven't joined you in my bed, so you should thank your lucky stars for that."

She bristled, and he fumed. As always they were getting along just splendidly.

"If you'd be so kind as to put me down, I'd love to take you up on that invitation for a hot shower."

His eyes twinkled. Seeing a vampire's eyes twinkle made her purse her lips. He was just full of surprises. She couldn't exactly say that she was looking forward to the next trick that he had shoved up his sleeve.

"I could join you in that shower."

"Yep, you could. And I could stab you while you sleep."

"I'll stay out here, then." His jaw clenched. Ever so gently, he placed her down on her feet.

"Was your mother pleasant like you, or pleasant like Grace?"

That got him. She smiled. His eyes lost their sparkle as he gritted his teeth together.

"My mother was just like Grace, in every single way, if you must know." He was becoming quite agitated.

"Every single way, eh?"

"Aye. Now you may be a good little girl, and get out of my eyesight before I rethink my opinion of you."

"What's that supposed to mean?"

"If I were you I wouldn't wait around to find out." As she recognized the heated passion in his eyes, she moved as quickly as she could toward the bathroom door. Once she had slept a bit, she'd get up and give herself a tour of Sutherland Castle. If her intuition were right, she'd find a portrait of Sean's mother, which would give her an idea as to Sean's real age.

"I hope I don't see you when I wake up."

"Oh, that I should be so lucky." His sardonic reply made her screw up her face.

"Good night!" She slammed the door in his face.

"Actually, I think you're supposed to say, good *morning!*" His laughter trickled through the door, and made her slam her fist down upon the vanity. She'd definitely enjoy damning him straight to Hell!

Chapter Thirteen

Sean inclined his head as Father Clancy rapped on the door to his sitting room. He unfolded his lanky form from his favorite chair, and walked toward the door.

"It's already open; you didn't need to knock to announce your arrival."

"Even though I know I'm always welcomed here, I still like to use some of the manners my grandmother taught me." Father Clancy's eyes lit up with good humor, and Sean had to clench his teeth to keep from groaning.

"If you're here to rescue Bridget from my clutches, you'll have to come back when I turn into another man, because she's not going anywhere."

"Actually, I came here to see Grace. But I can't seem to find her anywhere. Even Orla doesn't know what she's up to."

"No good, no doubt." He flung himself back down into his chair, and reached for his glass of brandy.

"Ah. Perhaps." Father Clancy's eyes followed him, and Sean fidgeted when he felt the man's eyes boring straight into him.

"I'd offer to go out and search for her, but since the sun is still fairly high in the sky, my hands are a little tied."

"I know. I did see Grace earlier today, but we never got to finish our chat."

Sean frowned. He watched with growing apprehension as Father Clancy rubbed his hands together. The man seemed quite excited about something, and he wanted to know what had gotten his spirits up.

"That's a shame. I assure you Father, when I see Grace I'll tell her to go and visit you straightaway."

"Oh, brilliant."

He expected the priest to leave after that verbal exchange, but instead Father Clancy settled himself down

89

upon Sean's sofa.

"Would you like a drink, Father?"

"A cup of tea would do wonders for me." Father Clancy smiled, and adjusted the pillow that was based at the crook of his back.

Sean didn't like the smile that Father Clancy wore. He hesitantly stood up and walked toward his small kitchen. Turning on the kettle, he began to pull out the tea and the milk.

"What have I done to earn such a pleasure?"

His soft-spoken question made Father Clancy jump, and then he settled back into his old relaxed self.

"Oh, nothing. Nothing at all, I just heard that Bridget was still recuperating from her injuries and I wanted to see if I could be of any assistance."

"Well, actually, she hasn't woken up at all. She's sleeping pretty soundly for being in such a strange place, with such a wickedly strange man."

Father Clancy harrumphed. "I don't think you're strange at all, Sean. Why you are as normal as they come."

"Normal. Aye. Except for the fact that I'm a vampire."

Father Clancy winced. "Aye, you are at that. But your curse turned out to be quite the blessing last night. You fought magnificently. You are a warrior at heart, Sean."

Sean chuckled. "That may well be, Father. Did I ever tell you what I did before I was cursed?"

"Well, come to think of it, I think you might've mentioned that you were in the same vocation as your father. But then I make it a point to never meddle in anyone's affairs."

Sean's thoughts strayed to Bridget. She had been poking her nose where it didn't belong, when she'd asked about his mother.

"I was a warrior. You are right. I certainly followed in my father's footsteps." He paused, as the kettle let out its loud whistle. As soon as he'd warmed the teapot with some boiled water, he moved to toss the tea into the teapot and then filled it up with the rest of the boiled water.

"Then that would explain the undeniable skills that you possess."

"Thank you, Father Clancy." He glanced at the clock, and began timing the minutes to when the tea would be ready to drink. Reaching into the cupboards, he pulled down some of his Aynsley china.

"My father taught me everything that I know." He smiled. He could still remember how his father had taught him to wield both a bow and arrow and a sword. He'd also taught him some other valuable fighting skills that helped him when battling his enemies.

Father Clancy cleared his throat. "I seem to recall the story of your father's last valiant stand."

Sean fought to keep his thought riveted on the here and now. "Aye. He lived as a warrior and died as one. My mother always said that he had a warrior's spirit, and yet he was a good, kind and considerate man."

"Then he showed mercy to his enemy."

"Oh, no. My father never showed mercy to any that stood in his path. You see he only fought..." Sean's voice trailed off as his keen hearing picked up on the rustling of bedcovers coming from his bedchamber.

Bridget was awake. And, if he his suspicions were correct, she'd be up and about soon, trying to eavesdrop on his conversation.

"We'll have to finish this discussion another time."

He arranged the teacups, teapot and plate of scones on his tray before he carried it over to set on the table in front of Father Clancy. Then, without so much as a break in his movements, he was at his bedchamber door. Pressing his ear against the door, he smiled. She'd surely get the shock of her life when he opened the door. Realizing that he couldn't harm her, he cleared his throat loudly, and then pushed the door open.

She stumbled back a few steps. Her hair looked windswept, and her eyes were slightly swollen from her hours of sleep. His nightshirt that she wore was tangled around her long shapely legs. He licked his lips, closing his eyes. Couldn't she learn to cover herself in a more decent manner?

"Good morning."

"Good afternoon." He grinned, watching her

uneasiness.

"I heard the kettle whistling. And then I heard my stomach growl."

If she tried to make excuses for eavesdropping he'd allow her to have her way just this one time.

"I have a plate of scones in my sitting room, if you're interested."

Her eyes lit up, and she was nearly at the door when he reached his arm out for her.

"You might want to don my dressing gown before you go out there. As you can see, I've had your things brought up from the village."

Strangely enough, Bridget's two large pieces of luggage had arrived early that morning. The man driving the cab was not a local, which had made Mary leery. Sean didn't want to think about it at the moment because he had far too many things on his plate. Maybe some day he'd investigate it, but for now, he chose to simply shrug his shoulders and get on with it.

"But since you're so utterly famished you haven't the time to change. So, make yourself decent and then come out to sit with Father Clancy."

"Father Clancy?" Her eyes widened substantially, and her left foot tapped the floor in an agitated manner.

His eyes dropped to the floor, and then ran back up the length of her body.

"Aye. He came to see Grace, but since she's not in residence, he decided to stay and visit me. You see, everyone in this village does not share your opinion of me."

He heard the tone of his voice become colder, and he took no pains to correct it. She had hurt him deeply, and he'd make sure that she knew as much before the night was out. His heart lodged in his throat.

She was a vision to be sure. She almost seemed ethereal to him in her sleepy state. He took a step toward her, and then thought better of it.

"You may hurry along. I'll just be a minute."

He met her gaze one final time before turning on his heel and heading toward the door.

"Sean?" He stopped. "You wouldn't happen to have some jam to put on those scones, would you?"

He rolled his eyes. He had been expecting a much more serious question.

"I'll see what I can find." His terse reply didn't even seem to rub her the wrong way.

"Thank you."

With a muttered growling noise, he walked through the door, and pulled it shut behind him. He didn't know if he wanted to throttle her, or kiss her until he was mindless with his passion. He'd have to see how the day went, and then he'd decide how he really felt about her.

Chapter Fourteen

Smiling, Bridget turned toward the end of the bed and reached for the dressing gown that was draped across the chest. She halted in mid-motion when the scent of heather tickled her nose.

"Come out from where you're hiding." She scanned the room for sign of the hidden faerie. A moment later the sound of fluttering wings filled her ears. "Why have you minimized your size?"

A rainbow streak flashed across her vision. "I was sent to check up on you."

"I know. So, why haven't reinforcements arrived yet?"

"We are preparing our forces for deployment. At the moment, we are still spread rather thin. Summons to other realms have been necessary. The vampire clans are stronger than we originally thought."

"Did my mother and father give you a message to relay to me?" Bridget reached for Sean's dressing gown.

"Your mother sent you this brew, to fortify your spirits." Iris pulled a bottle from the bag that hung on her hip. She dropped it into Bridget's outstretched hands, and it magically grew in size.

"Thank you. Did they send any other message?"

Iris tossed her long hair haughtily. "I am not a messenger woman! In fact, to my utter dismay, I have been ordered to remain here with you. I can't imagine why you'd allow that thing to keep you in his bedchamber. Your parents aren't too happy with the situation, you know." Iris sighed, and then sank down on the dresser in front of Bridget.

"I don't have time to play these weird games with you, Iris. I'm expected out there. You need to tell me everything that Intelligence knows about Sean Sutherland."

"Oh, he's special, that's what he is." Iris grinned, and

her purple eyes flashed merrily.

"Iris, my patience is wearing thin."

Iris's eyes snapped, and her multi-colored wings flapped in agitation.

"I am only following my orders. It seems as if you need to make some discoveries on your own. Certain faeries seem to believe that everything here has been predestined. We can't meddle in that kind of stuff as you well know." Iris brushed some dust off of herself, and Bridget sneezed.

"Iris, why don't you just return to your normal size?"

"I'm on orders to remain inconspicuous."

"You inconspicuous? That's a riot and a half." Bridget snorted.

"If Lord Sutherland saw me, what do you think he'd do?" Iris stood up and placed her hands on her hips.

"Well, at your size he might just eat you."

Iris shuddered.

"That's disgusting. It's either this, or I return to my normal size and remain invisible." Bridget tilted her head to the side.

"Hmmm...give me a moment. I can't seem to decide which way I'd like you better."

Iris huffed indignantly. "You know, I could leave you all alone here, and return to our faerie realm."

"No!" Bridget's genuine alarm broke through her voice.

"Bridget? Are you alright in there?"

Bridged groaned. Father Clancy must have heard her outcry.

"See what you just did?" Bridget muttered, moving toward the door. "You can bloody well stay in here. I don't need Father Clancy thinking that he's seeing things."

"Is Sean out there?" Iris asked.

"Yes." Bridget rocked on her heel, and stared severely down at Iris. "Unless you want me to lock you up in a cookie jar, you'll stay here until I return."

"I'd like to see this reluctant vampire," Iris said, fluttering her wings.

"What do you mean by reluctant vampire?"

"Didn't you know? Silly girl. You really should start doing your research when you take on an assignment.

Haste makes waste, I always say."

"Iris just cut to the chase, please; you're starting to give me a headache."

"Am I?" Iris asked. She raised her eyebrows in feigned innocence. "If you're that under the weather, you should go and drink that brew I brought you. Your mother was quite worried when you decided to heal Grace Sutherland. She said that it would nearly be the undoing of you. She also told me to make certain that you drank that stuff, so hop to it!" Iris turned her attention to the door. "And I'd be really quick, since Sean's getting impatient. If my eyes and senses aren't betraying me he is about to barge in here, again. He's rather rude, isn't he?"

Bridget rushed into action. She picked up the bottle of purple liquid, and popped the seal on it. A sickeningly sweet aroma wafted up to her. Moaning, she pinched her nose shut, and drank the offensive smelling stuff. As soon as she had downed the last drop, the bottle simply disappeared into thin air.

"How do you feel now?"

Bridget couldn't seem to reply to Iris's question. Everything swirled in front of her.

"Sean," she mumbled.

This wasn't right. Her mother would never have given her anything that would cause her harm. She sank down on the side of the bed. Swallowing thickly, she tried to curtail her nerves. She just had to wait for the potion to activate. With a few cleansing breaths, she began to feel a bit better.

"Are you feeling any better?" Iris asked. "I can only delay that vampire for so long with my magic."

"I'm feeling better, yes. For a moment there, I felt quite woozy."

"Ha. That must have been the effect your mother warned me to tell you about. She said that it might make you a bit light headed since you're not full faerie."

"I only have a smidgeon of mortal blood in me."

"For all intents and purposes, it seems to be enough, doesn't it?"

Bridget scowled. "Would you just get lost?"

Iris flew up into the air, and hovered in front of Bridget. "Don't you want your question answered?"

"What?" Then recognition dawned. "Yes, of course. Tell me why Sean is a reluctant vampire."

"Because he's never given into the stirring no matter how loudly it calls to him." With that, Iris floated away out of her line of vision. "I won't be far; you need only call for me. That potion won't restore you to your normal self for at least another few hours, but it sure does beat walking around half dead."

Bridget grimaced. Sometimes Iris really annoyed her. She didn't know why her mother had sent Iris to be her backup until reinforcements could arrive. Iris was a bloody nuisance! She'd never really made it out of huntress training; instead Iris preferred to remain in the land of Faerie, where darkness never fell. If they were to get entangled in another battle with the vampire clans, she didn't know if Iris would be of any help. Fighting always came as too much of an exertion for Iris.

She snapped her head to attention when Sean's booming voice swept through the room.

"Blast and damn woman, you can be a thorn in my side." The door swung back on its hinges. "I've been yelling myself hoarse in there, and Father Clancy was about ready to get a battle axe to take this door out. The bloody thing was jammed, and you sounded as if you were dying a horrible death in here."

Bridget narrowed her eyes. Hard as she tried, she couldn't remember making any noises.

"Iris!" She muttered beneath her breath.

"What did you say?"

"Nothing," she stammered. "I'm ready for that tea now."

"Why is there a rim of purple around your mouth?" He raised his index finger up to her lips, and trailed a circle around her mouth.

She shivered. "I don't know."

His eyes rested on her for a moment. She knew that he knew that she was lying, but for now she didn't want to try to explain anything to him. If she told him she had been talking to a faerie friend, he'd probably laugh her right out of the castle.

He opened his mouth to say something further, and then seemed to think better of it. "You know what? I don't want to know. Not right now anyway. If and when you're ready to tell me, then I'll be an avid listener."

"The same goes for you too, you know. You're going to have to tell me about yourself at some point, Sean."

"I don't have to do anything I don't want to do, Bridget Sinclair!" With that he moved past her, walked out the door, and into his sitting room.

Sighing, she moved to follow him.

For as long as she lived, Sean Sutherland would be the bane of her existence.

Twilight's Kiss

Chapter Fifteen

Sean followed Bridget with his eyes. She looked immensely better, better than when he had seen her when he asked if she'd like to join them for scones. It didn't make any sense whatsoever. How could one woman seem to perk up so much in a matter of minutes? He rested his chin on his hand, and riveted his eyes on Bridget as she settled herself on the sofa next to Father Clancy.

"Ah, my dear girl, you look none the worse for wear." He smiled at her, and a bright flush crept into Bridget's milky white complexion.

Sean remained silent. As far as he was concerned he had nothing to say to Bridget. Until Father Clancy left, he'd be sure to be on his best behavior. Bridget leaned forward, and began preparing herself a plate heaped with two scones, slathered with clotted cream and damson plum jam. Her appetite had returned in full force. He tapped his finger against the bristle on his cheek. He watched in rapt fascination as she took a large bite out of her scone. She chewed like a madwoman and swallowed with deep appreciation.

"After my long sleep, I feel much better."

"Well, you certainly look better," Father Clancy agreed, smiling in approval. "Would you like to ask us some questions about last night?" Father Clancy's eyes glittered, almost as if he was hanging on Bridget's every word. The old man knew something about Bridget, and he seemed absolutely delighted with the revelation. The inhabitants of his village always forgot one thing. He was an expert on human behavior. He had years of experience studying human nature...the best and worst. Whatever Father Clancy knew, it had to be big, and it was something that Sean needed to know.

Bridget's eyes filled with wariness as she dove into

the second scone. She swallowed and reached for her full cup of tea before speaking. After taking a sip, she breathed in deeply and sighed.

"Honestly, no. I've heard of things that go bump in the night before, and I've done quite a lot of research on vampires in relation to my romances."

"I bet you have," Sean muttered, without being able to help himself. Grimacing, he shut his mouth, and kept a watchful eye on Bridget's reaction. She did nothing but narrow her eyes at him. If she wasn't careful, she was going to give herself a rather good pair of crow's feet.

"Well, then perhaps you know a good deal more about their nasty habits than even we do." Father Clancy locked gazes with Sean.

"I doubt that," Sean remarked.

Bridget coughed, and her face turned a bright red. Father Clancy's brow furrowed, and he gave her a good thump on the back. "Better now, my dear?"

"Yes." Her hoarse voice made Sean uneasy. She didn't seem to be in any dire straits but he'd keep an eye on her anyway, in case she started to choke again.

"Father Clancy, I don't think that my expertise in the area of vampires could even come close to the knowledge that this little village possesses. After all, do you not have a council formed for battling the creatures?" Sean sat up straighter. She shouldn't have known that. This side of Bridget was really beginning to annoy him.

"Yes, of course we do." Father Clancy didn't seem the least bit perturbed. In fact he acted as if her statement had been expected. How did she know about the council when it had been Claire that had rescued her from the vampires? Too many things didn't add up.

"Well, then I'd expect that you all know how to hunt vampires. I have no idea what it takes to kill one, save for silver bullets, a nicely sharpened stake or holy water."

Sean began coughing. He hastily put his hand up to his mouth, as his eyes began watering. Bloody hell! What sort of a woman discussed killing vampires as easily as she would chat about tending to her flower garden?

"There are other ways my dear, ways that you no doubt know something about."

Sean cringed. The topic of conversation was

beginning to get to him. He didn't really like to contemplate all the different ways that he could possibly meet his demise.

"The next time that Claire visits the village Father, you can ask her if there are some ways of vanquishing vampires that we know nothing about. Until then, I'd really appreciate it if we could end this discussion.

A small smile tugged at the corners of Bridget's lips. Sean didn't like the look of it one bit.

"Then you wouldn't like to know about how flames can make a vampire go poof?"

"I think that's enough, dear." Father Clancy reached to pat her hand.

"That reminds me, has anyone located my camera and flashlight yet?"

Sean leaned forward. She seemed to be way too concerned about her camera and her torch. Good Lord, the woman's persistence was almost nerve wracking.

"What's the matter, Bridget? Are you hiding some sort of illegal film?"

"Certainly not! I need them because the camera belonged to my mother and the flashlight, well let's just say it has my initials inscribed on it. It too has sentimental value to me."

Sean wasn't buying any of her blatherskite. It seemed to be rather far fetched. He'd bet his money on the fact that Bridget's torch and camera did something else than simply taking photographs or lighting one's way. A normal camera and torch could be easily replaced, even in the secluded out of the way village that they lived in.

"You needn't fret Bridget, my luv. When I find your camera, I'll take a picture of you."

She looked at him with a horrified glint flashing in her eyes.

There. That was the kind of reaction he'd hoped for. Father Clancy didn't seem to notice anything. His expression still looked slightly dotty. For some reason, Father Clancy seemed to be flying high up in the clouds, and Sean didn't think he would be alighting anytime soon. Sean's eyes dropped to Father Clancy's hand. The priest still had his fingers tightly entwined with Bridget's slim and tapered fingers. He watched as Bridget gave

Father Clancy's hand a soft squeeze.

Okay, that was it. He'd seen about enough for one day.

"Father Clancy, I'd expect that Grace might be down in the pub."

"Huh?"

Sean shook his head at Father Clancy's dumbstruck reaction. The man had never been at a loss for words in all of the years that Sean had known him. Father Clancy was still relatively new to the village, but he had been here on assignment for nearly forty years. The Vatican knew of Sean's predicament. They also knew that Sean was a key force in their fight against the darkness that threatened all of humankind. Essentially, Father Clancy had been assigned to not only counsel him, but also lend a helping hand in the good fight. Unfortunately, Father Clancy was getting on in years, and as such a reassignment would soon be required.

Sean hoped that Father Clancy would choose to remain in the village. But the man might very well welcome the chance to retire from the life that he currently led. Vampires were frequently attracted to Sean, and because of this, the village was a nexus of paranormal activity.

"I said that Grace is probably down in the village."

"You don't say?" Father Clancy still seemed to be distracted.

"Aye. I could ring the pub to check and see." Sean stood up.

"No. Son, that won't be necessary. I do believe that a man of my significant age can take and recognize a hint when it is tossed his way. I'll just finish my tea, and go."

"Sean. You're being an awful wretch. You can't just throw Father Clancy out on his ear."

"Oh, I'm not throwing Father Clancy out. He knows that he's always welcome to visit Sutherland Castle just as I know I'll always be welcome to visit him at the church."

"Indeed," Father Clancy muttered, gulping down his tea. "Besides, I do have some rather pressing business to attend to. Tomorrow is Sunday; I must prepare for the coming Sabbath."

"Father, you needn't rush out, just because Sean chose to be rude." Bridget glared at him.

Sean smiled back. He would welcome some time alone with Bridget, and then he needed to gain some sustenance of the physical nature.

Father Clancy put down his teacup and stood up to his formidable height. "Good night my dear. I hope to see you tomorrow. And pray that I do not see you later tonight for various other reasons."

Sean frowned. If any other vampires chose to invade his inner sanctum this eve, he'd be bloody furious!

"Father, you have a good night. And remember, no matter what, I'll always be ready to listen to you."

Father Clancy chuckled. "You'll rethink that offer, my dear, in due time." He winked at her. "Sean." Father Clancy nodded his head at him, and Sean shuffled uneasily. He hadn't meant to offend Father Clancy in any way, but dire times called for dire measures.

"Goodbye, Father, until tomorrow." Sean followed him to the door, even though Bridget remained motionless on the sofa. "Tell me what you found out about Bridget today." His voice dropped to the faintest of whispers. At least Father Clancy's hearing was as keen as it had ever been.

"I can't. My faith and vocation restricts me from breaking the confidence of the person that confessed to me."

Sean pursed his lips, and folded his arms against his chest. "It won't go any further than me."

"Nice try, Sean, but I'm not that dotty yet. I know a trap when I see it. In due course, I think you'll discover what I already know. Go easy on the dear girl; she holds a burden that is much similar to the cross you bear."

Sean snorted. "I doubt that, Father."

"Do not be so quick to doubt my word. Have I ever led you astray before?"

"No, of course not."

"Right, then. Well, I'll be going now. For heavens sake, don't do anything up here that will cause improper gossip down in the village. I would not like it if I were forced to come up here and give you a long lengthy lecture."

"I understand, Father Clancy. Now, go. I'm sure that you'll still want to meet up with Grace."

"Oh. Aye. Grace. I'm off." He smiled again and then left Sean's quarters.

Sighing, Sean turned back around, and stared at an empty room.

Chapter Sixteen

Bridget gasped, and stared down at herself in dumbstruck horror. Sean obviously could not see her, so her suspicions were correct. She hadn't given the mental command to become invisible, which could only mean that the potion her mother had sent for her to drink was wreaking havoc when it came to side effects.

"Bridget?" Sean mumbled.

She watched as he carefully closed the door, and meandered further into the sitting room. She tried to still her breathing, and her eyes widened when she felt something tickling her nose. She was going to sneeze!

Clapping her hands up to her nose, she tried vainly to pinch away the feeling. This wasn't good. If Sean heard her sneeze, he'd be sure to figure out that there was more to her than just being human.

Clamping her mouth tightly shut, she tried to stifle the sneeze. As the spasm of the restrained sneeze worked through her body, she heard a rather loud popping noise. All of Sean's chinaware was blowing up!

No! She put her hands out and tried to keep her magic restrained. But it was to no avail. Tiny rivulets of sparkling light that slightly resembled orbs bounced around the room.

"What in all that is Holy?"

So, that answered her question. Sean could see her powers going wonky. The next thing she knew, Iris fluttered into her field of vision.

"What's the matter with you? You have to stop right now! There is light crashing out of the very crags of this castle. All I can say is that the village is getting quite the light show. Pluck up and control yourself!"

"I can't!" Her head was pounding. No matter how hard she tried, nothing would work.

"Are you doing the normal calming procedures?"

105

"Yes, damn it. That brew that mother made me must have been tampered with...either that or she knew this would happen."

"What are you suggesting, Bridget? Because if you're intimating that your dear mother and my most exalted Queen would deliberately booby trap your drink, then you'd better think again!"

"I'm not speaking against my own mother, Iris. You should know better than that. I know that she'd never dream of hurting me, but maybe she thought that a lesson needed to be taught in order for me to see the bigger picture."

"Well...perhaps. But I think you've just lost your wits. You've become too involved with that big strapping vampire over there. He's gone and muddled your brain."

"Iris. You have to do something! Anything! Whatever happens, Sean can't find out what I am!"

"What should I do? If you want me to stake him, I don't think I can."

Bridget rolled her eyes heavenward. "Oh, my stars! Do you think you could possibly distract him? Anything, do anything! Just get him off my trail. And for goodness sake, transport me magically into the bedroom, in case I become visible right before his very eyes!"

"Done!" Iris snapped her fingers, and in the next moment, Bridget was back in the bedroom lying flat out on the bed. At the next resounding crash that shook the floor, she bolted upright, and dashed toward the door. Slowly, she edged it open a crack, only to see Iris fluttering around the room, right in Sean's line of vision.

She slapped her hand over her mouth before the sound of her laughter could fill the room. The sight of Sean running around the room trying to snatch Iris right out of the air tickled her funny bone to no end. The swirls of rainbow light that trailed behind Iris probably blinded him, and yet he was still trying to catch her.

"Damn firefly."

"Firefly?" Iris's raised voice sounded more like a screech than anything else.

Bridget shut her eyes and grimaced. Sean didn't know what he was in for now that he'd insulted Iris.

"You'll pay for that, Sean Sutherland!"

Sean stopped dead in his tracks, and dropped the pot that he held. "I'm hearing voices now. I knew that Bridget would get to me sooner or later."

Bridget let out a shocked gasp. Why that no good idiot! She'd show him a thing or two. She bounded out into the room, and caused Iris to stop with her hand in mid-air.

"Uh, oh," Iris muttered, her eyes as wide as saucers. Iris and she connected gazes.

Then, Bridget's eyes dropped down to scan the length of her body. She gulped. Instead of seeing Sean's burgundy dressing gown, she was instead clad in her Claire regalia.

"Claire!" Sean's eyes nearly popped out of his head.

"Uh...hello."

Iris seemingly sensed that the time had come for her to find sanctuary over by Bridget.

"Nice touch," Iris murmured.

"I didn't consciously do this!"

"Well...now things might start to get really interesting."

"Do you know that thing that's flying behind you, Claire?" Bridget stiffened. She really didn't like the way that Sean had said *thing*.

"Iris isn't a thing. She's a faerie. And you'd do well to show her some respect!"

Sean dropped his jaw. She noticed with satisfaction the nervous bob of his Adams Apple.

"Faerie?" He looked even paler than usual.

"Aye. A faerie. One of the Little People, or Gentry, or Sidhe..."

"Aye. You can cease your blathering. I get the idea." He waved his hand impatiently in the air.

Iris tapped her lightly on the shoulder and then settled down on her shoulder.

"You may call me Lady Iris, vampire."

Sean didn't seem to like the tone in Iris's voice. "Iris..." Bridget warned.

"You tell him to call me my lady, or Lady Iris, or I will let your real identity slip."

"You wouldn't dare. Do you forget who I am?"

"Oh, of course I remember your true identity. But

you're only my princess when your name's Bridget, as far as I'm concerned."

"I should throttle you when we're alone together, you know."

"Perhaps. But you won't."

Bridget sighed, and then directed her attention to Sean.

"Sean, you must show this noble faerie some respect. Or else I can't promise what I'll do to you."

He glared daggers right through her. She laughed. Her sultry laugh traveled through the room, and changed the stony expression on Sean's face.

"Lady Iris," he said, bowing.

"That's more like it," Iris said, clapping her hands together in delight. "I'd like some cake now."

"Beg your pardon?" Sean's eyes widened.

Bridget grimaced. Why did Iris always have to push people?

"You're excused," Iris quipped.

"Iris. Shut your trap!" Bridget hissed.

"I can't. I'm having far too much fun!"

"Cake? My ears must deceive me," Sean said, shaking his head.

"Oh. That's right. Hospitality isn't a strong suit of yours, is it?" Iris remarked, as her voice tinkled throughout the room.

"Iris is talking rubbish. We're going to leave now," Bridget said, backing toward the door. Now was her chance. If she didn't take advantage of it, she'd be stuck with Sean.

"No, I'm not going anywhere. I've been told to stay at Sutherland Castle for the time being," Iris argued, staring up at her with mischievous eyes. "And you know I always do what I'm told."

Bridget narrowed her gaze. Iris grinned.

"No faeries are laying siege to my castle. Not while there's breath in my body."

Bridget watched with trepidation as Iris opened her mouth to respond. In one swift movement, she'd snatched Iris up, and cradled her in the palm of her hands.

"If I enlarged myself right now, the joke would be on you," Iris mumbled.

A strange sensation rolled over Bridget again. She had to get out of here before Sean saw her do something that would lead him to figuring out that she was both Claire and Bridget.

She raced toward the door. Without so much as a goodbye, she had darted out into the hall. "Okay, Iris. Now I'm going to get angry."

"You know, he might decide to pursue you. I think he's rather fond of you. The problem he's having right now is trying to decide which personality he fancies more. You or Bridget."

"I am Bridget."

"I know that and you know that, but right now he doesn't have a clue. Come to think of it, I'm not sure he's got a clue about anything."

"Iris, I don't have time for this. You have to scoot along, and get out of here before Sean comes out and finds us."

"I'm not leaving until I receive the order directly from your mother. So there," Iris said, slanting her mouth into a pout and crossing her arms over her chest. "I'll just tell Sean that Claire left me here to keep an eye on him. You're going to need me in the near future you know. And besides, I can help you until you regain control over your powers. Don't look now; dear, but you've become Bridget again." Iris sighed.

"Oh, no!"

"He's coming. I'm going to pop back inside there. I'll see you in a few minutes, Princess."

With that, Iris magically disappeared.

Sean wrenched open the door, and stared at her openmouthed for a few seconds.

"How did you get out here?"

"I don't know. I must have..."

"That faerie witch must've put you out here. Get back in here; you still don't look so good."

That was an understatement. She actually felt quite lousy. Here she was a faerie that had wayward powers. If the vamps attacked anytime soon, she'd be as useful as a leprechaun without his pot of gold. Sighing, she allowed him to touch her arm, and guide her back into the room.

"Sean, I'm fine. You don't need to get all mushy on

me. You're beginning to worry me. What did I ever do to get your sympathy?"

"I need to talk to someone that's normal, that's all."

"Me normal? Well then, buster, you're looking in the wrong place. Why don't you go down to the village and see Father Clancy?"

Sean tossed his head toward the window.

"It's still daylight." Then, he stopped suddenly. Obviously he'd just realized his blunder.

"Are you afraid of the daylight?" She smiled at his frustrated groan.

"No, of course not."

"Then, why don't you go and visit him now?"

"Because I want to stay here with you."

"Sean, oh be still my heart. I didn't think you felt that way."

"Actually, you still need to answer some of my questions."

"Goodness, you're like a dog with a bone, aren't you? You just clamp on, and hang onto something until you get your own way."

He looked down at her.

"Well...truthfully, I've never heard it put that way before." He smiled. So, the man did have a sense of humor after all.

Would wonders never cease!

Her stomach let out a loud grumble.

"Still hungry?" He glanced down at her midriff.

"I am," Iris called out cheerily, waving to them from the picture frame above the sofa.

Sean looked horrified. Bridget knew that she had to feign her surprise.

"I've heard of the Little People but I never dreamt that you'd have one as a roommate, Sean Sutherland." If only she had a camera to take a picture of the stunned look Sean wore. She stifled a chuckle.

He stared between them. "I...actually..."

"I've sort of decided to take up squatters rights," Iris said, chuckling softly. "But now that we're on the topic of food, I'm quite famished. I could go for a..."

"No one cares about what you'd like to eat, you little imp."

110

Bridget's eyes flew to Iris's face. Iris would consider the moniker 'imp' to be an insult. Briefly, she closed her eyes, and held her breath.

"FAERIE!" Iris clarified, accentuating her word as if she believed that Sean had suddenly gone daft.

"I could make you a steak, since I'm hankering after one." He offered, unaffected by Iris's somewhat irate reaction to his slanderous word.

Bridget shook her head. "Actually, the only thing I think I could possibly stomach at the moment would be some eggs." Her belly let out a loud gurgle. She actually felt a bit unsteady or topsy-turvy as her old friend Garrett would say.

"I could whip you up a cheese omelet."

Bridget didn't like the way that he was trying to be so accommodating. She almost wondered if Iris had sprinkled him with some pixie dust. She carried the mood altering magical stuff around in a pouch on her hip.

"That would be...nice."

"Grand. I'll get right to it." He strode toward the kitchen.

Inconspicuously, Bridget sidled over toward the picture frame.

"Did you blast him with some pixie dust?"

"No. Of course not! He seems to be happy, because he likes you. Fancy that, a genuinely happy and harmless vampire. Well, I never dreamt I'd see the day!" Iris said, swinging her legs. "And look! He cooks too! I think you've made the man lovesick. Did you notice the way he looks at you? He looked like he wanted to gobble you up with his eyes. Oh, this assignment is just too much fun!" Iris clapped her hands together. She was almost giddy with excitement.

Bridget sighed, and sank down into the plush sofa.

Her eyes fixed on his bottom as he moved about the kitchen. Why did he have to be a vampire? He seemed to be perfect in every other way. Well...there was his volatile temper, but she could deal with that. He'd never really lashed out at her in full terrifying glory anyway.

"Do you think your mother sent me to chaperone you two?"

She snapped her head up. "Of course not! Mama

111

knows how important my job is to me."

"She also noticed how wickedly handsome that vampire of yours is. Why, if she weren't so in love with your father, she'd probably already be here to gain a closer look at Sean. You know, if I am meant to be your chaperone, I'll have to watch you morning, noon and night...the way that he looks at you; he'll be sullying your honor before you can say faerie cake. Now that I think of it, I probably am here to protect your honor...if the court ever heard that you had been having some hanky panky with a vampire...well, that would certainly make the scandal sheets."

"He's a vampire. I'll have to stake him eventually. That's my job. It's my vocation in life."

"That's a shame. A crying shame. Such a good looking man, wasted."

Bridget watched as Sean plunked his steak into the pan. Only a few moments passed by before he pulled it out, and placed it dripping juices and blood onto a plate. Her stomach rolled.

"Please, tell me I don't have to watch him eat that." Her stomach gurgled.

"I'm afraid so, Princess. Maybe you should close your eyes while you eat that omelet?" Iris suggested helpfully.

"I think I'll just whip up my own food." Within a blink of an eye, Iris held a picnic basket heaped with food. "Tally ho!"

"I hate you." Bridget was tempted to conjure up her own food.

As if sensing her thoughts, Iris clucked her tongue in warning.

"I wouldn't do that if I were you, not with your powers on the blink. If you sent for chicken, you just might get the feathered and alive type."

"Iris, don't you have someplace to go?"

"Now that you mention it, the pub down in the village did look awfully attractive. I think I'll go and have a look see. Do you think they'll have any scrumptiously umptious men down there?"

"Iris, don't you stir up any trouble down there."

"Little old me?" She batted her eyelashes innocently. "If I didn't know better I'd think you'd just called me a troublemaker. I only make trouble for people I don't like. Fortunately, you don't fall into that category. Come to think of it, you should be thanking me for leaving. I'm giving you some precious time with that delicious looking man."

"Vampire."

"Aye. But by the looks of it, he's still in every way a man. Oh, what a manly man." Iris winked at her, and then in a flash of rainbow colored light, she vanished.

"The food is ready," Sean called.

Groaning, she stood up and arched her back. And now, the fun began.

"Oh, happy joy," she grumbled.

Chapter Seventeen

Sean still couldn't quite believe what had transpired between him and that faerie. No one in the village would believe that a member of the Little People had taken up residence in his castle. They would definitely think that he had gone barking mad.

Popping the last piece of steak into his mouth, he smiled. A contented feeling coursed through him. For the time being, his craving for blood had been sated. But there was still his craving for Bridget that he had to conquer. She looked all ruffled, and very attractive. In fact, he had never dreamt that a woman in such utter disarray could stir his blood so much. She had finished the last bite of her eggs, and had turned her attention to regarding him thoughtfully.

"Don't you want to tell me just a teensy bit about your past?"

"I've already told you, no." His gruff tone belied the pounding of his heart.

"If you tell me something I'd be willing to tell you something," She offered.

He brightened up. So, this was the catch she had been referring to earlier.

"My mother loved her gardens."

"Is that all?" She leaned forward on the table, and rested her head in her hands. "That really wasn't worth it you know." Wrinkling her brow, she sighed.

"Well, you'll have to take what you can get."

"Which isn't much. You skimp on almost everything."

"What is that supposed to mean?"

"Well, the eggs were good, but they weren't nearly enough."

"I'll make you some more."

"No. I'm fine. Watching you eat that bloody steak really didn't do anything for my appetite."

Sean folded his napkin, and slammed it down on the table.

"I'll keep that in mind. The next time I have a nice rare juicy steak, I'll make sure you're nowhere in the vicinity."

"Thank you." She reached her hand out, and had almost curled her fingers around his hand, when he jerked it away. "Why do you eat your steak that rare anyway? I can just imagine how healthy that is." She looked utterly disgusted.

"I've had a thing for them, for a very long time." He closed his eyes.

Usually, a rare steak would pacify his craving, and sometimes it lengthened the times between his feedings. If she thought eating rare steak was vulgar, then she would be absolutely horrified to learn that he had to drink bottles of animal blood. Her eyes roamed across his face, almost as if she were trying to read his thoughts. He stood up. Suddenly, he wanted to put some distance between them. Glancing up at the clock, he let out a low whistle.

"Where did the time go? I have to mosey down to the pub. I have an appointment to keep."

"Oh." If he didn't know better he would have thought that she was disappointed. "I could come with you. Perhaps I'll locate my missing torch and camera."

A slow small grin worked across his features. He let her comment pass, because he didn't have the heart to point out that she had just referred to her flashlight as a torch.

"Will you be comfortable here alone?"

"Alone? And here I thought I'd have your family ghosts to keep me company." Her good-natured approach to life was gradually returning. Somehow, someway, they were finding a way to get along. That was a miracle to be thankful for.

"I don't believe that there is much ghostly activity here in this castle. Most of my family members were fortunate enough to pass onto to the glorious hereafter. But then, some of us were cursed to roam this earth for what seems to be eons."

"You talk as if you've experienced it first hand."

Her remark jarred him, and hit him down to his very

Marly Mathews

core. Perhaps she was more insightful than he had originally given her credit for.

Clearing his throat, he grimaced. "Sometimes, my life does seem difficult." He struggled to get that last word out.

"Yes. You must have an awful time coping with your responsibility. After all, you can hardly live the life of a swinging bachelor."

"Aye."

"How long have the vampires been visiting your village?"

Their conversation had gone on long enough. Her attempt to ease her way into this territory caused him to get his guard up.

"For as long as I can remember. But this is none of your concern. You'll be leaving this village in three days time."

"Oh, no I won't."

"But you were only booked into the B&B for five days. I checked."

She smiled. "Yes. That doesn't surprise me. You never fail to make sure that you know almost everything. Actually, I was intending to buy that cottage on the edge of the village."

He furrowed his brow. The old healer Lavinia Nelson had lived there for forty years. She had been taken down last summer by a rogue vampire.

"Oh."

Then he thought of another way to dissuade her.

"I own that land. That means I control that land."

"But the cottage is for sale."

"Is it? I'll have to contact the estate agent, and tell them, that I've reconsidered. I was going to sell the cottage, and the property that surrounds it, but you know what? I think it should remain in control of the Sutherlands."

"You're a dirty bastard."

"I know." He held her gaze, and then just to infuriate her further, he winked.

She let out a frustrated oath and jumped to her feet.

"I think you should follow through on your earlier promise, and go and take your ass down to the village.

116

They can have the sheer pleasure of your company for a few hours."

"Fine. I will." He moved to the door. "If you get a headache, you might like to rest. Take a load off." He smiled, and then left his quarters.

He jogged through the hall down the steps, and out into the front entryway. Twilight was creeping across the landscape, but he still didn't want to take any chances. He reached for his dark cloak, and whisked it around his shoulders. Then, he headed for the tunnels that led down to the village.

It didn't take him long to reach the pub. As he stepped into the pub, he pushed his hood off of his head.

"Uncle Sean!" Grace called, waving to him from their table. "I thought you'd never get here," she murmured, as he came toward the people that were gathered around Grace.

"What's going on?"

"The Council decided to have an emergency meeting. Ridley received a phone call a while ago from Father Munroe. He called to warn us of an impending attack." Grace's eyes widened, and she clenched her knuckles so tightly that they had turned pure white.

"Attack? Didn't anyone tell him that it was a little late for the warning? We've already been attacked."

"Sean, I don't think you get the gist of what Grace here is saying." Father Clancy's brow was furrowed, and each and every line in his forehead was visible. "This warning is about another impending battle. They're trying to assemble a team of reinforcements, but they don't know if they can spare them. Vampire attacks are on the rise. Trouble is brewing, to an almost catastrophic proportion, and that trouble is coming to our doorstep."

"Bollocks!"

"No, Sean. It's true. This came through that new fangled fax machine that Ridley bought over an hour ago." Mary sat down on the empty chair beside him and handed him the sheet of paper she held in her hands. He scanned the message quickly.

"Shit!"

"My sentiments exactly," Father Clancy murmured, reaching for his glass of whisky. "We've all been trying to digest the news. It's an impossible force to go up against. If those numbers are accurate, we don't stand a chance."

"Aye. Not even if Claire emerges again, which I know she will," Grace added.

"How can headquarters expect us to go up against this?" He threw the paper on the table, and grunted.

"Father Aidan and Father McNeil are on their way as we speak." Father Clancy reached for his whisky glass again, and downed the last of the swirling liquid.

"As are Sister Agnes and Sister Mary Clarence. Let us pray that they get here on time," Mary murmured.

"Four people? That's hardly enough." He pushed his chair up, and stood. Things didn't look good. If he thought that he had a problem on his hands with his feelings toward Bridget, then he could think again. Now, he had the weight of keeping his entire village alive.

He heard Father Clancy's familiar gait. "I also talked to Father Monroe. Our sources seem to believe that one of the vampire clans is coming for you." A shiver ran up and down his spine.

"Bullshit!"

"But we should take that into consideration. Maybe you should make yourself scarce when they arrive. The villagers and I will do everything in our power to keep them at bay. Remember, we have the daylight on our side."

"Aye. And the days are getting shorter as the time goes by. No. I will not run from them. I've never run from anything in my life, and I'm not about to start now. Besides, where would I go? You know as well as I do that the curse keeps me from leaving Sutherland land."

"I'm sorry for that." Father Clancy's face fell.

"Have heart, Father Clancy," he said, slapping his hand on the older man's shoulder. "You've been at my side for years, keeping the darkness at bay. I won't allow the clans to get this village. This is *my* village."

"What if you're seduced?"

"Do you honestly believe that they could tempt me into betraying my values, and my beliefs?"

"Temptation is a hideous monster."

"Aye. And some would say I am a monster. I think we're pretty evenly matched, wouldn't you agree? I have

118

some thoughts on how we should set up defenses. It might take the entire night, but we don't have much time to prepare. I think we should gather the entire village together and transplant them to Castle Sutherland. It will be safer there. We can buckle down for an all out siege."

"Siege? You make this sound as if we're on the brink of war." Father Clancy shook his head, and wiped his spectacles with his handkerchief. Positioning them back on his nose, he turned his blue eyes on Sean.

"We aren't on the brink; we're already past the line of no return."

"I don't know about your idea, Sean." Father Clancy frowned.

"Actually, I think it's a pretty good one." All heads in the pub turned to stare at the person that had voiced that. Sean didn't need to look, but he did anyway. He already knew the voice.

It haunted him. It was Claire, but this time she'd brought along company.

"Hello!" A life-sized version of Iris waved exuberantly.

Claire walked slowly toward him. If he wasn't mistaken he could have sworn that she looked unusually pale. As Ridley had said during the battle, her glamour seemed somehow dimmed.

"Claire! We thought you'd never get here," Grace said, bounding toward them.

"It's good to see you, Grace." Grace boldly put her hand out, and touched Claire on the shoulder. Claire didn't even start. Sean couldn't understand their familiar interaction. Yet another mystery for him to solve, they seemed to be piling on top of each other. Sure, Claire had saved Grace's life, but their personal interaction had been kept to a bare minimum.

"Aren't you going to introduce me?" Iris interjected, staring at Claire in impatient expectation.

"Of course, this is Lady Iris. We both hail from the land..."

"Of Faerie. We know," Mary murmured, staring in adoration at Iris.

Sean couldn't understand Mary's reaction. Sure, Iris

was a sight to behold, but couldn't everyone see that Bridget's beauty far surpassed that of Claire and Iris put together?

He groaned. And nearly slapped his head. Why in all that was good and glorious did his thought always stray back to Bridget? Claire could very well be the one sent to break his curse, and yet his heart yearned for Bridget. As if she sensed that he was thinking about her, Claire pinned her glorious eyes on him. He hadn't noticed before how peculiarly close they were to Bridget's. They sparkled with the same animated life.

Curious. What was even more curious was the way that she looked at him. It was as if she knew him inside and out. He swallowed, and moved away from them toward the back of the pub.

"We have come to aid you all in your fight against the army that is coming this way. First off, the vampires will begin to fight amongst themselves, and then when they grow weary of that, alliances will be forged, and the time will come for them to take their wrath out on everyone in this village."

"We are not afraid," Ridley spoke up, and valiantly held up the stake he held in his hands.

"Everyone is afraid. It is how we deal with that fear that truly counts." Claire smiled, and stretched out her hands. "My kind is at this moment sending out reinforcements, but they will not arrive for a while. Therefore, we must go to great pains to make sure that we are as prepared as we can be."

A keening wail ripped through the pub, and struck everyone silent.

"What was that?" Mary asked. Her face was blotchy, which indicated that her nerves were up.

Sean looked around. They had no weapons. He watched as Claire moved to the window.

"Everyone remain still. It could be naught but a banshee."

"And that's supposed to make me feel better?" Mary shivered. "Death is near, if that's a banshee."

"Shush!" Claire murmured, holding her hand up.

In the next moment, everyone seemed to regain his or her composure. Then, in what seemed to be a millisecond, the same keening wail filled Sean's ears. He moved toward Claire. Whatever was out there was perilously close. He was just about to reach out to pull Claire away from the window, when shards of breaking glass flew into the pub. He raised his hand to shield his vision from the broken glass.

As he lowered his arm, he saw a sight that made his heart cease to beat. A hand reached in through the open window, and latched onto Claire's shoulder. In the next moment, she had been pulled from the pub. Without thinking, Sean rushed to the door.

Ripping it open, he stuck his head out, and was meant with the coldest pair of eyes that he had ever seen. Mass chaos had engulfed the pub. If Father Clancy was thinking properly, he would already be leading the villagers to the tunnels, so that they could make their way onward to Sutherland Castle and then on toward the armory.

"Greetings, Sean Sutherland," the vampire witch murmured. "Allow me to introduce myself. My name is Queen Catherine."

He looked toward Claire. She seemed none the worse for wear. He didn't know where Iris had gotten off to, but he could only pray that she had a trick hidden up her sleeve that could get them out of this predicament.

"I do not believe you understand how fortuitous our meeting is." Catherine held her manicured hand out for him to take.

He stepped back. As far as he was concerned, he wanted Catherine as far away from him as was possible.

"Why don't you shove it?" He should have brought along his supplies. Hell, he'd give an eyetooth for his claymore right now, because if he had it, he could simply lop off their heads. The idea was a very agreeable one to him, since he knew that Catherine and her posse would show them no mercy.

"Ah. Your reputation has not disappointed me. I see that now. You will however be very interested when I tell you the next part of why I have come."

"And why have you come?"

"I've come for you." Her words pierced right through his skin, and caused his stomach to roll. "You are the man

121

I have chosen to become my husband."

"Well, I must respectfully decline."

"No one says no to me, and lives to see another night. I know you can be persuaded." She moved toward him. She moved like the snake she was. He couldn't do anything, for fear of getting Claire killed. Could faeries be killed? He didn't know. He really should have paid more attention to Ridley, when he used to go into great lengths about the powers of the Sidhe.

He would definitely need a miracle in order to save his hide from this bitch.

Chapter Eighteen

Bridget closed her eyes. She really wanted to jump into action, but she was still giving Iris some time to prove herself. Hopefully her friend would mount a distraction big enough to give her the time she needed to deal with Catherine and her horde. She still felt unusually sluggish. But since Sean didn't have a stake to his name, she'd have to save the night.

Figured.

"Iris," she called out mentally. "Give me a great big rainbow."

Sean looked pointedly at her. If he thought she had a plan, then he'd better think again. Right now, all she wanted to do was go back to Sutherland Castle, and crawl into bed. His eyes widened, and he tried to mouth something to her. Problem was, she wasn't all that great at reading lips.

Sparkles of light started to envelop the landscape. She smiled. Now all she needed was for Iris to light up the night sky, and then she could go about her own business.

"Actually, I'm a fairly determined kind of fellow." Sean smiled, and then looked at her again.

Okay. So she normally saved the day. But right now, she was at the disadvantage. In her weakened state, she needed some help to take out the bad blood suckers.

"Well, in that case, perhaps I can use this lovely...faerie is it?" Bridget wrinkled her brow. She didn't like the way that Catherine licked her lips.

Come on, you bitch. Just try to suck the life out of me, she mentally intoned. If Catherine did try to have a feeding, well, she'd get one hell of a surprise. Bridget tried to wriggle out of the young vampire's grip. He bared his teeth at her, and she cringed.

"You know what; you really should go and see a dentist. And maybe this time, you could try leaving him alive afterward. And, you could also buy some breath mints." The vampire hissed in response and she shrugged her shoulders. "You really should tell me your name, so that when I kill you, I can mark your name in my records."

"Kill?" Catherine turned her attention to her. "Tell me, how does one kill a magical creature such as yourself?"

"Well, I can tell you one thing. We don't die from getting a wooden stake through our heart." She smiled serenely at Catherine.

"You are quite the mouthy little faerie aren't you?"

"I try." She smiled, and finally managed to rip her hand out of the one vampire's grasp. She gasped when she finally caught sight of Iris's familiar rainbow streak.

Thank the heavenly stars that she hadn't abandoned them. Bridget could hear voices in the distance. She licked her lips. They were human voices. Obviously Father Clancy had gotten the villagers up to the castle, and they were now coming back fully armed, and prepared for battle. She had to give them credit. They were impossibly brave for mortals. With one loud resounding crackle that shook the very ground, Iris lit up the sky with thousands of exploding fireworks. They were multi-colored and the light nearly blinded her.

The vampires began to shriek in agony. Her heart leapt when Sean grimaced. Dear Lord, he was in pain as well. For some weird reason, she felt for him. Her heart actually went out to him.

She elbowed the last remaining vampire that still managed to cling to her. He grunted in pain, and fell to his knees. Then, in the same fluid motion, she summoned her Elvin blade. The sword that had been dubbed Ceridwen hummed in her hands. She skewered the fallen vampire. He let out a bloodcurdling wail as he burst into flames and then his ashes sprinkled upon the ground.

"Now, then. Who's next?" she asked, turning to the remaining vampires.

Sean struggled to remain upright. His valor impressed her. Alarm rang through her when she noticed Catherine moving toward him. Inexplicably, Catherine was barely managing to hold her own against Iris's light.

Bridget took a few precious seconds to star up at the heavens. Iris hovered high in the sky. Her lavender colored hair billowed around her, and her rainbow colored wings were outstretched, and looked as if their tips were touching the stars in the sky.

Iris was magnificent.

Wrenching her attention back to the spectacle that unfolded before her, she dashed toward Sean when Catherine clamped her hand onto his shoulder.

"No, let me go." Beads of sweat glistened across his brow. His teeth were chewing on his lower lip.

"Sean, you needn't fear. Iris's light is not intended to cause you harm." She met his gaze, and nodded toward Catherine.

Recognition dawned in his eyes. The other vampires backed off, but they seemed reluctant to leave their new queen.

She trudged toward Sean, and took down any of the vampires that moved to block her path. Her strength was ebbing. It seemed to be pouring out of her, as if she had an open wound and she was gushing blood. She swallowed, and swayed when her vision doubled. She couldn't lose control. If she passed out now, Sean would be doomed. For the life of her, she couldn't figure out why he wasn't putting up a good fight.

"I deserve to die." Sean's softly spoken admission hit her like a punch in the gut.

What?

Whatever he was thinking of had to go. He definitely needed to get himself a new attitude.

"Hey, I spared your sorry ass thus far, and you have to repay me by staying alive."

"Do not listen to the little faerie witch. You shall feel much better once you align yourself with my clan, and become my lover. You need a woman in your bed. I can see it in your eyes. The hunger is there. And if you think the stirring is hard to resist, then fighting the call to bond with another of your kind is much harder to defeat." Catherine's voice sent a chill down Bridget's back.

"Don't listen to her, Sean. She's trying to brainwash you. She needs your strength in order to become dominant among the other clans. She wants to rule the proverbial roost. Don't throw everything away by giving into her. If you do, I'll be forced to vanquish you. I can't afford to lose such an old and powerful vampire such as you to the dark side."

"Come to me, Sean, and I will show and give you pleasures that you can only dream of." Catherine had her fingers under his chin, and she turned his face so that he would stare up into her eyes.

"Don't meet her gaze. She'll mesmerize you!" Bridget tried to move quicker, but even Ceridwen began to feel heavy in her grip.

"Must fight it!" Sean struggled to his feet.

"That's it, Sean." Hope flared in her heart. She fell to her knees as her another dizzy spell overcame her. Plunging Ceridwen into the cobblestones, she leaned on her blade for support.

She was so tired! If only she could fall asleep for just a few minutes. Drowsiness tore at her very being. She looked to the night sky, and felt the tingle of Iris's thoughts brushing against her mind.

So tired.

She could sense the two vampires that remained lunging toward her. But she could do nothing. Her magic would not respond to any of her commands. She was a Huntress of Hell, and yet her strength had abandoned her in her darkest hour.

"Bridget!" Iris's voice ripped through her haze.

She looked up. Two of Iris's fireballs arced toward her. They were large. Iris had evidently overestimated the size. If they struck the ground they would take out not only the two male vampires, but Sean and Catherine as well. She couldn't be killed by faerie fire. But Sean, well he would perish.

"No!" She didn't know why. She couldn't explain what motivated her.

Keep the villagers at a safe distance. She prayed that Iris would hear her mental plea. Summoning strength from out of nowhere, she pushed herself to her feet, and pulled her sword out of the ground. She sheathed it at her side, and propelled herself toward Sean. She pushed him to the ground, and without another further thought, she managed to wrap her long faerie wings around him.

"What's going on?"

"Stay still." Out of the corner of her eye, she caught the silhouette of Catherine slinking off into the darkness. She couldn't go after her. She didn't even have the energy to move them to another location. Opening her eyes, she stared into Sean's dark orbs.

"What the...Bridget?"

She opened her mouth to reply, but her voice was lost, as the two fireballs hit right on their target. Faerie fire engulfed her entire vision. She did all that she could in her power to protect Sean.

He deserved to live.

Then, as the colorful flames began to disperse, she felt herself slipping toward unconsciousness. Gasping for air, she closed her eyes, and fell into a pitch-black void.

Chapter Nineteen

Sean could barely believe what had just happened. His eyes still burned from the faerie light, and he felt ready to retch from the smell of the incinerated vampires. He coughed, and then tried to budge the woman that was lying on top of him. He still couldn't see properly through his burning line of vision. He felt as if he'd swallowed a fireball.

Iris.

He could see her out of the corner of his eye. Hell, even if he couldn't see her, he would've known that she was there.

"Bridget?" Iris dashed toward them, and gently pulled Bridget or Claire, or whoever the woman was off of him.

"Is she alive?" He went into a coughing jag and when he came up for air, Iris had her sparkling violet eyes pinned on him.

"Her glamour is weak. I'm sincerely worried about her. I don't know if I'll be able to heal her, I may have to take her back to our lands."

"No!"

"That is not your choice to make, Sean Sutherland." Iris had Bridget/Claire cradled in her lap. "Her mother will be worried to the point of distraction about her daughter. And in my experience you don't make my lady worry needlessly."

"You can't take her. There are a few things that we need to get straight between us. And besides, she said herself that the people of this village needed her." Sean gasped when Iris pulled Bridget/Claire up to her so that she could kiss her forehead.

That birthmark. The half-moon glowed in the moonlight. He reached out to trace his fingertip over the outline of it, which sent a shiver coursing through

Bridget/Claire's body.

"Who is she, really?"

"She is Bridget. Claire is her Huntress of Hell persona. I do not believe that she wished you to know that she and Claire were one and the same."

"Then Bridget is... a faerie?"

"Aye. A very highborn faerie, Bridget is special."

"I know. She risked her life for me."

"A risk that she should not have taken. I simply don't know what possessed her."

"But it's okay, because she can't be killed, right?"

"When she moved to protect you from my faerie fire, she was in a highly weakened state. As such, I do not know what will happen to her, if I don't do something for her. She is not in the undying lands. And no faerie has ever been this badly wounded in this human realm."

"I'll carry her back to my castle."

"Bridget needs much more than just a bandage and some rest. Bridget needs something that even I may not be able to give her."

"I'll do whatever I need to. Bridget is the answer to my prophecy. She is my savior."

"I know that, you silly man. She just saved your cursed life."

"No, you don't understand. Bridget could give me back my soul. She could save me from this living Hell I exist in."

Iris's eyes welled with tears. "I can't remain here. We must leave."

"Sean?" Grace hurried toward them.

A look of utter horror had enveloped his niece's features. "Uncle Sean, are you okay?"

"Fine. I'm fine. I need Bridget."

"Bridget?" Grace clapped her hand against her mouth and stifled the scream that she had almost let out.

"Please, I implore you; you must give me a second chance with her." Sean could feel desperation pouring through him again. He had to convince Iris to leave Bridget with him. If she left now, he'd die from the disappointment and from the separation.

"No. You have no second chances. You are not worthy of Bridget."

"I know. I'll never be worthy of her, but I'll do my best to be good to her."

"You do not understand. One such as you can never hope to be loved by someone such as Bridget. It is just not meant to be." Anger boiled within Sean. Fire coursed through his blood.

Grace knelt beside him, and turned a worried face his way.

"She doesn't look so good, Uncle Sean. Maybe you should let Iris heal her, like she healed me." Grace reached out to tenderly stroke Bridget's arm.

"I am not up to the task." Iris bowed her chin, and her eyes glazed with helplessness.

"How do you know if you don't try?" Grace demanded, piercing Iris with her stern gaze. "Now hop to it. I expect to see Bridget's color improve within a few moments. She healed me. That is why she's so weak. Why can't you just heal her enough so that she doesn't die of her wounds?"

"I...I shall try. I don't know why more of my kind hasn't come to help us."

Sean could see that Iris was not accustomed to responsibility. No matter what he had thought of Bridget before, he had never seen her balk at the possibility of being responsible for someone. Nor had he ever witnessed her ready to shirk that responsibility, as Iris seemed to be. Evidently, Iris needed to learn how to be more than just a fun loving faerie.

"Well...you are a faerie. You can do it." Grace nudged Sean with her elbow. By now, the rest of the villagers had entered the square.

"Bridget?" Mary moved forward, but Rupert pulled her back.

"Not now, Mary," Rupert whispered.

Sean would do anything. He would beg Iris to heal Bridget if it came to that. He knew now that Bridget was the woman that was meant to save him.

"Bridget is Claire. They are the same woman." Sean's gruff announcement earned gasps from everyone.

"Bless my soul!" Mary murmured. "The poor wee one. We should've guessed. Why Claire and Bridget were so wonderfully giving and kind, we should've made the connection."

Sean didn't know why he hadn't figured it out sooner. Mary spoke the truth. Bridget and Claire did share a lot of the same shining qualities. Qualities that he sorely lacked. But his redemption was at hand.

"Sean?" Bridget moaned, stirring from her induced sleep.

"Aye. I'm here." He reached for her hand, and gripped it between his two hands.

"I think I would like to go back to the castle now. We must prepare for the attack. We only have two days. And those days will go by sooner than you think."

A smile touched his lips. "You are in no condition to think of battling vampires."

"Oh, yes I am!" Her confidence rang through her voice. "I'm feeling much better. Something sort of clicked inside of me. I could feel it as I was waking up."

"The potion. It must have taken a few hours to take effect." Iris breathed.

Bridget looked absolutely radiant. Sean wanted to gather her in his arms, and make sweet love to her.

"I am now this village's protector. It is my destiny."

"No. You aren't the only protector of this village."

"Will you be able to resist Catherine without my assistance?" Bridget stared at him.

She did have a point. Sean paused. Indeed, he didn't believe that he could withstand anything if Bridget ever left him. She was his shining star. She would bring him back into the light and into the land of the living. It had been foretold, and he was so close to it coming to fruition that he could nearly taste it.

"No. I need you." Bridget smiled. It had been a wane smile, but it was a smile nonetheless.

"May I gather you into my arms?"

"Please." Her encouraging response made his heart skip a beat.

He didn't know if he'd ever truly been in love, and he'd always scoffed at the notion of soul mates. But with Bridget, things seemed to be different. She was like no other woman that he had ever known.

"Come with me, Bridget. I'll give you the world that is at my fingertips."

"I never knew you were a poet."

"I'm not. But with you I think I could be anything."

"How about being something other than a vampire?" He took her from Iris, and gathered her close to his chest.

"If you stay with me, then I might even be able to accomplish that." He wanted to kiss her. But he would not kiss her while they were on display in front of all of his family and lifelong friends. The sooner he got them up to Sutherland Castle the better, as far as he was concerned.

Chapter Twenty

Every single bone and muscle in Bridget's body seemed to cry out in burning agony. She wetted her lips, and looked up at the glowing moon. Soon, it would be dawn. And they would be safe from the vampire clans for another day. But she knew from first hand experience that one day could pass by in the blink of an eye. She groaned as the sound of a crow cawing filled her ears.

First a banshee, and now a crow.

The villagers believed that the sound of the woman's scream had been courtesy of Catherine, but Bridget knew better.

The thick smell of the sea air tickled her nostrils. This place had an ancient mystical quality to it. Her people would be quite happy that the vampire clans had decided to converge here as the ground nearly bled magic.

She sighed. Her eyes followed the sight of one lone butterfly. The sign of the Elves. Perhaps, they were coming to help as well. If they were, then she'd be all the happier for it. Elves, like Faeries, were fierce warriors, and nearly unstoppable when it came to combating vampires.

"Bridget?" Sean's whisper sliced through the stillness of the night.

"Yes." She moaned. Even though her strength slowly returned, she still felt rather crummy.

"Thank you, for saving me."

She smiled, and felt a single tear trail down her cheek. "You deserve a second chance. You were willing to give up everything for a good cause. That should not go unrewarded."

Sean's grip upon her tightened for a few moments and then relaxed. "I suppose we have a lot to learn from each other, don't we?"

She laughed, and then coughed. Smothering her gasp

133

of pain, she caught the outline of his face as it had been illuminated by the moonlight.

"Definitely. But not tonight, for tonight I just want to relish the here and now, and try not to dwell on what tomorrow might bring."

"My sentiments exactly. Perhaps my long years of tortured suffering will soon be over."

She frowned. What did he mean?

"Sean, I don't understand what you're referring to."

"You mean you don't know?"

"Of course I know that you're a reluctant vampire but beyond that, I have nothing."

Silence loomed between them.

"For now, let's just heed your earlier advice. I'd far rather just enjoy the here and now instead of thinking of would have, should have, and could haves."

The lines in her forehead deepened, and she raised one eyebrow. The rest of the villagers had returned to their homes for the night.

"Will you be evacuating the village tomorrow?"

"I'm mulling it over. We've never made a stand at Sutherland Castle before. Well, that is to say not for a few hundred years."

She chuckled. He was right. Perhaps they did need to think things through a bit more, before they jumped head first into something that they might later regret.

"We should take a vote from everyone and listen to whatever ideas they might bring to the table."

"What ideas? They won't speak against mine. Well, no one but Father Clancy would contradict me. Not even Grace or Orla. They know that my decisions are always in their best interest. My family and my friends are loyal to me. Maybe they are loyal to a fault. I cannot say. But I've guided the inhabitants of this village for many years."

"How many family members and friends have you loved and lost?"

Sean clenched his jaw. "Too many. I've fought the battles with the vampires and other dark creatures of the night here on my home turf, but never have I been able to venture further than the borders of my land. I can defend my home in only one way." He sounded bitter. "Do you know that I have watched brothers, nephews, and cousins march off to countless wars? And yet, I have always been doomed to remain here."

"But you have a point. A purpose. That is nothing to be ashamed of."

"I don't know if you would really call it a purpose. Sure, with my vampire strength and ability to fly, I make a very formidable adversary, but there are days when I almost go stir crazy. I live on stories and pictures given to me by my family. Perhaps, if I had the choice of leaving this land, I would not yearn to flee so much."

"How long have you known Father Clancy?"

"For a relatively short amount of time."

"Tell me Sean, what do you measure as a relatively short span of time?"

"Forty years."

"Is that all? For mortals that is sometimes half of a normal lifespan."

"I know. I've lost a lot as you can well imagine." The cynicism in his voice made a shiver creep along her back.

"So I can imagine that you and Father Clancy are very close."

"Aye. We're friends. But in some ways, in some matters, he's still learning how to be my advisor. I think at times that I intimidate him."

"What in the world would make you think that?"

"You don't know how I struggle with the stirring. Sometimes it pulls at me with such intensity that I feel as if I am a caged monster that is battling to be released."

"But so far you have managed to control it," she pointed out.

"Barely. If you knew how many times I've almost come to the point of no return. I feel as if I'm always standing on the edge of a craggy cliff, waiting until the time comes when someone will shove me falling to my doom on the rocks below."

She bit her lip. His inner turmoil was immense. She had never dreamt that he would be this haunted. She had to change the subject. Perhaps, if she did she would ease his worries.

"How many siblings did you have?"

"Is this in any way relevant to our preparing for a battle in two days time?"

"No. But it is relevant to the success of our relationship. I need to know that beneath those multi-faceted layers of indifference that you actually possess a heart." She winced. In hindsight she probably shouldn't have used those words. She could tell that he was sensitive to the pain of others, but she wanted to know more of the man he had been as a mortal, as she already knew the man that he was as a vampire.

"If you are still unsure of that, then why in God's name did you save me tonight?"

Silence stretched between them. She inwardly chided herself for trying to push past the carefully erected boundaries that Sean had created. The man would never back down or give in. Truthfully, she didn't know for the life of her why she had saved him. At the time she had experienced a strong sense of desperation. Instinct had called out to her. Telling her that no matter what she had to save him. That his being alive would be critical to the success of her mission in life.

"I saved you because I thought at the time that I had feelings for you."

"And what do you think now?" His eyes glistened. In this light, they looked as if they were a smoky cobalt blue.

"I'm thinking that I'd like to get some sleep."

He clamped his mouth shut, and nodded to Grace when she opened the side door into the castle.

"I think that's the best idea, Bridget. You look like you need a good long sleep."

Orla nodded her head in agreement. "Aye. It would be the best medicine for you. I can't suggest anything else, because I've never treated one of your kind before."

"Speaking of that, where did Iris disappear to?"

Bridget shrugged her shoulders, and then grimaced ruefully. She really shouldn't have moved.

"I expect she's not even in this realm. She's no doubt gone to report back to my mother."

"Who is your mother?" Grace inclined her head to the side. Her eyes shone with hope, and Bridget didn't have the heart to snap at her.

"Yes, Bridget. Do tell us more about your family." Sean's eyes glittered mischievously. No doubt he greatly enjoyed this sudden turn of events. After all, now he could relish in her discomfort.

"I'd warrant that you wouldn't be at all interested," she muttered, clamping her mouth shut. Rolling her eyes, she sighed, and prayed for some patience.

"Oh, you'll find that Grace, Orla and I can be quite the captive audience." His silky smooth voice irritated her to no end. He definitely was not playing fair.

"You really don't want to know. I'm insignificant. You needn't fret about knowing all there is about my family. They are...different. But in some ways, they are the same as all families. We care for each other deeply, and I know that we can rely on each other when things get tough. But I haven't been home in years. I don't really know what they'd think of me now. I've lived here on Earth for so long."

"When did you come to our realm?" Grace's eyes brightened with excitement.

"I'd say about..." She shut her mouth suddenly. She couldn't tell them. That would give away all of her innermost secrets. Secrets that were best left undisturbed. "I've been here ever since I graduated from the Academy."

"Academy? You mean they actually have our form of schooling in your faerie land?" Grace sounded perplexed.

Wearily, she closed her eyes. "Yes. We have many things that are similar to your world. But the Academy is a special training institution. At the Academy I learned how to be a certified Huntress of Hell."

"Oh." Grace's eyes bulged, Orla coughed, and Sean, to his credit, didn't drop her. She could at least be thankful for that.

"Huntress of Hell?" This time it was Orla's turn to act as if she were at a loss.

Bridget smiled. "It is a high honor to be chosen to be trained. Our masters have seen things that even the inhabitants of this village haven't been privy to." She watched with growing apprehension as Sean clenched and unclenched his jaw. The muscle in his cheek bobbed rapidly. She'd apparently hit a nerve. Describing him, as being disturbed didn't even hit the nail on the head.

"So, you came to this village because you believed I was one of those creatures." Now Sean sounded as if he'd just sucked on a great big lemon.

"Yes and no. I sensed you; I won't deny that." She gulped in a fresh breath of air before continuing. "However, I also knew that this village needed me. I don't think that you've grasped the full extent of the battle we face."

"Oh, I've seen bloody fantastic battles before. Might I remind you that I'm a vampire?"

"No need of that. I will always know. Don't worry, it's not about to slip my mind."

A loud howling wind echoed outside of the castle. Bridget turned her head to the side. She didn't like the sound of that howl one bit.

Grace jumped. Orla placed a comforting hand on Grace's shoulder. "No need to worry m'dear. It's just the wind."

But Bridget wasn't as sure of that as Orla seemed to be. She really wished that Iris hadn't taken off when she did. Even though Iris wasn't as highly trained as she, Iris still had a fair amount of oomph when it came to her faerie powers. She could really use that extra comfort right now.

"How highly trained are these reinforcements that Father Clancy has called upon?" Bridget asked.

Sean trudged up the stairs, with Orla and Grace trailing behind them.

Stony silence resonated between them. She shivered. Maybe she shouldn't have asked that particular question.

"They are the best in the world," Sean said.

She tried craning her neck to look behind her at Orla and Grace, but only ended up with a crick in her neck for her troubles.

"Do you think that one of the priests will be Father Clancy's replacement?" Grace sounded as if she dreaded the possibility.

"Replacement? Whatever for? Sometimes your mortal ways confound me to no end. I mean I think I've picked up your customs, and speech fairly well, but sometimes mortals do something that blows me right out of the corner. It's as if the idea comes in from left field."

"Left field?" Sean muttered.

"Never mind. Just answer my question about Father

Clancy."

"They think that he needs to resign his post. He's becoming rather old, and they don't want him to jeopardize the team." Sean sounded as if he wanted to beat someone for having that sort of mentality.

Bridget shook her head. "In my land, age is a quality of distinction. The older you get, the wiser you get, and the more beautiful. Here the aged are viewed with contempt or with pity. I do not understand. To me, Father Clancy seems as robust as a thirty-year-old man. His sense of adventure is certainly still there, and I don't recall seeing him do anything that would indicate otherwise. You should speak to his superiors."

"Sean's sort of on probation right now," Grace muttered, rolling her eyes.

"What? What do you mean? I thought that they needed you here and on their side."

"They do," Orla answered. Her voice was calm, and tightly controlled. "The thing is, they sent a replacement up here three months ago. Sean didn't like his attitude and socked him one."

"Uh, oh." Bridget grimaced. "I'd bet that went over like a lead balloon."

"You'd be right. Father Clancy had to fight tooth and nail to convince his superiors that Sean had just cause for his actions."

"Yeah. That little toad had it coming to him," Grace piped up. "If Uncle Sean hadn't done that, I would have blackened him from head to toe."

"Taking liberties with my niece can't be tolerated." Sean grumbled.

A slow smile spread across Bridget's face. Realizing that he was that protective of his own kith and kin made her feel strangely contented.

"What did you do to him?"

"He scared the living daylights out of him, and then he punched him so hard that he knocked his two front teeth loose." Grace muffled a giggle.

"Ah. So you gave him something to remember you by, eh?"

"That was the only time that I was ever tempted to fly him to a high altitude and then let on that he'd slipped out of my grasp."

Bridget closed her eyes.

"I did that once to a rather unsavory man. But not to worry, I caught him before he could go splat. But I think it sort of affected him, because he kept on going around afterward, telling people that he could fly."

"I thought you were supposed to be the protector of the innocents?" Sean scoffed.

"Oh, I am. But sometimes, Sean, darkness comes in all shapes and sizes."

"Ain't that the truth?" He snorted, and then turned round the bend toward his own quarters.

"Hey, hold up. I thought you were going to take me to stay in my own quarters tonight." Her ears blazed, and if she'd been right back to her old self, she would've given him a good what for.

"You stay with me. Always with me, got it?"

"Sean..." Orla cautioned. "Perhaps you should stop being so high handed."

"Orla, keep out of this. Do I nose into your affairs?" He turned on Orla with his eyes blazing.

"Every damned day, Sean. Every damn day. I think that you need to afford Bridget with some respect. She did just save your arse. If it weren't for her efforts, I'd be placing you in an urn in the front parlor."

Sean was about to explode. "She stays with me. No room for any more arguments. I'm fagged. I need to get some rest, at least for my mind, if not for my body."

Bridget pursed her lips. "Have you ever been anything but a spoiled little brat?"

He didn't answer her.

Grace patted her arm. "Good luck. Don't worry, he doesn't bite." She gave her a reassuring smile, and then tramped down the hall toward her own rooms.

"Sean, if you're not careful you will rue all of the decisions that you have chosen to make." Orla looked as solemn as Bridget had ever seen her.

"You look utterly exhausted; go to bed, Orla."

With that the subject was closed. In her head, Bridget could almost hear an imaginary gavel slamming down to end their discussion. She stuck her tongue out at him. As soon as she was better, she'd give him one hell of a good fight.

Sean kicked the door open to his quarters and gave her a wolfish grin.

"Welcome home, my sweet."

Chapter Twenty-One

Octavia LaCroix eyed the man that was chained in the corner. "Who is he?"

"Someone who spoke out against you, mistress," her handmaiden murmured.

The smaller female vampire stared up at her in complete adoration. That was how Octavia liked her subjects. Submissive and blinded by complete love for her. She waved her hand, and the handmaiden stood up, and scurried from the room.

"How are the plans going for the grand battle?" She turned to her second in command. Catherine DuLaurent's eyes flashed with fire.

"They are going along as you intended."

"And does Sean Sutherland suspect anything?" Octavia walked through her dimly lit lair and headed for her throne. She dropped into the black velvet chair, and sighed.

"No. He'll have no warning for when you strike him."

A slow contented smile worked across Octavia's face.

"Splendid. Simply splendid. I've worked far too long to bring him to my service. When he took my Boris away from me, I cursed him. But never in any of my long years of dolling out pain did I ever dream that his salvation would find him. He can't be saved. That just will not do. He is strong. I can feel his strength, even from this distance."

"The woman that matches the prophecy is strong and resilient. She saved him once already, though she has not cured him of being one of us yet. But I fear that given time, she will profess her love for him."

Octavia raised her hand. "Do not speak of such depressing things. I will be tempted to run myself through if that man ever finds his way back to being human." Octavia pursed her lips, and resisted the urge to spit.

Sean Sutherland deserved to be tortured for all of eternity. However, since he was growing in strength by leaps and bounds, she had to make certain that he never fell into her enemy's hands. She had far too many enemies.

The vampire clans were not as harmonious as they had once been. Now, since the various hunters and Huntresses of Hell had taken so many of them out, they had to fight amongst themselves to decide whom the strongest and weakest members were.

Her position as the true queen of the European clans had already been challenged. Fortunately for her, the challenger had been vanquished by the one they called Claire. But soon, the forces of good would come knocking at her door, and she had to strike back while the iron was hot. If she failed to commandeer Sean over to her side, she would lose what precious advantage she still had.

She stared down at Catherine. Catherine was her daughter. She had made her into a vampire during the time of the French terror. That was when she had still been lost. Boris had been everything to her. Losing him had nearly taken her viciousness away. She had almost lost her reason for being until she had come across Catherine. Catherine had brought her back from the edge, and now they would triumph over all of those that would see them damned straight to Hell.

Catherine settled herself beside her, and Octavia watched mesmerized as she repositioned her silky black dress across her legs.

"The faerie that saved Sean will be hard to defeat," Catherine stated. Her voice was calm though her eyes were wide with trepidation.

Octavia reached out toward Catherine and cupped her chin in her hand. Tilting it upwards, she let out a silvery sigh.

"Don't concern yourself with such trivial matters, my dear. I will take care of this creature of the light. She will be no match for me. I have come across others of her kind. There is a way to kill them. Ah, oui ma chere, there is a way. And I shall take extreme pleasure in watching her wither away."

"I'm glad to hear it. As always mistress, you take my

143

worries and smother them with your words of comfort."

"Oui. That is what I am here for." Narrowing her eyes, she turned her attention back to the man that was strapped in the corner.

"He's ready for punishment, mistress."

"I know. I can feel his fear. I can taste it." Octavia licked her lips. "Do you know that I once had sympathy for my common man?"

"Did you?" Catherine's eyes lit with anticipation. "What happened?"

"I was turned. Taken by one of the elders. He had been following me for days. At that time in my mortal life, I was working as a prostitute. I was a camp follower. He snuck into our encampment during the night, and I was taken by surprise when he walked into my tent. He wanted services from me that I could never give him. That is, until he turned me, and showed me what the stirring could do. My Boris taught me everything. He even taught me in the ways of the dark arts. I always had the promise you see, but he had the ability to foster it, and make it grow. That was the golden age of the vampire clans. We were a force to be reckoned with; we hid in the shadows and gained power with every battle we won. It was an age of barbarism, and I loved every single second. The entire known world was in chaos...and yet, Boris and I were so happy."

"Why have you never told me that before?"

"Because ma chere, some things are best left for the right time to say them. I try to not remember the time I spent with Boris. We had almost one thousand glorious and bloody years together. When I lost him...when Sean vanquished him...I wanted to die with him. But I fulfilled the promise I had made to him long before that. I owed him that much...and much, much more."

"The promise?"

"Do not act so daft, Catherine. I have told you of the promise before. You are growing a bit daft, ma chere. Perhaps you need to pick smarter victims." She watched as Catherine's eyes sparked with dawning recognition.

"Ah. Now I remember."

Reaching out, she patted Catherine's cheek affectionately. Then, with the long fingernail on her pinky finger, she scraped a jagged thin line along Catherine's cheek. Blood trickled from the cut, and spattered onto Catherine's dress.

"You must learn to recall the things I tell you. You make me quite sore at you when you act so tres stupide."

"I'll endeavor to please you in the future, mistress."

Octavia smiled. "Endeavoring and doing are two completely different things. Do you wish to end up like that man over there?"

"No," Catherine stuttered.

"Then, be a smart girl, and listen to what I say. Heed my words, ma chere, or suffer the consequences. I like to make the consequences severe." She stopped and tapped her fingernails on the armrest before continuing. "As I was saying, the promise forced me to continue on, even during my greatest moment of distress. Boris was dead before me. Sean had beheaded him. I was inconsolable. I didn't know what to do. And then I remembered the promise, and I set about fulfilling my vow. Several of Sean's family members were with him that day. His father and a few of his siblings. Blast the whole lot of them I say. Those damn Sutherlands. So, I emerged from my hiding space. They were quite shocked to see me I can tell you that. I don't think they dreamt that Boris had taken a queen. But there I was in all of my terrible glory. I had even surpassed my master in the ways of my dark magic. I lit up the room. Everyone scampered for cover. But they could not hide from my wrath. I sought them all out. And I even incapacitated Sean and his siblings for they had been foolish and naive enough to believe they could defeat me. Me!" She grinned. It felt so good to recall the way that she had inflicted horrible suffering that day. It made her feel warm all over.

"What happened next?" Catherine was on the edge of her seat, enraptured by Octavia's stunning story.

"Well, ma chere, I cursed the whole lot of them. But I saved their father. He deserved to die. Their father had been the greatest vampire hunter that the world had ever seen. But even he couldn't stand against me. And strangely enough, he knew he was doomed. I could see it in his eyes. Those eyes. Sean and he shared the same eyes. Come to think of it, they were nearly carbon copies of each other, right down to their bloody heroics." She spat.

"Yes, he is quite yummy," Catherine agreed.

Octavia sighed.

"What did you do to Sean's father?" Catherine asked eagerly.

"Ah, I gave him the greatest treat of all. I fed upon him. By the time I was done, he was dead."

"Oh, mistress you are wonderful!"

"I know. But now the tide has turned. It would seem that I require Sean's assistance. Yet, there is one thing that I must do to him, before he will ever come over to my side."

"And what is that, mistress?"

"I must destroy him. He is holding onto his Catholic faith with all of the fervor he has in his body. I must start upon him this day. I must make him see. I must make him understand that he his not meant for a life of piety. I must show him how magnificent it is to be like us! Once he gives in to the stirring, he will never be able to turn back."

"He will revile himself," Catherine murmured. She clapped her hands together with smug delight.

"Ah, but there is more beauty in my plan. Once he loses hold on his reality as a so-called reluctant vampire, and he gives into his cravings, he will be just like us. I knew a few vampires that were reluctant to feed upon human blood. Once they fell, they become most foul."

"As did I. They were murdered by members of their own clan as I recall."

"Oui. Those two were. But the ones that I speak of are not like those men in any way."

"Who were they?" Catherine's dumb and dull eyes lit with anticipation.

"I was one of them. And my dear sister, Grunhilda was the other. Grunhilda was killed in the first Crusades. But before she was vanquished, she too had given into the stirring, and when she did her entire personality changed. The woman she had been was lost forever."

"Oh, mistress, you are wicked! You've definitely surpassed yourself this time!"

"Ah, oui. And as the day dawns, Sean Sutherland's

nightmares will begin!"

"May we punish him now, mistress?" Catherine stared at the man shackled in the corner, wetting her lips.

Octavia smiled and tousled Catherine's hair.

"Of course we can ma chere. You may have the first bite."

"Oh, mistress, you are too good to me."

"No. I'm too wicked to you." She laughed, and stood. Linking her arm through Catherine's, she guided her toward the man. She would have her fun, but before the day was out, she'd ensure that Sean Sutherland was given a little taste of what he was capable of.

And a sweet taste it would be.

Chapter Twenty-Two

"Welcome home?" She stuttered. Her mind whirled. She couldn't believe that he was actually up to his old tricks again. "Aren't you ever put off?"

His eyes glittered. He flipped the switch to the lights in his quarters. The lamplight flickered, and then illuminated his face. She sighed.

Cobalt blue. That's what they were. Her heart skipped.

"I'm never swayed when I want something. And, in case this comes as a shocking surprise to you, Bridget...I want you!"

She shivered. If she hadn't known better she would've thought that someone had jacked up the heating, because it was almost becoming stifling. She let out a shaky breath.

"All talk, and no action, eh?"

"You want action?" His voice was gruff, but his eyes filled with tenderness. Rocky sensations spiraled through her. She tried to fight the tantalizing allure that danced in his drop-dead gorgeous eyes.

He was to die for!

"We can't do this, and if you'd just start thinking with your brain instead of..." She cleared her throat. "Is it getting hot in here or is it just me?"

"Oh, I find it quite comfortable in here, but we could heat things up a bit more, if you'd like." His breath brushed her face, and fluttered her hair.

Swallowing thickly, she adamantly shook her head. "No. I'm fine. I just wondered if maybe you'd turned up the heat. That's all."

"Hmm...Well, I didn't." He flashed a deliciously wicked grin.

Her heart pounded loudly. She turned her head when she heard the haunting tune of the bagpipes.

"Don't pay that any mind. It's only Ridley's brother Rowan. He's practicing for the big battle."

Her thoughts were all a jumble. She couldn't seem to focus on anything save for the way that Sean looked at her.

This felt right. Being in his arms, so close to him, seemed as natural as flying. He permeated warmth, and love, despite what he was. She took another shuddering breath.

"We can't do this. We can never be."

"Why not?"

His question nearly made her flip. Was he out of his frigging mind?

"Sean, I'm a faerie. Furthermore, I'm a Huntress of Hell."

"Aye. I know that. I'm not the village idiot. Actually, now that I think of it, we haven't had a village idiot since Old Man MacKay. Now, he was off his rocker." Sean's eyes sparkled. His eyes. She couldn't believe that Sean was the kind of creature that he was. It wasn't fair.

"Sean, listen to me!"

"I am listening." He chuckled. For the first time since she'd met him, he actually seemed full of happiness. Usually, he was a big old grump.

"We can't happen. It's best to stop it before we do anything we'll later regret." At her words, he pushed the door open to his bedroom, and dumped her on his bed.

"Regrets? I'll tell you a thing or two about regrets. I have exactly…"

"Sean, you know I do realize what you are. You don't have to hide your age from me. How old are you?" She sat up, and shimmied closer to him, when he sat down on the bed. He hung his head morosely in his hands. When he next spoke, there was a definite catch in his throat.

"Too old." He groaned. "I'm too damn old. You're right. We can't work. I'm like an old man to your young fresh vivaciousness." Her heart went out to him. He sounded so pitiful. If Sean thought that his age was the main factor for why they couldn't be together then he couldn't be farther from the truth.

"Well," she coughed. "I'm no young chicken either. At least, not when you measure it in mortal years."

"Huh?"

Her announcement seemed to have taken his mind off his own worries. She smiled. Then, she inched toward him, thereby crossing what little distance there was between them.

"What? Are you becoming hard of hearing, old man?"

He grinned. "Ha, ha. Very funny." Gradually, his visage sobered. "Actually, it isn't funny. This is no laughing matter."

She snuggled up against him without even really realizing what she was doing.

"You know what? You need to loosen up a bit. Learn to enjoy life. Look at me, I embrace it fully, and I cherish every day. And, before you say anything, I'm immortal just as you are."

"Aye. But you can go out in the sunlight. Sometimes, I want to punch holes in my wall, because I ache for the heat on my face."

"Well, you could stick your head in the oven. That might recreate the effect for you." She chuckled. "All I'm trying to say is that I'm three hundred and twenty-five years old, and I'm still finding the beauty and wonder in life. My mother's much older than me, but I don't think you want to hear about that."

"Are you close to your mother?"

"Always." She patted her heart. "And I can visit her whenever I want, even though we do live in different realms."

"I wish I could visit my mother."

She tilted her head to the side and chewed her lip.

"You know, she is always around you. The spirit realm is just another plane of existence. There is a way to receive visitors from there."

"I don't want her to see me as I am now. It was bad enough when she was alive. It broke her heart when she found out what had befallen me."

She wrapped her arm around him. It would probably turn out to be the proverbial kiss of death for her, but she had to give him comfort somehow. "Was she still alive when you were cursed?"

"Aye." He closed his eyes. Deep lines of pain furrowed his brow. "She lived a long life. Even in the face of danger, she retained her unflappable calm. She was the perfect wife for my father." His throat constricted.

"I take it that your father didn't live as long as your mother?"

"No." Now, he was bunching his hands up in fists. She kissed his cheek. A shudder ran through him. He had borne a cross of great magnitude for far too long.

"Care to give out your age, old man?" She nudged him gently.

"You must already have an idea. I'm fairly certain that you've come across my mother's gravestone."

"I have?" She wracked her brain. The potion that her mother had given her had nearly returned her to her optimal strength. She felt as if she could fly from here straight over to Nova Scotia without breaking a sweat. "Let me think."

"I think you might've come across it on your first night here."

"Yeah, well, don't get me started on that first night, buster. A lot of strange things happened to me that night." She wrinkled her brow. Then, she dragged in a long breath of his scent.

"What are you doing?"

"I'm smelling you."

"Thanks. Do I need a shower?"

"No, you jackass. Well, maybe. But that's not what I was checking your scent for."

"Then why pray tell were you checking my scent?"

"Ah, ha! That was you!"

"I don't know what you're talking about. Will you please stop talking in gibberish?" He grunted when she nudged him again.

"It was you. That first night. You were the force that I collided with."

"Oh. Aye. That was I. You stepped on my foot by the way. It hurt like a bloody bugger."

"You're a vampire, get over it."

He moved away from her, and caused her to nearly fall on her side.

"I wish...I wish that you would stop bringing that up. What I am makes no difference to how we feel about each other."

She batted her eyelids innocently. "I'm obviously not following your train of conversation."

He glared at her.

"Oh, that's just brilliant. You're in my bedroom, sitting on my bed with me, and you don't want to discuss your emotions."

"Most men don't like to talk about such things."

He threw his arms up in the air.

"Well," he scoffed. "I'm apparently not your run of the mill man! Vampire, remember?" He thumped his chest to accentuate his meaning.

"Yes." She scooted to the edge of the bed. "That brings me back to my other question. How old are you?"

"If you'll just humor me and remember my mother's gravestone then you might be able to take a guess at it yourself!"

He seemed pretty positive that she'd come across his mother's gravestone. But she only remembered reading one gravestone. She'd seen it just before taking shelter inside of the village church. The bunch of Lily of the Valley had caught her attention. She had a strange fondness for that particular flower. They stood for eternity, and since she was a faerie, she could connect with that.

"Lady Janet Sutherland. She was your mother, wasn't she?"

"Aye." His voice was unusually gruff. The look on his face made her want to move across the bed and kiss his sorrows away.

"She must have been a wonderful woman." She could still remember the heartfelt inscription. Though for the life of her she couldn't recall the dates of birth and death.

He turned to her and stared at her in expectation. Then, shrugging his shoulders, he sighed.

"I'm three hundred and sixty-five years old, if you must know. I became a vampire three hundred and thirty years ago."

She stood up, and took a step toward him. "So, since our ages don't seem to be an issue, where do we go from here?"

"We go nowhere. As you said, I'm a vampire." He seemed utterly defeated. His slumped shoulders made another pain shoot through her heart.

She could feel the indescribable attraction that burned between them. Never before had she felt such urges. She wanted to take him to the bed, and never let him leave. She shivered. Could she in all good conscious tempt fate? When she looked at him again, his eyes were hooded. She took another step toward him. He still wasn't telling her something.

"You're still hiding secrets from me. Are they about the curse?"

"I've told you all that you need to know."

She crossed her arms. "Gee, thanks." Narrowing her eyes, she bridged the gap between them until she could feel his breath on her face. She looked up, and caught his gaze. "I need you to trust me. Place your undying faith in me. You have to tell me everything about the curse. If you don't and I find out something that you've neglected to fill me in on from someone else, I'll be furious. Seriously. You haven't even begun to see me angry."

He held her gaze. "As I said, you know all that you need to. Anything else would only give you heartache."

She searched his face. Biting her lip, she rested the palm of her hand on his chest, and almost drew back when electricity charged through her hand. His eyes twinkled. Wrapping his arms around her, he gave her a heart-stopping smile.

"I know you just felt that." She smiled. Even though something still gnawed at her, she'd drop the subject for now. Besides, he might just be keeping something that was equivalent to stepping in cow muck. Messy, but you could still clean it up.

"Sean, if we do more than just talk here…"

He pressed his fingertip to her lips. "I know. It's not as if I'm going to claim you as mine. But know this, Bridget Sinclair, if you wanted me to, I'd claim you in a second."

She swallowed. Now, she definitely felt hot. In all of her years, she'd never felt anyone that had stirred her passions so much. He made her feel as if she were on fire with her need.

"Would you just put a lid on it, Sean Sutherland and kiss me?"

Any further words were lost between them, as he willingly obeyed her command.

Chapter Twenty-Three

Visions of unspeakable horrors plagued Sean's dreams. He tossed and turned in the bed, and finally sat up. Wild-eyed, he stared around at his surroundings. The calming sound of Bridget breathing next to him didn't even help him. He shuddered. Touching his hand to his forehead, he found that it was drenched in sweat. He took a ragged breath. His nightmare had been one of his worst. At the end of the nightmare, right before he'd started himself awake, he had been about to give into the stirring.

He muffled an agonized cry. He wanted to howl at the moon. Chaotic emotions rolled through him.

Reaching for his dressing gown he stood up. He couldn't bear to be near Bridget for much longer. The beast coiled inside of him, getting ready to strike. He needed to get dressed, and leave his quarters.

Restlessness surged through him. He feared that nothing could sate it this time. Making sweet love to Bridget had only caused his heart to ache. He knew that she would never confess her love for him. And it made him feel so despondent.

The curse would never be broken. At this rate, he would be doomed for all of eternity.

"Sean?" Bridget rolled over, and reached out for him.

He moved away just in time. Her eyes were still closed, which meant that she was still half asleep and half awake.

"Go back to sleep, love. I'm just off for my nightly jaunt. I'll be back in about an hour."

"I should go with you," she mumbled sleepily.

He smiled. Despite the wildness that crashed through his being, her soft smile could still make his knees weak.

"There's no need. I'll return to you in a while." Resisting the urge to lean down and kiss her, he turned

155

his back. Her even breathing filled his ears, and he sighed. At least she'd fallen back asleep. If she'd woken up, and seen how miserable he was, she would've become alarmed. It was times like these that he wished he could see his reflection.

Within minutes, he'd donned some clothes, and had fastened his cloak around his shoulders. He glanced at his bag of hunting supplies, and on a whim, he reached for them. It would be better to be safe, rather than being sorry.

Coupled with the stirring was the wanderlust that had always filled his blood. As soon as he'd been old enough to leave he had done so. His entire family had been seasoned travelers. His mother had loved Paris and London, and they had frequently visited both cities.

He had been a rake at Court in his day, and when he'd been cursed, he had struggled with being confined to the borders of his own land. Even though Sutherland County stretched over quite a lot of land, he still could not fulfill his want to travel.

He stepped down into the tunnels, and pulled his hood over his head. It would be nearing twilight soon. But he could still visit the village even when the sun was high in the sky. Fortunately, for him, the tunnel led into the MacKay pub. Another entry had been redirected into the village church as well. It had been a cunning plan that one of Father Clancy's predecessors had invented.

He swallowed. His mouth had become dry. Thinking of that man always made a lump lodge in his throat. Father Clancy had not been the only priest that had been a close confidante of Sean's. Sean's brother Declan had also been a priest and like Father Clancy, he had been a keen warrior.

Declan.

Shaking his head, he opened the trap door, and climbed up the ladder into the pub. Mary stood with her back to him, flipping sausages on the grill. He licked his lips. She swayed her hips in time to the Celtic music that streamed out of her stereo. Her bright red hair was piled on top of her head, leaving her long, creamy white neck exposed. Silently, he shut the trap door. She still had not heard his approach.

Good old reliable, Mary.

"Mary, are the bangers and mash almost ready?"

Sean halted in mid-stride.

Rupert.

He stared toward the kitchen door, almost expecting the man to come rushing through it. Mary stopped, and reached for the volume control on her stereo.

"They'll be ready in two shakes of a lamb's tail, so hold your bloody horses." Smiling, Mary turned the volume back up, and began to reach for the warmed plates.

Beads of sweat popped out on his forehead. He clenched his hands at his side. They shook horribly.

He had to control himself.

A woman's voice filled his mind. Clasping his temples, he moaned and turned away. Then, something snapped inside of him. Careful to not make so much as a peep, he moved toward Mary. He felt like a wolf, stalking its prey.

Mary's neck was almost as beautiful as Bridget's.

Bridget.

Blast and damn, how he loved that woman. Images swam before his eyes.

"Do it." The seductive voice inside of his head murmured.

Groaning, he fell to his knees. Strangely enough, Mary had still not heard the ruckus that he inadvertently created. He reached for the wooden table that stood near him, and let out a grunt as he pushed himself to his feet.

He could not give in. Defeat had never been an option for him. Closing his eyes, he tried to remember the light. An instant image of Bridget's smiling face filled his mind. Had he been able, he would've already had his rosary in his hands. Convulsions ran through his entire body. He had never felt so helpless. He felt as if he were about to explode. Turning into a monster seemed to be the only way to make the pain go away.

Something brushed against his temple.

"Please, God. Help me to endure!" His familiar plea sounded more like a restrained growl.

Breathing deeply, he meandered toward Mary. She still danced in time to the music. By now, she had moved

the bangers to a plate so the grease could drain. He
watched as she piled a good dollop of mashed potatoes
onto the warmed plates. Swaying slightly, he nearly lost
his footing. If he had, he would've gone careening to the
floor.

Suddenly, Mary stopped.

He held his breath. Then, she shook her head, and
began singing the tune that blared out of the stereo. She
reached for the salt and sprinkled it onto what was
obviously her plate.

"Rupert?"

He could sense her trepidation. He was just about
there. Another step and he'd be near enough to her neck
to kiss it. Reaching his arms out, he pulled her against
him.

She laughed. Evidently, she believed he was Rupert.
He bared his vampire fangs for the first time in his life.
As her merry laughter trickled over him, a chord inside of
him snapped back into place. Dragging in a heavy breath,
he twirled her around so that she could see who it was.

"Sean!" She wiped her hands on her apron. "You
nearly scared me half to death! I've never had such a
fright." Placing her hand on his shoulder, she smiled.
"You shouldn't sneak up on people, you know. One of
these days you're going to give me a right and proper fit."

Grinning foolishly, he reached for one of the steaming
plates.

"Sorry, Mary."

She reached out, and patted his cheek.

"Never you mind. You know, I can't stay sore at you
for long." She shut off the stereo and then turned her
attention back to him. "Now, then. Would you like me to
whip you up something?"

He knew what he craved, but he could never partake
of it. Never!

"Och, no. You and Rupert should eat. I'm not that
hungry anyway."

"Well, you seem to have an added spring in your
step," she remarked, as they emerged out into the pub.
She put the plates down on the table, and plopped her
bum into her chair. Looking up at him with her intense
eyes, she frowned. "Sean, are you sure you're not sick?"

"I'm fine." He sagged into a nearby chair. In truth, he felt as if he were dying. But that certainly wasn't possible.

"Mary does have a point. You don't look so hot, your lordship."

"Rupert, did you tell Sean about Father Aidan?"

"No. Actually, I haven't seen Sean at all, since last night."

Sean gulped.

Then, Mary's eyes lit up knowingly. She winked at him. Of course, in a village this size word would soon spread that he and Bridget were now an item. Excitement would then spread like ripples in water, as they all knew that Bridget was his savior.

"What's this about Father Aidan?"

"Well, he's a lovely young lad. Rather keen and well…" Rupert shrugged his shoulders, and stuffed his mouth full of potatoes and sausage.

"He doesn't have much experience, does he?" Sean groaned. That's just what they needed, someone that didn't know his arse from a hole in the ground when it came to fighting.

"Now, Sean. Don't be jumping to any far-fetched conclusions. Father Aidan is still a bit green, but that doesn't mean that he won't make a fine replacement when Father Clancy retires."

"What?" he stood up so suddenly, that his chair crashed to the floor. In his current state of distress, he certainly didn't need this bombshell dropped on him.

"Sean…"

"Be quiet, Rupert. I thought I had this all straightened out. Father Clancy isn't going anywhere!"

"Sean, collect yourself. You know that Father Clancy is getting on in years, and a man of his age, just can't be expected to…" Mary's eyes glittered.

"What? To take care of a monster like me?"

"Now, you're just twisting my words around."

"I don't think I am." He wanted to throw a chair across the room.

"Sean."

They all turned at the sound of Father Clancy's voice.

Sean's jaw dropped when he caught sight of the young priest standing next to Father Clancy.

"Tell me that what they're nattering on about isn't true." He leveled his gaze at Father Clancy.

The older man crossed his hands in front of him, and sighed. "Sean, this was inevitability. Try as I might, I can't live as long as you will."

Sean's shoulders slumped. Mortality was the only enemy that he could never defeat when it came to his family and friends.

"You aren't that old."

Father Clancy chuckled. "Maybe not in your way of reckoning, Sean. But aye, I'm getting on in years. I'll be moving on to greener pastures before you will, my son."

"So, I expect you'll want to return to Dublin."

"I beg your pardon? What ever gave you that idea? Heavens no. I'll be staying here. There is still work that needs to be done in this village, and as long as there is breath in my body, I will endeavor to do it. But I must begin Father Aidan's training."

Father Aidan grinned. Sean snorted.

"Then, you can tell your bloody superiors that this village no longer requires a priest."

"Sean!" Mary and Rupert exclaimed in unison.

"I will do no such thing, Sean. Stop acting like a petulant child. You have gone through this process many times before."

Sean puffed.

"Kill them. Kill them all." The voice filled his brain again. It sounded like a chant.

Where had he heard that voice before? It unsettled him. Something had changed in the cadence of the voice, but it was still the same. She camouflaged the sound of it somehow. His world swayed again, and this time, he crashed onto one of the nearby tables. It collapsed beneath his weight, and before he knew it he was sprawled out onto the floor.

Mary screamed. Father Clancy issued orders. He knew he could count on him to remain calm.

He moaned. A tingly sensation raced through him.

"Bridget," he gasped. Whatever had taken control of him was strong. He needed Bridget. He felt certain she would be able to help him.

To save him.

"Mary, run and fetch Bridget. She just might know what to do."

"What's happening, Father Clancy?"

"It's the stirring, I'm afraid. God help us." Father Clancy knelt down beside him, and reached out to feel his forehead. "Sean, you're raging with fever. What should I do?"

"Lock me up." Sean rolled over to his side, and groaned as another painful spasm ripped through him.

This was the closest that he'd ever come to truly losing his grip on his reality. In one startling move, he reached out, grabbing onto Father Clancy's frock. Gripping it tightly, he pulled him down so that they were eye to eye.

"My bag. I left it in the kitchen. Get it!"

"What's he on about?" Father Aidan asked, coming toward them.

"Father Aidan, dash into the pub's kitchen and bring me out the black knapsack."

"Why?"

"Just do it." Father Clancy smiled. "You'll be fine, Sean."

Shaking his head, Sean struggled for his breath. "I fear I won't be. Some foreign force has overtaken me."

"I know, Sean. It's the stirring. You just hush now, and save your breath. You look terrible."

"I feel worse." Sean laughed, and then groaned as another painful spasm wracked his body. "Someone is controlling me like a bloody puppet. I'm trying to fight it but the pull is too strong. If I'm completely possessed...if I snap, if I lose it, you'll have to stake me."

"I will never do that, Sean. As we speak, Mary is getting Bridget, and the Council is assembling. In no time at all, we'll have this under control. But I must say, Sean, this is a fine time to go berserk on us."

Sean smiled at the teasing in Father Clancy's voice. "The next time this happens, I'll try to schedule it around the impending battle against the forces of evil."

"Aye. That would be better for me." Father Clancy sighed. "Sean, it is not your time yet."

"Bullocks. Sometimes, I think it's been my time since I died."

"You're alive, Sean."

"Am I? I'm a vampire, Father Clancy. I haven't been alive since the day my father was murdered, and I was cursed."

"You have Bridget, now. She is worth the fight."

"I don't think she'll ever say the words. I can't tell her that she's my savior."

"Aye. But I can."

"Don't you dare! If you do, I'll never forgive you."

Father Clancy's eyes flickered with doubt.

"I have it!" Father Aidan ran back toward them. He tossed the knapsack at Father Clancy.

"Thank you, Father Aidan." Father Clancy smiled down at Sean. Then, he stood up, and pitched the knapsack across the room. "We won't need those, Sean. I trust you. I know that you're a good, strong man. You'll fight whatever is controlling you."

"You shouldn't have done that." Sean gritted out.

"Sean, you need to calm down."

Swallowing thickly, Sean tried to sit up.

Father Clancy reached out, and tried to give him a helping hand.

"Stay...away!" He needed to get out of the pub. An inferno pulsated inside of him. He'd never felt this hot. The tether on his control was about to snap. Hurting Father Clancy or the new priest was out of the question. If he didn't make haste, he'd be doing something that he'd never be able to atone for.

"Give into it." The voice inside of his head chanted.

"Shut up!"

Father Clancy's eyes widened.

He darted his eyes to the side, and caught sight of Father Aidan sidling toward the discarded hunting bag. Sean licked his lips. Then, he took in a shattering breath.

"Father Clancy, if I were you, I'd be leaving this pub, now!"

"I won't leave you. I promised to take care of you when I first came to this village. Do you know why my superiors keep sending out Jesuit Priests to this sleepy little village?"

"Why?"

"Because they know that you are a force of good.

They know that you always fight the good fight. Without you, without the Sutherland family, the forces of darkness would've gained the upper hand a long time ago. I've read through the whole history that we have on your family. There are scads of documents. You need to fight this. Warrior blood pulses through you, Sean. Embrace it!"

He let out a shallow laugh. "That's true. We Sutherlands are a stubborn lot. I can do this." He reached out for Father Clancy's outstretched hand. Then, as if someone else had suddenly stepped into his body, he stopped. His body went rigid. "No!" He tried to move his arm. He couldn't. The puppet strings were being pulled.

"Sean?" Father Clancy's grip slackened.

Hissing, Sean tore his hand out of Father Clancy's hold and backed away toward the nearest corner of the pub.

He had to regain control. Whoever was trying to possess him needed to be repulsed.

"Help me!" Sean's plea came out sounding strangled.

Father Clancy's eyes lit with determination. "Father Aidan, get out of here."

"I'm supposed to stick with you."

"Well, not tonight, lad."

"I..."

Sean could hear retreating footsteps. He groaned. Fire spiraled through his veins. He needed Bridget. Why hadn't she come yet? He slid down the side of the wall, and collapsed. Finally, he had regained control. But he knew that it would only be a brief respite.

Father Clancy extended the cross that he wore around his neck toward him.

"Don't come any closer," Sean rasped. The last person he wanted to lash out at in his current state of confusion stood in front of him. He sighed with relief when he heard the familiar tinkling sound of the bell above the pub door.

"Bridget."

"Take him." The voice reared up inside of his head again.

"Sean?" Bridget's voice soothed him.

But Father Clancy still approached him.

"Don't come any nearer." There was a battle of wills between him, and whoever tried to commandeer his body.

In one blinding flash, he sprung toward Father Clancy and knocked him to the ground. Then, he bent his head, and leaned in for his first taste. And oh, how sweet it would be.

Chapter Twenty-Four

Bridget watched almost spellbound as Sean leaned in to bite Father Clancy. Reacting completely on instinct, she summoned the full strength of her powers.

"Get away from him!"

Raising her hand, a gale of wind swept through, and pitched Sean across the pub. She dashed to Father Clancy's side, and knelt down to take his hand.

"He wouldn't have hurt me." Father Clancy's bright blue eyes filled with certainty.

She smiled. A catch formed in her throat. Wild-eyed, she stared over at Sean. She had knocked him senseless.

"Are you unhurt?" She brushed her fingers across the place where Sean had been about ready to sink his teeth into.

"Aye." Father Clancy's voice shook. In the short time that she'd known the man, his voice had never wavered. His eyes still widened in disbelief. He looked as if he'd aged a few years.

"Father Clancy, I think Mary should take you back to the church. I'll deal with Sean." She helped him to his feet, and placed her hand on his shoulders. Uncertainty rioted through him. Sucking in her breath, she nearly collapsed when she sensed his loyalty. Even after what Sean had almost done, Father Clancy still seemed willing to stand by him.

"I'll be right as rain in but a moment." He mustered a smile for her, and she tilted her head.

"Father Clancy, I must insist. What I have to do will not be pretty."

At her words, renewed strength seemed to flow through Father Clancy. Gripping her shoulders, he turned her to face him.

"You can't kill him!" His eyes went wild.

Indeed, Father Clancy was gripped by the deepest of

emotions. If she didn't know better, she would've thought that Father Clancy had known Sean while he'd still been human.

"I'm afraid that I must. I'm sorry, Father Clancy. I had hoped that he would..."

"You don't understand, lass. He wasn't in control when he attacked me."

She shook her head. None of this made sense. Didn't Father Clancy know that when vampires were in the grips of the stirring, they sometimes didn't even know who they were? Really, she thought he had been better trained.

"Father Clancy, I understand that your loyalty knows no bounds, but you mustn't invent such nonsense. It was to be expected. A vampire can't resist the stirring for long."

"My dear, lass, I can barely believe my ears. Would you turn your back on him so quickly? After all that the two of you shared, I thought you would've been willing to open your heart to him. You are the key to his salvation, after all." His words weren't fully registering. She had inadvertently distanced herself as soon as he'd said *turn your back*. She clenched her hands together and bit her lip. The feeling of Sean's passionate kisses still lingered there. And if she concentrated hard enough, she could recall the feeling of his gentle hands on her body.

They had made love. It hadn't just been mindless sex. She had connected with Sean on a deeper level, and as loathe as she was to admit it, she loved the man. He had been the only man that she'd ever let herself get close to. And now she was willing to damn him straight to the fires of Hell.

"I have a job to do." Her voice belied the helplessness that she felt.

Couldn't Father Clancy see that she didn't want to kill him? It wasn't a question of what she wanted. It was a question of what was the best choice. The only sensible choice had to be death.

"And so do I." He moved around her, and she wondered at his swift agility. "I won't let you kill him. You'll have to go through me first."

"Father Clancy, please be reasonable. Sean would

want this. He knew what he was capable of."

"If you must, my dear, you may keep telling yourself that. But I know better. I know the kind of man that Sean is. He would give up his life for anyone in this village. And even though you have only known him for a few days, you have become part of his small isolated world. He cares deeply for you. He'd brave the very fires of Hell for you if it ever came down to it. Sean deserves better. He deserves our loyalty. Have you never heard the expression love is blind?

She swallowed. A tear slipped down her cheek. Raising her hand, she wiped it away. She would mourn Sean after she killed him, but she had to do it. Soon, the villagers would see that her choice had been the right one.

"I must fulfill my destiny."

"Aye. You must. And your destiny is right over there." Father Clancy turned and pointed at Sean.

Again, her heart jumped up into her throat.

Why was Father Clancy torturing her so?

"Father Clancy, please. Let me do this, while I still have the strength necessary."

"No. Do you know who he called out for when he knew he was slipping?"

She looked Father Clancy straight in the eyes.

"Who?" Tears filled her eyes, and soon she'd be shedding a bloody storm.

"You were the only person he could think of. Not me. Not Grace. Not Orla. You. His heart is already yours. I beg you; try to see past what the curse has done to him. Give him a second chance. In all of his years as a vampire this is the only time that he's come this close to giving into the stirring. I should know. I've been counseling him for forty years. He is a good man. With a good heart, but then you should already know that, shouldn't you?"

"Why are you doing this?"

"Because when you are someone's true friend, you'll fight tooth and nail for that person. Sean has been my true friend ever since I set foot in this village. These people may have their own quirks but they are the most loving people that I have ever met. When they call you friend, they mean it for the rest of their lives and beyond, I expect. As soon as you stepped foot into this village, you were welcomed with open arms."

"I could not gain access to any of the buildings, save the Church."

Father Clancy shrugged his shoulders.

"That night there were...extenuating circumstances. We were in lock down mode. But as soon as we'd discovered our blunder, we took you under our wings. That night, how do you think you made it up to Mary's guestroom?"

She didn't want to answer any more of Father Clancy's questions. Try as she might, she had to follow her gut instinct. She had been trained to fight and defeat creatures of the night. Curse, or no curse, Sean was still a vampire. And vampires only deserved one fate.

Death.

But a little voice inside of her head told her to humor Father Clancy.

"I don't know. Someone must've carried me."

"Aye. And who do you think that someone might have been?"

Her heart skipped. "It was Sean." Her eyes flew to where he was just coming round in the corner.

His groans of anguish cut her down to her core. She closed her eyes. The whirlwind that continued to blow through the pub suddenly died off. Father Clancy was a brave man, for the full force of her powers of intimidation hadn't even affected him.

"He needs your loyalty and your love, my dear. And if you're only willing to give him the first and not the latter yet, then you must make him believe that you trust him."

"I should kill him."

"No, you must show him mercy. He was not in control of his actions. I don't have your powers. If I did, I'd be already on the scent, trying to figure out who is controlling Sean."

Her heart thumped in her chest. She couldn't do this. Sean had just proven that he was unstable. He needed to be put out of commission for good. But the thought of actually going through with vanquishing him terrified the living daylights out of her. She had never felt this kind of fear before. If she did kill him, it would be akin to killing a part of herself. She might as well admit it.

Sean Sutherland had stirred emotions within her from the get go. She'd never even dreamt in her wildest dreams that she'd fall for a vampire. But she had. Now, she had to do as Father Clancy advised. As soon as she found the root of Sean's problems and after the battle had been fought and won here in the village, she'd leave. She couldn't stay with Sean. It would go against all that she had ever believed.

A faerie simply could not fall in love with a vampire. It was sacrilegious!

"Bridget, you must promise me that you will give him a second chance." Father Clancy's eyes bored holes into her.

"I promise. But if he ever does this again, I will kill him. Even if he is being controlled, make no mistake I'll stake him, sure as looking at him."

"Fine. I don't think you'll have to worry though, my dear. If he ever comes that close to the brink again, I fear he'll find a way to do himself in."

Sighing, she moved toward him.

"I'll just leave the two of you, so you can have a private moment."

She was about to tell Father Clancy to stay, when she heard the pub door click shut.

"Sean?" She hesitated.

He had buried his head in his arms, and had somehow pulled himself into a ball.

"Leave me. Tell the Council to bring the silver shackles."

"No one is going to tie you up. In the future, I might be inclined to lock you up and throw away the key, but for now, you're stuck with me." She crouched, and reached out to touch him.

"Don't. She might return. I couldn't bear it if I hurt you. I'd rather die."

"I'd like to see you try and hurt me, Sean Sutherland." She snorted. Then, she leaned forward as his words hit home. "She? What woman are you referring to? Is the person controlling you a woman?"

"Aye." His face had turned a violent red.

"Sean, you have to let me help you."

"You were going to kill me just a short while ago."

She fell silent. "You don't need to apologize. If I'd been in your shoes, I'd have done the same thing. But unlike you, I wouldn't have given it a second thought. Mercy. I had no mercy, before..."

"I didn't expect Father Clancy to jump in on your behalf. He's one in a million, that's for bloody certain." She had lowered her voice to a silky whisper. She gasped when he finally riveted his eyes on her. They were bloodshot. She studied his tortured eyes. He held the anguish of too much heartbreak in his eyes. He had soulful eyes...and yet, he was a vampire. She shivered. He looked as if he'd been to Hell, and had come back, burned down to his very core. "Oh, Sean." She touched him again, and frowned when he drew back. "I'm here now, Sean. I'm not going anywhere. You do know that I have the powers to drift inside of your mind, and root that woman out."

"She's powerful. You won't be able to fight her."

"Well, *thanks* for the vote of confidence. I'm a faerie. I wield unimaginable powers. I can fight that entity that has possessed you. I promise; I won't let her walk away. I'll fry her brain."

He locked gazes with her.

"This is not your battle. You should leave this village. We don't need you."

She rolled back on her heels at his coldly spoken words. "Why, Sean Sutherland, I didn't think that you'd play that card. It's the oldest one in the book. You may have thirty years on me Sean, but I still wasn't born yesterday, you know. I'm not the naive little woman that you seem to think I am. I can see through your façade."

"I don't know what you're going on about."

"Oh, you don't." She pursed her lips. "I made a promise to Father Clancy, and come hell or high water, I'm going to fulfill that promise. A faerie never breaks a promise." She planted both of her hands on his shoulders and stared straight into his eyes. She bit her lip. For having already lost his soul, Sean's eyes were filled with spirited suffering. This man did deserve more than what she'd originally been willing to give him. "Thank Heavens, for Father Clancy." She rested the flat of her palm against his hot cheek. "We're in this together, buster! Don't ever try to turn me away again. It isn't going to fly with me. I can match you tit for tat. The sooner you realize that, the easier our relationship will be."

Fire sparked inside of his intense orbs. "What relationship?"

"Well...let's see. We did sleep together, and I am going to see you through a living hell, so I think we can say that we're fast friends."

His shoulders slumped. "So, I'm your friend, eh?" He laughed.

But the sound of it was hollow, and struck something deep inside of her. She couldn't be anything more to Sean. If he were human, if they'd met in another time, then maybe...she couldn't think about what might have been.

The mortal world was a cruel place. Sometimes, true love triumphed, and won the day, and sometimes hearts were broken. She would never find another man like Sean Sutherland, but she'd always have the memory of him.

"Yes. Now come on, let me help you up."

He wobbled slightly as he stood up. Then, in a swift motion, he pulled her against his chest.

"You shouldn't stay. I can't...I can't have you with me, and then lose you. We should cut ties, before those ties become knotted."

She sighed. He smelt like Heaven. For being a vampire, he sure did exude the most wonderful aroma. She felt as if she floated on a cloud of ecstasy whenever she was around him. A jolt of lightening ran though her, and she looked up into his eyes.

"Don't worry. When I leave you, you'll have better things to fret about. You want to put me up on a pedestal, but really, I'm just a normal run of the mill woman. Nothing special about me at all."

"Aye." He snorted. "Except for two things. You're a faerie, and you're the love of my life."

Her heart stopped.

"Gee. Thanks." She stepped away from him. She felt miserable. He'd just professed his love for her, and she'd cut out his heart, and handed it on a platter back to him. She punched his arm playfully. "Now that you mention it, I'm rather fond of you myself."

His eyes dimmed. She groaned. She liked to see his eyes sparkle. They reminded her of precious jewels.

"Fondness can only stretch so far."

"Yeah, so don't push it. Sean, we have other things to think of. First off, I have to find a way to keep you from…" She couldn't seem to finish her sentence.

"From going berserk again?" His face mottled with fury.

"No. There you go again. Putting bloody words in my mouth. You make a habit of doing that to me, and I've had it up to here." She pointed at the ceiling, and watched as that all too familiar muscle in Sean's cheek twitched.

"I don't want to have a row with you."

"Well, do you think I was itching for a fight? Get real. I don't want to fight with you. I just know that we're both on edge." She felt something prick the back of her mind. Widening her eyes, she looked around the pub. "Shit!" She backed away from him.

"What's going on?" He stepped toward her.

"Sean, do you feel the way that you felt before you attacked Father Clancy?" He shook his head. Then, his eyes rolled back in his head. She rushed toward him. "Sean! Sean, do you hear me? You have to fight it!" She reached her hand up, and pressed her fingers to his temple. Breathing deeply, she tried to enter his mind.

A loud, anguished scream tore through the pub. She didn't realize it came from her, until she slammed against the far wall. She shook her head. Moaning, she tried to stand up. Whoever was inside of Sean's head was highly skilled. The blasted bitch had erected shields inside of his mind.

Damn, how she hated fast workers.

"Bridget?" Sean's softly pleading voice made her heart flutter.

Cursing a blue streak, she fought to pull herself to her feet. Why did it seem as if she was always getting the shit beat out of her? Oh, yeah. She was a Huntress of Hell. That explained it.

"Sean? Can you hear me? You have to push her out of your mind."

"Keep away." Sean put his arms out, and she wisely kept her distance. "No! You can't make me do it."

"What does she want you to do?" Bridget's eyes nearly fell out of her head, when Sean's voice faded away only to be replaced by a woman's voice.

"I want him to feed upon every last person in this village."

Chapter Twenty-Five

Sean was dying from the inside out. He hadn't meant to give into the woman that had suddenly regained control. The crumpled form of Bridget nearly made him lose his mind. Relief the likes of which he'd never felt before filled him when Bridget fought to regain her composure. He could feel the entity inside of him.

It was pure evil. Even though he struggled like mad to take back his mind and body, the woman had a firm hold on his strings. He looked to the side, when the pub door opened, and rattled back on its hinges. Surprisingly enough, the bell didn't even chime.

"As far as I'm concerned, you can go straight back to the fires of Hell, you bitch!" Bridget raised her hands, and light danced around the room.

He heard the woman howl in pain. For some reason, he had become detached from the physicality of his own being. And funnily enough, he was eternally thankful that he couldn't feel the excruciating pain that Bridget's faerie fire created.

"I shall have him! Make no mistake, faerie. There is nothing that you can do to stop me! I've had my revenge upon him before. I will not allow him to step out of the dark and into the light. The promise must remain fulfilled!"

Sean halted. Now he knew whom he was dealing with.

Octavia.

He picked himself up, and fought like a true warrior of the Scottish highlands. He wanted his body back, and he was going to get it no matter what he had to do.

Sean Sutherland was no bloody puppet.

Give me back my body, he mentally intoned. He fell into a void and pushed himself to his feet. When he next looked up, he stood on a battlefield.

"Choose your weapon, Sean Sutherland." Octavia stood before him. She looked like a Roman Soldier.

"Where are we?"

"We are in a reality of my own making. Well, perhaps there's a bit of your consciousness here as well, but for the most part it's all mine."

He stared down at himself. He was garbed in a kilt and a white shirt, with his plaid and family brooch pinned on his chest.

"This can't be happening."

"Oh, it is. If you want your damn body back, you'll have to fight me."

"Bridget."

"I've taken care of that little faerie shrew for now. She won't be bothering us."

Apprehension rolled in his gut. He shook his head. What she said had to be lies.

"You speak with a forked tongue."

"Ah, Sean. You still have not lost your ability to amuse me." Octavia smiled.

He looked to her short sword and shield that she carried. In his mind's eye, he pictured his father's Claymore.

Oh, what he would give to have that as his battle companion.

"Sean?" Bridget's voice spiraled across the dark landscape.

He turned to follow the sound of her voice. She was his salvation. His only hope was in clinging to her voice. She would lead him home.

"Bridget." The sound of her sweet name rolling over his tongue nearly caused his knees to buckle. He wanted her so badly. Why could she not come to him? For once in his life, he would gladly accept her help. He swallowed thickly. He had gone up against Octavia once before, and the outcome had led him here. He hated being a vampire. He hated himself. Octavia wore a grin that seemed to encompass the whole terrible landscape.

Red and black swirls collided in the sky above him. There was no sun, and the moon was gone. Yet, as he searched the stormy clouds above him, he could just make out the slimmest outline of a half moon. It glowed brightly. The clouds parted. His father's claymore floated down toward him. He raised his hand to receive it. It felt warm against his bare palm. His eyes filled with tears.

Bridget.

Her birthmark symbolized the moon in the sky. She would always be his beacon of hope, even in his darkest of hours. She had used her faerie magic to send him his chosen weapon. For that, he would be eternally grateful.

"I will be the victor this time, Octavia."

"I see that your head is just as swollen as it was three hundred and thirty years ago."

"Damn you straight to Hell."

"You, first." Octavia charged him, and he pivoted to the side.

The Claymore he wielded should have needed both of his hands, but in this world he could easily hold it with one. The wood on the grip still felt warm beneath his hand. If he didn't know better, he could've sworn that the sword began to sing as it arced through the air.

"When I'm done with you, Octavia, you'll not only be out of my head, but you'll have lost your head as well."

Her laughter made his flesh crawl.

"You insipid man. Whatever happens on this plane of existence is only an illusion. We are not really here."

His jaw dropped.

Damn.

For some reason, he had hoped that she had used her sorcery to wrench him out of the pub and into her own lair.

"I will defeat you."

"You shall never defeat me. I am the one that cursed you and yours. I will never go away. The largest battle you have ever seen will be raging in less than forty eight hours, and I will be there to see you lose everyone you love."

"No, you won't. Because I'm going to take care of you here and now."

"No matter what you do, or where you go, I'll always be able to find you. Call me your vigilant companion. My eyes will always follow you."

His heart stilled.

"Sean?" Bridget's voice ripped across the landscape

again. The fervency in her tone made him tilt his head to the side. Genuine concern had been in her voice. What was happening in the waking world?

"I grow tired of your parlor tricks, you old hag." He charged toward her, and by some twist of fate, her shorter sword held it's own against his great Claymore. The two blades met, and the resulting cacophony nearly rendered him deaf. The force of the connection sent him hurtling into the air. He hit the mist-enshrouded ground with a great thud. The bones in his body cried out in agony.

"And when you're at your darkest hour, Sean, I will be there to nudge you over the edge. You will betray Bridget, and the resulting agony from your deception will kill her."

"No!" He stood up, and charged Octavia like a madman.

But she had disappeared. Something pulled at him. He could feel it latch onto him, and suck him through the great tunnel he had first come through. He didn't want to leave. The need to know how Octavia would kill Bridget made him want to scream out in frustration.

Soft cool hands pressed against his temples. He moaned. Pleasure rolled through his body, coupled with that now familiar tingle. Electric bursts rushed through his body.

"Hello." His greeting made the lines in Bridget's forehead relax.

"I thought I'd lost you."

He was sprawled on the pub floor again. It seemed as if everyone from the village had gathered around him.

"Oh, look at the braw man. Why, even after all that he's been through, he still looks…"

"Mary, shush!" Rupert's loud exclamation made him wince.

Bridget reached down to clasp his hand.

"I don't feel her presence anymore. Did you drive her back to her place?"

He looked at her through hooded lids. How could he in good faith answer her?

"Sean!" Father Clancy's voice distracted him and thereby kept him from having to answer Bridget's question. He grinned like a manic fool when Father

Clancy's shadow draped over him.

"I'm so sorry."

"Apologies are not necessary, Sean. I've known you long enough to realize that you'd never intentionally hurt anyone of us. Isn't that right, Bridget?"

"Aye." Sean closed his eyes.

"Sean, once you feel well enough, we must start making plans for the battle."

Sean winced. He hadn't thought of that.

Octavia's words echoed though his brain. His very presence in the village could turn the tide of the battle. He couldn't compromise whatever strategy they concocted. In all likelihood, if Octavia had been speaking the truth then that could only translate into one thing. Whatever he knew, she would know too.

He had to leave. Post haste.

Whatever reservations he had would have to be set aside for the greater good. He had now become a liability. He would not be used as Octavia's secret weapon. Not in a million bloody years.

He rose to his feet. Silence stretched through the pub.

Grace and Orla stared at him, almost as if they could sense his thoughts. Grace stepped forward, but Orla pulled her back. The rest of the reinforcements would arrive soon. It would be better if they never caught sight of him. He could survive with little out in the wilderness. He would travel up to Sutherland Castle. Gather what few supplies he needed and then he'd be off. For the first time in his entire lifespan the village would be better off without him.

Declan's voice resonated through his brain, even after all of these years.

Sean, you can't ever leave this place. Even without the curse, we Sutherlands are a part of this majestic land. We can't deny the way that it calls to us. We'll always be the monarchs of this land.

A salty taste filled his mouth. Bridget cocked her eyebrow. Blast and damn, she could sense his intentions. He smiled at his family and friends.

"I'm sorry, Father Clancy, but before we start strategizing, I must go up to Sutherland Castle. I need to fortify myself." His lie seemed to hit it off with Father Clancy.

"Ah. Of course, of course, off you go. We shall wait for you, and meet you in the Church. I will hold a short Midnight Mass, and then we will get to it."

"Thank you, Father." He smiled.

"Don't be late, Sean," Mary quipped.

His gaze engulfed them all. As long as Bridget remained here, the odds were still stacked heavily in their favor. And if his suspicions were correct, he had no doubt that Bridget's kind would be sending in troops. The question that still nagged him to death was how the vampires would be able to come to their village in such great numbers. The day was against them. Even he would have to take shelter in the old hunter's cabin in the woods when the sun claimed the day.

"Sean?"

He turned.

That voice.

Bridget stared to the doorway, and her eyes widened. His heart had now been put to ease. As long as William was here, his people would be well set. He embraced the man that had just walked through the door. Cries of excited greetings rang through the pub. Orla and Grace rushed forward to hug William. Sean didn't have time to tarry long. They were now in good hands. William would only be able to stay for a fortnight, and then he would be forced to resume his endless wandering of the globe.

In the ensuing hubbub, he was able to slip unnoticed from the pub. He strode toward his castle. Anguish tore at his being.

"Sean?"

He could hear Bridget's soft footsteps pursuing him.

"Go away. Leave me alone. I don't want to be near this village anymore."

"Why you stubborn ass! I know why you're leaving, you know."

"Aye. I'm leaving because I'm no longer needed."

"Who is that man?"

"He is William. William Sutherland."

"Yes, I heard everyone nattering that. So, tell me, why didn't anyone mention him before? The whole village seems to be nutters!"

"We didn't mention him before, because he rarely visits. But when he does, we all celebrate."

"Sean, you have to slow down. On foot, I can't keep up with you."

"I'm in a hurry. The village can't have me around for much longer. I could cost them everything."

"I highly doubt that." The scorn in her voice seared him. "I mean, you have been their protector for over three centuries."

"Please, Bridget. Could we not speak? I already told you; I'm in a hurry, and this cold night air is burning my lungs." The next moment, he heard the fluttering of wings, and then he nearly collided with Bridget.

"I'm not letting you get away with this, buster! You might've pacified Father Clancy, but the gig is up with me. Spill it or I'm just going to have to do some digging."

"Where do you hide those wings of yours...I didn't see them last night."

She frowned. "Sean..." She raised her hand.

He sighed. "I wouldn't do that if I were you. Don't you recall what happened the last time you tried to invade my brain?"

"Sean Sutherland, you're straining my patience. First off, you refuse to tell me how William is related to you, and secondly, you won't tell me why you find the need to leave the village."

"I'm not required to tell you anything. You said yourself that we are just friends." He shrugged his shoulders, and then tried unsuccessfully to move her out of his way.

"Damn you straight to Hell, Sean Sutherland." Her angry outburst fell away as she realized what she'd said. "I'm sorry. Forgive me."

Every which way he dodged; she was there to meet him.

"Bridget, there is nothing more to say. You will leave this village after the battle. Why should I let myself get attached to you? In the long run, it will be better this way."

"Sean, I'm not letting you run away."

He straightened. "A Sutherland never runs away. We

stand until there is no longer breath left in our bodies."

"You could've fooled me." She crossed her arms. "So, when one Sutherland flees, does another come to pick up the slack?" Her taunting finally hit home.

He gripped her shoulders, and pulled him to her. A wild wind howled through the open landscape. He wanted to kiss her and...

"You don't know what you're talking about. It would be better for you if you just dropped it."

"I looked into William's eyes. Why do they look just as haunted as yours?"

"Drop it." This time it was a demand more than a request.

"You know, if you ever hope for us to be more than just friends, you'll have to give a little. Like say, opening up to me a bit."

"I know almost nothing about you. So, why do you want to know anything about me?"

"Because, you jackass, I'm in your village. I need to know why I've been summoned here. It obviously wasn't to kill you. So, why? I mean, I would've probably just come with the reinforcements, but for some reason unbeknownst to me, I was sent ahead."

"Well, maybe you should ask your superiors why." His voice turned flat. He still held Bridget, and he fought the urge to kiss her with every fiber in his being. It was the hardest battle he'd ever fought.

Her nostrils flared. "Is William more closely related to you than Orla or Grace?"

He sighed. "You never give up do you, Bridget?"

"Well, hot damn! You hit my motto right on the head. Never give up, never give in, I always say."

"In this case, you're fighting a losing battle." He tried to move around her again, but this time she grabbed a hold of him.

Reaching up, she pulled his head down to meet her lips. Her kiss was long and languid. Fire dipped down into his belly.

"Does that feel like a kiss between friends?"

He shook his head. "Hey, you said it, not me." He grinned. He looked toward his castle. She was stalling him, and thinking that she could get away with it. "Nice try. But unless you're about to have your way with me here on the open road, I'm not going to be distracted."

"Sean, you make me want to scream! You close yourself off from everyone. You won't even let me touch your heart. So, tell me, how do you expect us to be more than just friends?"

"You've already touched my heart. That's my ruddy problem. I can't stay, and watch all the people I love die before my eyes. I've been there, done that, and I'm sick and tired of it. I've had it! I can't lose anymore."

"Yes. I understand. But if you don't stick it out, you'll keep yourself from gaining. Love is a wonderful force; it can rock worlds, and it can conquer nearly everything."

"Are you saying you love me?" Hope flared in his chest.

She scraped the ground with the toe of her boot.

"Now, don't go putting words in my mouth, Sean Sutherland. Just because I mentioned it, doesn't mean I have to declare it. But yes, I do care deeply for you."

"Care deeply?" He grunted. "Everyone in this blasted village cares deeply for me."

"I care for you in a romantic way."

That made him look up. "Huh. Well, you sometimes have a funny way of showing it."

"A faerie must be able to embrace love fully when it comes to taking a mate."

"We've already slept together."

"I know that you fool! I was there. I'm talking about taking a life mate. I have to feel as if life wouldn't be worth living without you. Faeries take love and they make it soar. I must be certain."

"Well, I already am. So, maybe we're just not meant to be. If you'd kindly step out of my way, I'd be most appreciative."

"Oh, no. You're coming back with me to the village. No ifs, ands or buts. I'll have none of that malarkey."

He eyed her warily. "You will be the death of me. I already told you, now that William has come; the village no longer needs me."

"Are you out of your mind? Those people will always need you. Mary adores you, and frankly, I'd be a wee bit jealous if I didn't see how much she loved Rupert. Grace's world revolves around you, and Orla thinks you're the greatest thing since sliced bread. And don't get me started on Father Clancy. That man would walk to the end of the world for you."

"Get off it."

"No. I won't. Everything I say is the God's honest truth. William's help might be appreciated, but they still want you around. I mean you're just such a joy to be with, they can't help themselves!"

He laughed. "William has it all in hand."

"Would you please stop preaching the wonders of William to me? I don't even know him."

"Well, you will soon enough. He'll be sure to make a great impression on you. He always has that special touch when it comes to the ladies. He's quite the ladies man…a regular Casanova."

"I'm not interested in him."

"Oh, you will be, when you find out who he is."

"Well, then. Enlighten me. Who is this William Sutherland?"

"He's my younger brother."

Chapter Twenty-Six

Bridget couldn't quite believe her ears. "Pardon me?"

"I didn't think you were becoming hard of hearing." He smiled. "William is my younger brother. He's three years younger, actually."

She swallowed. "You didn't tell me that you had any siblings left alive." Her eyes stung.

"You didn't ask." In her moment of confusion, he managed to slip past her.

She darted after him. "Wait a darn tooting minute. You just can't drop a smoking gun like that and then go on as if nothing happened. You have way too many secrets, Sean."

"Oh, and you don't?" He pivoted back on his heel, and raked her with his eyes.

Clearing her throat, she tossed her head. "Not as many as you do, apparently. You already know that I write romance novels as my cover, but I didn't know anything about you. You're wound tighter than a bloody clock!"

"And you wormed your way into this village, under false pretenses. Now, you've wound me around your pinky finger, and..."

"And what?"

"I can't decide whether I want to tear your clothes off of you, or smack you silly!"

"Well, if someone smacked you silly, it would be a huge improvement."

He let out a growl, whirled around, and began trudging up the steep incline toward the castle.

Her breath came out in shallow puffs. Glancing up at the moon, she groaned. If she didn't work quickly, she'd have to track Sean across Hell's half acre. Personally, she wasn't into that. She'd rather just do it the simple way. She'd talked people out of making rash decisions before, and this instance wouldn't be any different.

"You know what? I feel like a dog chasing my tail here. I'm not going to shut up until you return to the village with me. Your brother returns home for a visit and you reward him by running away?"

"William understands. He knows what makes us Sutherlands tick."

"Oh." She stopped. "So, I guess you're telling me that I don't know you, huh?" She narrowed her eyes. "Well, you're probably right. I don't know what has gotten into me these past few days. It's almost as if an invisible force has taken hold of me. And don't worry; when I say invisible force, I'm not referring to the sort of entity that took control of your body."

He halted in mid-stride.

"You never cease your prattling, do you?" He tossed her an irritated glance over his shoulder. The lines in his forehead showed that he was annoyed...and yet, the twinkle in his eyes told her another story.

"Oh, good one. I'll give you a perfect ten on that insult." He began muttering under his breath. "You do realize that I can hear you, right?" She raised her voice an octave on the last emphasized word.

Suddenly, he fell silent. She stared back up at the moon, feeling a knot slowly forming in her belly.

Coiled around the moon, was a thin sliver of crimson. Blood on the moon.

Her heartbeat quickened. Her palms grew sweaty. She didn't need this sign of foreboding.

She hastened her step, and let out a curse, when she tripped on a rock. Before she knew what was happening, he had locked his hand around her wrist. She'd been about to fall on her knees, but his grip kept her from sinking to the ground.

"Thank you."

An owl hooted off in the distance. A shiver ran up her spine, as he caressed her with his eyes. Who was he trying to kid? The man was head over heels for her. It didn't take a rocket scientist to deduce that.

"In the future, do try to watch your step. I won't always be around to catch you."

"Well, if I'd fallen, I wouldn't have done any lasting

damage anyway. So there." She groaned. "Lord knows I can take one hell of a licking and keep on kicking. The day I need you to keep me from falling, will be the day I need a hole in the head!"

Good Lord, they were acting like frigging teenagers! How could they have resorted to acting in such a juvenile manner? If some of her instructors could see her now, they'd be thoroughly disgusted with her bad behavior.

"Perhaps you're right. In the future, I will let you go ahead and fall."

"Fine."

"Right, then." He released her wrist, and began his ascent again.

"Tell me, what's up with your brother?"

"I don't follow. There is nothing up with William. He's as normal a man as you'll ever find."

"Well, I could say the same thing about you, except when you're taking a walk on the wild side."

"You're a barrel of laughs, Bridget."

She nearly bumped into him when he abruptly stopped.

"What's going on?"

"Did you leave the castle lit up like a Christmas tree?"

"Well, give me a minute to mull that over. I was sort of in a hurry to get down to the village and save you from your crazy assed self. So, as you can well imagine, the events following Mary bursting into our quarters freaked out of her wits are a just a wee bit sketchy."

He snorted. "Our quarters?" His eyebrows rose.

She cleared her throat. "Your quarters...what was I thinking?"

For a few seconds, silence fell between them. Sean glanced back up at the castle and grunted. "In any case, my castle seems to have every single light turned on."

"That is strange."

They had finally reached the castle.

As they entered, a great flash of light nearly blinded them, and then they were draped in darkness.

Moving forward, she bumped into Sean, and nearly sent him hurtling. "Sorry."

"Don't you have special vision for the dark?"

"Yep. But that still doesn't take care of the fact that I tend to be a bit klutzy."

"Wonderful." He grabbed her hand and guided her past the furniture. "I sense something. But they're obviously, trying to cover their tracks."

"Do you think it's a vampire?" Here she was, a Huntress of Hell, and she was asking Sean if he thought his inner sanctum had been invaded by vampires. She really had to get her act together and focus!

"I don't think so. But what are your keen senses telling you?" He made a shushing noise.

Her eyes widened. "Did you happen to bring your hunting bag with you? I can summon my weapons, but I don't think you have that handy dandy ability."

"Hush up!"

She closed her mouth. Nervousness rolled through her. She hated the unknown. This didn't make any sense...she should be able to sense danger.

"Do you smell that?" She whispered.

He groaned. "Do you ever listen to me?"

"Only when I feel like it. Just focus. Now, breathe in deeply. I think I've got your mystery solved."

"What mystery?" The lights turned back on at full force.

"Iris," they both said, in unison.

"You didn't actually think that I'd gone for good, did you?" Iris floated in mid-air with a cheery expression plastered across her face. For once, Bridget was actually glad to see Iris.

Bridget shuffled and Sean cleared his throat. She really hoped that he didn't say anything to set Iris off. She could be very touchy, and very sensitive.

"Of course we didn't, Iris. But we weren't expecting you to bring company with you. Well, you did say your castle was lit up like a Christmas tree...there are your faerie lights." Bridget stared around at the faerie warriors. She could feel Sean getting ready to have it out with Iris.

"Unbelievable!" She turned in time to see him shake his head. "I've been invaded by faeries that look more dangerous than I am!"

She closed her eyes. Suddenly, she felt a whopper of a

headache coming on. "Sean, I think you should go upstairs and...well, occupy yourself."

"Oy! What does he think he's doing?" Sean started toward the nearest male faerie.

She looked to what had alarmed Sean. Rolling her eyes, she stepped in front of him.

"Don't worry about it, Sean."

"Don't worry about it?" Pointing angrily, he cursed. "Where do you think you're putting that tapestry? That's a valued family possession! Bridget, they're turning my castle into a bloody war room!" His bellow made her hair ruffle, as if a breeze had rushed through the castle.

"Only for the time being. Once the battle is over, they'll get up and leave."

"Damn straight, they will. Or I'll make them leave!"

"Besides, you don't have to worry about that, now do you? Aren't you going to be off in the wilderness when the village is attacked? Go ahead, go and play the role of eccentric loner...see if I care."

He bit his lip. The muscle in his cheek twitched. "Well...I might decide to stick around."

"Are you sure about that?" She gestured toward the assembled faeries. "The elves will no doubt be here soon, even though their numbers won't be as great. Since they've decided to use Sutherland Castle as headquarters, you might want to run off and chase the ghosts that are haunting you. I saw a few on my way up here...go and have tea with them, will you?"

"You're enjoying this, aren't you?"

She folded her arms across her chest, and rolled her eyes. "I don't know what you're hinting at." She grinned.

"This." He waved his arm. "You're enjoying my discomfort!"

"Well, maybe I am. Just a little. Just a wee bit." She muffled a chuckle.

He stormed toward her. "This is my home. You can tell everyone to get up and shove off."

"What did he say?" Iris asked.

The great hall fell dreadfully silent. Bridget sidled over to him, and tugged on his arm.

"Apologize!" Even though she was highly respected by the warrior faeries, they just might decide to put Sean out of their misery. They viewed him as just a vampire...and the only good vampire to them was a vanquished one.

"I'll do no such thing."

"Sean, if you don't apologize, they'll take offense. Remember what Iris almost did when you called her a firefly? Rule number one, don't insult a faerie."

"Now that we're on the subject of rules, I'll give you one. Never piss off a vampire! This castle happens to belong to me. I want my damn privacy."

"Do you want help fighting the scads of vampires that are on their way here even as we speak?" Iris demanded.

Bridget had to give Iris some credit. She actually seemed a bit stronger. She'd never seen the faerie this passionate before.

"Sean?"

The sound of a door slamming shut jarred Bridget's already strained nerves. She turned and groaned. Just what they needed, it seemed as if the entire village had trudged up to conglomerate in the castle.

"William." Sean nodded his head.

"What's going on? Mary started to tell me a tale that would put our curses to shame..." William's voice trailed off when Sean and Bridget both stepped aside. "Holy Smokes. It is true."

Bridget looked between the two brothers.

William bore a striking resemblance to Sean, and he exuded the same warm magnetism. Obviously, it was an innate family trait.

"Aye. It's true," Sean muttered. "As you can see, Sutherland Castle has been invaded by faeries."

Bridget sighed.

"And," Sean said, whirling back to Iris, "I do want the help of the Gentry against the forces of darkness that are set upon destroying us."

Iris's face lit up. "Good to hear." She clapped her hands. The great hall cleared, and lavish chairs of all shapes and sizes filled the great space. "Sit, sit. We all must start planning!"

Bridget's eyes narrowed. She watched as Sean slunk into the shadows. He was trying to make a fast getaway.

She crossed the distance, and pulled him back by the arm.

"Where in the blazes do you think you're going?"

"I'm leaving this room. I can't hear the battle strategy." The sound of drums, pipes and a horn filled their ears.

"The elves," she murmured. "Why do you feel the need to leave? You should stick around...you're about to get the sight of a lifetime."

"It would be better for me to be in the dark. Octavia told me that she would always be keeping an eye on me. I can't risk her spying on us, and setting up counterattacks."

"Do you know how well protected this castle is now that the faeries have arrived? If you think that bloody sorceress's magic is any match for the magic that we wield, then you can think again."

His eyes clouded. A storm raged inside of their depths.

"I'd prefer to not take any chances, if that meets your approval."

William had made his way over to them.

"I don't think we've been introduced. I'm William Sutherland." He flashed a heart-stopping grin, but to her it was dimmed in comparison to Sean's.

She glanced down at William's outstretched hand. "I'm pleased to meet you. As you probably already know, I'm Bridget Sinclair."

"Aye. I know. I've heard some pretty fanciful tales about you, courtesy of Grace and Mary."

She smiled. "Hopefully, they all put me in a favorable light."

"Oh, aye. An angelic light, come to think of it." He seemed transfixed by her eyes. She glanced over at Sean, and her heart fell at the morose expression he wore.

"So, when did you two last see each other?"

Sean moved to the side. He was still trying to get away. Whatever was she going to do with him? Sometimes he made her want to scream!

"Where are you going?" William turned to his brother and frowned. "If you try to take off on me again, I'm going to have to deck you one."

"I can't stay here," Sean mumbled.

190

"Oh, aye. Father Clancy told me about your wee little episode. Don't worry about it, Sean, you came through it with flying colors, and the village is none the worse for wear."

Bridget looked over to Iris. She seemed to have everything in hand.

"Since the elves are coming, no one will require my services. No doubt, their fighting skills will far surpass my own...so I'll leave them to get their jobs done. I'm due for a holiday anyway."

"Oh, but we will need you in the fight ahead. You're one of the best damn warriors I've ever known," William remarked. "Besides which, you still owe me a pint at the pub." William's green eyes sparkled.

Bridget felt like a third wheel. She wanted to crawl into a hole.

"You should've forgotten that. It would've been the decent thing." Sean chuckled.

Bridget smiled. It was good to see that someone could make Sean happy, even if she couldn't. She wandered away, thinking it best to leave the two brothers alone. If they hadn't seen each other in ages, they needed the time to become reacquainted. Now, more than ever, she wanted to know how William had been cursed. No doubt he was also a vampire. The only thing that rattled her was the fact that he could only remain in the village for a fortnight. Did his curse keep him from being near his loved ones? Before she knew it, she had walked over toward Mary.

"They are beautiful." Mary sighed. She looked like she was in seventh heaven.

Bridget glanced toward where Mary's eyes were fixed.

"Oh, aye. But get out of their way when they're fighting; if you think I had the moves, you haven't seen anything yet. They have far more years of experience...they're the best of the best. They're our crack troops."

"Sean is looking better, isn't he?" Mary fixed her eyes on Sean, and smiled.

"Yes. Seeing his brother seems to have done a world of wonders for him."

"It always does. It's such a shame. The curses have nearly torn their family asunder. But they still somehow make their way back here. I suppose the land gets into your blood and calls to you."

"This land does have a certain quality to it."

"Oh, you mean like being out of the way?" Mary's eyes twinkled.

"No. It is magical."

"Oh, aye, it is at that." Mary redirected her attention to the faeries at the front of the great hall. Suddenly, the haunting elvin melody drew nearer. "That ethereal music can touch you right down to your soul. I've never felt so at peace. I feel as if I could face a thousand battles." Mary's eyes brightened.

Bridget could feel the elves drawing near. The mortals in the great hall would be quite surprised to see how the elves would make their entrance. They always preferred to enter in style. Her people liked to be subtle, but the elves...well, they loved drama.

Pipe music filled the air, and the wall to their left suddenly opened. Elves came marching through the opening. A shiver raced up and down her spine. She recognized many of them. Fair-haired and raven-haired elves marched shoulder to shoulder. They too, were dressed for battle.

They looked determined. If she were a vampire...she'd be scared. Elves were unfailingly kind and loving to the innocents, but to the creatures of darkness, they had no mercy. They exuded the same glamour that her people possessed. A human that set eyes upon a true faerie or elf were said to be charmed for the rest of their days.

She locked gazes with a few of the elves that were her friends. Smiles shone in their eyes. She suddenly felt a bit more at ease. She wondered how the battles with the other vampire clans of this world and other realms were going. They had to triumph in the battle that was ahead. If they didn't, it could lead to a strategic victory for the vampire clans...a victory that they couldn't afford.

Mary gasped, and clutched onto Bridget. "I've never seen anything so extraordinary."

Bridget smiled. The leader bowed to Iris, and then

pinned his eyes on her. No, he couldn't recognize her. She nearly panicked.

Shaking her head, she hoped he would understand her message. This elf she knew well. He'd been at her mother's court many times before. Damn. Her rotten luck just kept getting progressively worse.

Not now, she mentally intoned.

He shook his head and strode toward her.

She wanted to flee the room. Jumping to her feet, she whipped around, intent upon finding the nearest exit.

He was about to blow her secret...he'd ruin everything.

"Where's the fire?" Sean asked.

She slammed into his rock hard chest, and he righted her before she could fall to the floor.

"Um...I have to go. I think..." her voice trailed off, when the elvin music stopped.

This couldn't be happening! Now, everyone in the village would know who she was. Why couldn't she ever seem to catch a bloody break? She really liked her anonymity...with it; she could pretend she was just a normal mortal. What a joke that was!

"What's gotten into you?"

"You wouldn't happen to feel another fit coming on would you?" She cringed. She'd almost sounded hopeful.

"No. I thought you said the castle was protected at the moment."

She bit her lip and sighed.

"Oh, it is. I don't think anyone could breach the magical shield that has been erected."

"Bridget, you've gone quite pale? Are you sick?" He gripped her shoulders.

His concern touched her, but still...she wished she could just transport herself upstairs and lock herself in Sean's domain.

No one would dare go there. Not even an elf.

She darted her eyes around the room. All of the visible exits were covered, and the gap in the wall had been restored.

Damn.

"Sean, there's something I neglected to tell you about myself."

"Oh, I'd rather think that there are a lot of something's that you've forgotten to tell me about yourself, but I'd rather not nitpick, at the moment."

"Sean," she looked him squarely in the eyes. "I'm..." She halted in mid-sentence when she was rudely interrupted.

"Princess!"

She gasped. All heads in the room turned to look at her. She felt as if she'd suddenly been put on display. Sean would definitely have a heyday with this one.

Why did Owen have to be so insistent? She'd specifically requested him to drop protocol in order for her to save face. Didn't he know that she'd initially been sent on assignment here? When she was on an assignment, her position as a faerie princess always had to be put aside. Sometimes there was greater work to be done than being part of a royal family. That mindset always seemed to exasperate her mother to no end.

Of course Owen would refer to her title. What else could she expect? He always valued the ranks of the magical hierarchy. But he too was born royal...so in essence; they were sort of on equal footing. She let out a heavy sigh. How did her simple life as a Huntress of Hell, suddenly become so damn complicated?

"Sean, I can explain."

But when she turned to face him, he was gone.

Chapter Twenty-Seven

A burning lump lodged itself firmly in Sean's throat.
He still couldn't believe what Bridget was capable of.

"Princess!"

Sinking to the ground, he looked up at the moon.
Reaching out, he picked a bunch of heather and crunched
it beneath his fingertips. He loved Bridget, but there were
times when he wished he'd never met her.

After years of waiting and wishing for her, she'd
stormed into his life like a bat out of Hell. He'd known
from the first moment he'd met her on that wild night
that she had been predestined for him. Even though he'd
fought admitting it, he'd loved her since first sight.
Actually, it had been more like first touch.

He swallowed. Sweat glistened on his brow. He had
to concentrate and will himself not to dash back into the
castle. She was just beyond his reach. He'd never be able
to attain her love. No matter what she did, she bravely
clung to the belief that he was a vampire and therefore no
good for her. And now, he realized why she wouldn't go
against her beliefs. She wasn't just a faerie. She was a
faerie princess.

Bile rose in his throat.

"I thought I'd find you here."

Sean didn't need to look to see who it was. "You
should go back inside the castle. You don't need to fret
about me."

"Well, why do you think I came back?" The rustle of
William settling himself on the ground beside him filled
his ears.

"William, how is this possible?"

"What, you falling in love?"

"No. You just visited us not three months ago."

"Oh, that. Well, let's just say some really nice faerie
arranged this for me. I won't be seeing you for a long time

though, because I had to borrow it against my next trip."

"I'm sorry."

"Don't apologize. I couldn't just stay in a Paris hotel wiling my hours away while you went up against the very face of evil."

"Do you ever think of what might've happened to us, had we not gone with father that night?"

"Never. We Sutherlands live by the motto *without fear,* so why should I think about what might've been? Our fates are as they are. And right now, I can see that you're about to throw everything away, because of another Sutherland curse."

"You mean our inability to find love."

"No. I'm referring to your blasted pride. I think you're surrounded with love. But the sort of love Bridget can give you is much different from the love anyone else can. I haven't known her for long, but her eyes are steadfast, and filled with emotion. She hides nothing from you. And it's only your pride that has forced you to flee from her. Look at yourself. You're acting like a little boy. I would've thought that three hundred and some odd years would've been enough for you to grow up. I guess I was wrong...will you need another three hundred to get your act together?"

"I've been grown up for as long as I can recall."

"Really?" William snorted. "Then, prove that to me, Sean. You have a great thing in Bridget. She's the answer to your curse. Would you honestly jeopardize everything that she could give you just because your pride is hurt? Face it, brother mine. You're sulking. We could see the smoke all the way up at the castle...you'd better be careful; I wouldn't want you to accidentally combust."

"You know, William, if you weren't my brother I'd be forced to do something drastic right now."

"Ah. But I am your brother. And since we're sort of in the same boat when it comes to this curse thing, I can tell you that you're a bloody idiot. If you don't allow Bridget to make your life richer, than I'll never speak to you again. And frankly, if you screw this up, you should stop calling yourself a Sutherland. We might've made a lot of bad mistakes in our lives, but we always put love before anything else."

"How can you give me advice? You haven't been that fortunate when it comes to the love game either."

"Aye. But I sure as hell wouldn't push someone like Bridget away. I mean, I put on my best charm for her, and she didn't even go for the bait. Whether she realizes it or not, she loves you. Now it falls to you to make her see just how much. Pursue her, and never let her go."

William placed his hand on Sean's shoulder and sighed. "Do you remember when we used to come here as children?" Sean's voice turned wistful.

"Aye," William murmured. "No amount of time could cause me to forget our childhood." A star streaked across the night sky. "Make a wish, Sean. Maybe it will come true."

"I'm sorry that I found the…"

"Don't worry about it. I can take being cursed for a little while longer. But I can see that it's getting to you. You look pretty bad, Sean. And whatever you might believe, I want the best for you. If Bridget can save you from your living hell, then I say all the power to her. So, she's a faerie princess. Live with it. I don't think that it'll make any difference. Besides, you fell in love with Bridget, without even knowing what she was. Let alone who she was. She's a lovely lass, take her as your own, and never let her go."

"Words of wisdom coming from my baby brother."

"Sorry to break this to you, Sean, but I haven't been a baby for a long time."

Sean breathed in deeply, when moonlight illuminated William's hand. The Sutherland ring that their father had worn during the hunt glistened on William's finger. William followed Sean's gaze and swore.

"I'm sorry. I forgot to take it off before I arrived. I'll take it off now."

"No." Sean reached for William's hand, and held it so that he wouldn't touch the ring. "Keep it on. It belongs to you. Not me. It was never mine."

"When you become human again, you'll want it. I'll put it in your rooms before I leave."

Sean grunted. "I already told you, no. You've had it for the last three hundred and thirty years, what sort of a man would I be if I made you give it back now?"

"Sean. I'll understand. It was always meant to be yours."

In the crest on the ring, there was a Celtic cross, with their clan motto etched around it. Their father had always worn it, and it had come into good use whenever they'd been fighting the creatures of the dark. But when Sean had become a vampire himself, he had been forced to give it to William.

"You've worn it well. It belongs to you. I won't hear anymore of it."

William's eyes glittered. "Well, are you going to go back into the castle and tell Bridget that you're a fool, or should I go back in there and tell her for you?"

"If they're strategizing, I'd really rather remain out here. Bridget doesn't seem to understand. Try as I might, I can't convince her that Octavia is a force to be reckoned with."

William nodded his head. "I wish someone had told us that before we decided to go after Boris."

"We couldn't have been expected to know, we didn't even know that Boris had taken a queen; he kept that really well shielded."

"Aye. But we'll get through this one together. I have a good feeling that everything will turn out right. It's your time, Sean."

"I hope you don't mean it's my time to die." Sarcasm dripped through his voice.

"Nope. Never that. You're too surly to go. You have to stay around and make life worth living."

Sean reached out to pummel William, when the smell of Heaven wafted into his nostrils. Bridget smelt like no other woman. She just made him feel good, right down to the tips of his toes.

"Penny for your thoughts?"

"I'd wager they're worth a good deal more than that." He glanced up at Bridget, and grunted when William went striding off into the distance.

"You're brother is a good guy."

"One of the best."

"Can he fight like you?"

"No. He can fight better." Sean dropped the crumpled heather that he held, and rolled his hands into tight fists.

He fought the urge to pull her down into his lap, but if her scent came traveling on the wind; he'd be a goner for sure.

"Sean, I should've told you about myself. But it didn't seem to be an issue."

"It's alright. I can understand why you did it. After all, I wouldn't want a raving monster like myself knowing about my nearest and dearest."

"That isn't fair." She snapped her fingers, and a blanket appeared on the ground beside him.

He narrowed his eyes when he recognized his family tartan.

"I wouldn't want you to get comfortable. You have work that needs to be done back up in my castle."

"Oh, don't worry about it, as you told me before, they all have it well in hand."

He slanted his mouth into a lopsided grin. Perhaps William was right. He shouldn't allow his pride to debilitate him when it came to Bridget. He could sense her drawing nearer to him. As soon as she was near enough, she snuggled herself up against him, and rested her head on his shoulder.

"You should leave."

"I'm not going anywhere. I need to be with you at the moment. And besides, it's a beautiful clear night. Look at that sky. I think that if I just reached up, I'd be able to snatch a star out and keep it for wishing on."

He smiled. She was a faerie. She could do anything she wanted, and yet she still found the beauty in nature.

"If I could, I'd give you anything. But it's pretty hard to surpass what you already have." He felt her stiffen and frowned.

"I don't have it all you know. When you took off on me, without even giving me time to explain, I felt like the floor was wrenched out from beneath me."

"You don't need to feel as if you have to tell me anything. I've decided that I just want the ability to love you." The sound of her breath catching in her throat made a warm pulse go through him. "And before you say anything, I don't expect anything in return. I've waited for ages just to meet you. Now that I have you, I wouldn't want to do anything that might cause you to run away from me. I can bear almost anything, but losing you isn't on my list."

Silence stretched between them, except for the occasional sound of nature.

"You'll never lose me. I'll always be someone that you can count on."

"Good to hear."

"Are you nervous?"

"Nervous about what? Loving you, or fearing that you'll never return that love?"

She looked away, and sighed. He groaned. He'd enjoyed feeling the nearness of her, resting her head on his shoulder. And now that it was gone, he felt strangely bereft. Before she could stand up, he enclosed his hand around her wrist.

"Stay with me." He pulled her against him, and arranged it so that she was lying across his lap looking up at him. A catch formed in his throat. Her eyes would always be able to make him weak kneed.

"I just remembered something."

"Well, that's always good. Shows that you're not quite over the hill yet."

"Don't be a smart ass. I'm serious. It's about something that Father Clancy said to me. About your curse."

He pursed his lips. "Don't fret your little head about it. It makes no difference. We are what we are. Strangely compatible for each other."

"No, he mentioned that I was the key. Tell me, what does that mean exactly? What am I supposed to unlock? Sean?"

He cleared his throat and then coughed. He couldn't tell her that she was the key, because she met all of the physical requirements. He couldn't tell her that if she professed her love for him, by saying 'I love you' that he'd be set free, and returned to what he was before being cursed. No, the curse precluded all of that. He'd seen what had happened to William when he'd tried to fight the curse.

Sean had come too far to risk losing it all.

"It doesn't mean anything." The look she gave him plainly told him that she knew he was avoiding telling her the truth.

"Sean, Father Clancy had a reason for telling me that. And I'd like to know what it was. Is there something that I can do to free you from your chains? If there is you need to tell me...and I'll do it."

She didn't understand. It wasn't that simple. He wanted her to mean the words when she said them...he wanted her to mean them for the rest of her life. And, since she was a faerie that was one long lifespan. He had to distract her, before she could go any further with her interrogation. "You could kiss me."

"If kissing you freed you from the curse then you would've been freed a long time ago."

He grinned. "Nothing ever escapes your attention, does it?"

He trailed a tender finger along her cheek. Her skin was silky soft. He could drown in her eyes, and forget himself whenever he made love to her.

She bit her lip. No matter how hard he tried dissuading her, she still kept to it. Maybe, they couldn't get along at times, because they were just too damn alike.

"If there is something that I can do, you have to tell me." She sat up, staring him straight in the eyes. "I've been asked by the elvin and faerie commanders if I've seen the way yet. When I inquired, they shut their mouths. Then, someone else whispered, *nope he's still a vampire.* So tell me, Sean Sutherland, what exactly are you hiding from me?"

"You already know everything that I can tell you. You're the key. But you'll just have to figure out how to unlock my curse on your own, because my hands are tied when it comes down to telling you. If I do, something terrible could befall us both."

"How terrible?"

He sighed. "Only you would ask a question like that."

"Well, can you give me a hint? On a scale of one to ten, how horrible would it be if you just let it slip out? We could always blame it on a slip of the tongue. You could say that you forgot you weren't supposed to mention it. I've never been one for rules anyway. Let's just say...I've been known to rebel from time to time." She smiled.

"Trust me, if I told you, it could put everything we've strived for at risk."

"Oh. That's a no go then?"

"Yes, it's out of the question. Not going to happen." He tried to put a severe look on his face, but he could see by the light in her eyes that she wasn't buying it.

"I guess we could call this the calm before the storm. By tomorrow night, everything could be much different."

"Aye."

"But I'll still have you, so everything will be okay."

"As long as you're with me, I can face anything."

Her eyes softened. He could nearly see her soul reflected in the sparkles that danced in her eyes. He'd never let her slip out of his grasp. She contained a quality that no other woman he'd ever met had held.

Simply put, she was a force of good. She definitely had all of the right stuff to free him from the darkness that plagued his life. He yearned to be kissed by sunlight again, but as long as he had her, he could bask in the most glorious light of all.

"Without me, you seemed to face down a lot of bad stuff," Bridget pointed out.

"Before you came to the village, I had been nearing my most desperate hour. I was in deep pain."

"So, I guess your grouchiness could be explained. Is that what you're saying? That's good though, I'd hate to have a lover that's a bear with a sore ass."

"I hate what I am. I had been feeling the stirring pulsing inside of me like it was going to rip right out of me. As you can well imagine, the hopelessness and helplessness I felt considerably added to my pain."

"Well, I'm here now. You can use me like a painkiller. I'm rather good at making people feel better."

He closed his eyes. "Aye. You are the answer to my prayers. I didn't know it at first, and I know I acted like a right proper prick, but I'm very glad that you stuck it out. Now, don't get me started on those romance books you write."

She arched her eyebrow. "Have you even read any of them?"

"No. But let me tell you, I've nearly tripped over a few of them. Grace is mad about the ruddy things."

"Well, at least someone in your family has good taste."

"Oh, you wound me!" He laughed. Everything seemed almost too good to be true. Somehow, they had found a way to work. Despite herself, Bridget seemed to be falling for him. But he needed her to tumble at a faster velocity. He wanted her to be his in every sense of the meaning. He wanted to be able to tell her that he loved her without getting a *thank you* in return. That still galled him. He clenched his jaw and ran his fingers through her hair. He was about to lean down to kiss Bridget when she bolted upright.

"Do you remember seeing Father Clancy in the castle? I don't." She chewed her lip.

He shrugged his shoulders. "I don't think I did see him, though it seemed as if everyone and their brother had come up from the village."

"Yes. Strange indeed, that isn't like Father Clancy. I know he would've wanted to..." Her train of conversation ran off the track as fire lit her eyes.

"What's going on?" He watched her warily when she jumped to her feet.

"Those bastards. How they thought they could away with this is beyond me. The nerve! I'll have to teach them a thing or two." She started to walk away from him.

"Where are you going? Whoever ruined our moment is going to get an ear full."

"I'm going to dash down to the village. I think that it would be better if you stayed here."

"Well, you can go and pound salt on that one. I'll do no such thing. I'm coming with you. Is it vampires? Have they infiltrated the village, unbeknownst to us?"

"No." She moved so quickly toward the village that her feet barely touched the ground. He sped up his pace, and had almost closed the distance between them when the village came into view. "It isn't vampires, and whatever you do, Sean, you have to keep yourself from losing your control."

"I never lose my control, unless properly provoked or possessed." He rolled his eyes. Then, he skidded to a halt when his eyes took in the scene that unfolded before him. "Blast and damn. Those stupid buggers. I'm going to..."

"You'll let me handle this, Sean Sutherland."

He glowered at her. Pulling his hood up over his

head, he snorted. "I've dealt with them before, and I've done okay."

"Oh, yeah. You really made an impression. So much so, that they put you on probation."

He narrowed his eyes to thin slits. "I only did that, because the man was a lecherous pig."

"Maybe so, but with what's coming, we can't afford for you to get yourself in any more hot water. Let a professional deal with this...besides, I'm not quite as hotheaded as you are."

Grumbling, he followed Bridget as she made her way over to the front of the church. Glancing down at the suitcases that were on the ground, he cleared his throat.

"Going on holiday, Father?"

"No." Father Clancy's eyes darted everywhere but to meet his gaze.

"Well, then what do you need that luggage for?" Sean crossed his arms. He was stewing for one hell of a row. He looked around, and his eyes nearly popped out of his head when a large black convertible pulled up.

The door opened, and he groaned. "Not you, again. I thought I told you that you were welcome to keep yourself out of my village? Do you have a hard time remembering things or what?"

Father Monroe looked at him sternly. "I see that you haven't changed, Sean."

"Aye. But you've gotten older and fatter."

Bridget gasped. Father Clancy made a weird choking noise.

Sean moved forward. "If you think that you're going to ship Father Clancy off then you can go jump off a really high cliff."

Chapter Twenty-Eight

Octavia looked into the deep black pool. Voices rose out of it. She raised her hand when Catherine entered her lair. "Shush. I need to concentrate. Things are not going as I expected."

Catherine's high heels clicked on the stone floor as she made her way over to her side.

"Are the odds stacked against us?"

Octavia pursed her lips. "Not yet, ma chere. Not yet. I am biding my time. Sean is harder to manipulate than I had originally thought. Things could get interesting but they are in no way undoable. I will crack him soon enough."

"He does have that faerie, and our spies say that their reinforcements have already begun to fill the village."

"Oh, I know. I've seen it all." She waved her hand across the pool, and smiled when the images popped up in front of her.

Catherine gasped. "How is this possible?"

"Many things are possible, ma chere. But I can see that I must up the ante now that those blasted humans and faeries are anticipating our arrival. Perhaps they should expect the unexpected; what do you think, ma chere?"

"I think you have outdone yourself."

"Are the forces ready?"

"Oh, yes. But our generals still fear clashes from other clans. We may not be able to wipe out the village as you had hoped."

"We need to destroy Sean's people. If we can obtain Sean Sutherland's holdings as our territory, our power will increase tenfold."

"What will Sean Sutherland's land do for us?"

"It will tip the scales of magical power in our favor.

The land is enchanted. We must have control of it. Once our darkness seeps across the territory, we will be nearly unstoppable. Our enemies will not be able to prevail against us."

"And if we lose, will we not..." Catherine clamped her mouth shut, as Octavia looked her way.

"Finish your thought, ma chere." Octavia's eyes narrowed.

Catherine might be close to her, but if she doubted her in any way, she'd make sure that Catherine paid for her disloyalty.

"I can't remember what I was about to say." Catherine's eyes flashed with fear.

Octavia sighed.

"Ma chere, in the future, do not lie to me." She raised her hand, and Catherine crumpled onto the floor writhing in agony.

"Mistress, please."

"And, do not beg for mercy. I don't admire that in anyone, especially someone as dear to me as you are."

Catherine's anguished cries filled Octavia with pure unadulterated joy. Silence suddenly draped her lair. She glanced over at the striking portrait of Boris. Stepping over Catherine, she moved to the painting.

"Ah, Mon amour. How I miss you." She reached out, and touched the canvas. Hatred filled her heart. Sean would either cross over to her side, or she would see that everything he loved was destroyed.

The curse had not been punishment enough for him. With every day that he spent with Bridget, he came ever closer to breaking the curse. Whatever happened, Octavia could not let his suffering end. Raising her finger to her lips, she kissed it, and then pressed it against Boris's lips.

"I will not fail you." She whisked around, smiling when she caught sight of Catherine.

"Mistress." Catherine's feeble voice barely reached her ears.

Octavia glided over to her, and held her hand out for Catherine to take.

"Get up, ma chere. We have work to do. I must begin the incantation to open the portals."

"So, we are moving ahead of schedule?"

"Ma chere, we will plant ourselves in strategic positions. We just have enough time to strike once this night. It will throw our enemies off, and while some of our troops are in attack mode, we can set the others up to strike tomorrow night."

"How will they take shelter against the sun?"

"Ma chere. Do not fret. I have taken care of it all. They will never see us coming. This I can assure you." Reaching for Catherine's hand, she gripped it tightly.

Sean Sutherland would lose everything that he held dear. And she would stand by and rejoice in every single aspect of his misery. He wouldn't see them coming, and by the time her people struck, there would be no way to escape.

And, so it begins.

Chapter Twenty-Nine

Bridget shivered. Sean pulled her close to him. She felt uneasy. Staring up at the sky, she searched it for any sign of activity. She didn't like the feeling that had just washed over her. Wrinkling her brow, she moved closer to Sean, and waited to see how Father Monroe would reply.

"Well, Sean, I can see that you haven't lost that silver tongue of yours."

"I'm serious, Father Monroe. Father Clancy isn't going anywhere."

"Could I please have a word with you, Sean?"

Sean looked between Father Clancy and Father Monroe. "Fine," he grumbled.

He stared over at Father Monroe. Bridget sighed.

"I'll humor you this time, Sean." Father Monroe climbed back into his vehicle and slammed the door shut.

Bridget looked to the side, expecting to see someone. She still felt antsy. Licking her lips, she sniffed at the air.

"Are you alright, my dear?" Father Clancy asked, staring intently at her.

"I think so."

At her words, Sean glanced her way.

"What's gotten into you? You look as if someone just walked over your grave."

"Don't worry. I'll be okay in a second."

Father Clancy hesitated and then started his diatribe. "Sean, you really must stop interfering. If you must know, this isn't my luggage."

"It isn't?" Sean's jaw dropped.

Raising her hand to her mouth, Bridget coughed.

"No. I would've told you if I'd decided to just get up and leave. But as I've already expressed to you on numerous occasions before, I'm in this for the long haul."

"Father Clancy, I don't know what to say."

"Well, that's a first. Saints be praised!"

Bridget couldn't help herself. She laughed.

"I'm glad to see someone's finding this amusing." Sean gave her a glare.

"Sorry," she mumbled, clapping her hand over her mouth. Out of the corner of her eye, she could've sworn she saw a shadowy figure. Suddenly on alert, she glanced toward the open door that led into the Church. "Father Clancy, who does the luggage belong to?"

"Eh?" Father Clancy also seemed to be on edge. "Those would belong to Father Aidan. He's requested a transfer. Right as we speak, the others are trying to convince him against it. They keep telling him that this is a prime parish, a great opportunity to prove himself, and that he shouldn't give it up. But I rather think he's a little overwhelmed, and a little unprepared. In theory, it's a walk in the park to prepare in countless simulations to meet up with vampires, but being faced with a real one can knock one for a loop. Father Aidan just doesn't seem cut out for the task at hand. Oh, aye, he's a great priest, but...well, some things just aren't meant for all people."

"The others?" she shook her head.

"Father McNeil, Sister Agnes and Sister Mary Clarence have arrived. They'll be staying with me."

"What about Father Monroe?"

Father Clancy chuckled. The smooth warm sound of it eased the chill in Bridget's bones. "Ah, he wouldn't be caught dead here in this village. He and Sean never have hit it off."

"Ah." Bridget jumped when another shadowy figure whisked by. "Did you see that?"

"What?" Sean turned around.

"I could've sworn that I just saw...but it couldn't be."

"Bridget, you have to tell us what's going on. We aren't mind readers you know."

Bridget watched in dumbstruck horror as Sean's eyes rolled up in the back of his head.

Not good. Damn.

"Sean?" She clutched onto his cloak, pulling her close to him.

He growled, and threw her off of him. She hurtled through the air. Just before she was about to hit the ground, she took control of her actions, and slowed her

Marly Mathews

momentum. Levitating herself, she created a great gust of wind. Thunder rumbled through the landscape. Shadowy figures begin to drop from the sky in the dozens.

"No!" Her eyes widened. Through the haze of her disoriented vision, she could see Father Clancy pulling Sean into the church.

Father Monroe had hold of the door, and he slammed it shut, just as Bridget began to fly toward them. As much as she didn't want to admit it, she couldn't trust Sean in his current state. She feared that Octavia had repossessed him.

As a horde of vampires moved in on her, she lit the sky up with the full force of her faerie fire. It took out a few of the stragglers but not enough to put a dent in their lines. Fortunately for her, her conjured faerie fire would be seen by all of the inhabitants of the castle, and reinforcements would soon arrive.

Lightening streaked across the sky. She swallowed. In her days as a huntress she had faced many vampires in battle but there was something oddly different about these vampires. In a flash, she summoned her blade.

Working quickly, she took out several vampires before they could close in on her. Battle cries filled the air, as warrior elves and faeries charged to her rescue. She closed her eyes. A searing sensation entered her left shoulder. She plucked a dart out of it and grimaced.

"What in the world?" She couldn't seem to recall when she'd been hit with the bloody thing. Drowsiness bled into her veins.

She yawned.

She had to get to the Church. Sean needed her. She could feel him pulling her to him. Her heart hammered inside of her chest, as fire raged through her. Why had she become so damn hot? Dizziness threatened her vision, and blood pounded in her ears. She flew toward the church.

The elves and faeries seemed to have the fight tipped in their favor. As soon as her feet touched the ground, she moved to the Church door. Stumbling, she fell against it with a loud thud.

Voices raised in their urgency.

"Sean," she whispered.

Weakness traveled to every corner of her body. Whatever had been in that dart had been made specifically to debilitate her. Even though she was a faerie, some rare and ancient poisons could still affect her kind.

Invisible hands pulled at her. She tried to brush them away. No one seemed to see that she needed help. But then, why would that even occur to them?

She was after all a Huntress of Hell. Through her clouded vision she could see Mary, Grace and Orla running toward her. She slumped into a cross-legged position in front of the church. She couldn't give into the lethargy that pulled at her.

If only Sean could fight Octavia. She needed him, no doubt more than he needed her. A familiar sensation brushed against her temple. She smiled. At least someone from her own kind realized she had fallen into a perilous state of affairs.

A portal opened in front of her, and before she could react, the yawning whirlpool sucked her in. The last cry she heard before she lost all coherent thought came from Sean's mouth.

Chapter Thirty

Sean lunged toward Bridget. He watched in desperation as she faded before his eyes. He hit the ground face first.

"God help us!" Father Clancy muttered.

Sean closed his eyes. His heart pounded so loudly that he feared everyone clustered around him could hear it.

"Uncle Sean?" He could feel her hand on his back. "Come on, you have to get up!" He wanted to die. Bridget had been taken from him. Helplessness seeped into every one of his pores. "Uncle Sean, please, you have to take control of your senses. Uncle William's on his way over here as we speak." In one last ditch effort, Grace knelt down beside him, and pressed her hand against his cheek. "We have to find a way to rescue Bridget."

He looked up. During his moment of emotional turmoil, he could've sworn that his mother stared at him. Buoyed by the comforting emotions that rolled through him, he sat up. Rubbing the back of his head, he grimaced. He could only recall a few snatches of what had just happened.

"Father Clancy, what just went on?"

"You had another fit, my son."

He groaned. A burning sensation kept prickling at the palm of his right hand. He turned it over and snorted.

"Thank you, for doing what had to be done to get Octavia out of my head."

Father Clancy nodded his head solemnly. "You are more than welcome, Sean. I thank the Lord that Octavia finds the touch of the cross even more painful than you do." Father Clancy offered him his hand, and Sean gratefully accepted it.

"Do you think that it was Octavia that took Bridget?" Grace asked.

He nodded his head grimly. "Who else could it be? I know of no other that wields such terrifying dark magic."

"Did you see her face before she disappeared?" Orla cut in.

"Aye." Sean's stomach churned just thinking about it.

"No, I didn't," Grace murmured. "Was she frightened?"

"She looked pale." Orla chewed her lip. "I don't think that turning that pale is a good sign for mortals or faeries."

Sean kicked the ground. The battle still raged above them, and in the street. But he couldn't seem to get his thoughts off of Bridget.

"Sorry, I took so long." William shouted above the noise. Just as he approached them another vampire skulked up behind him. Without even turning to stare down the vampire, William took his stake, and plunged it into the vampire. William's keen senses almost gave the impression of having eyes in the back of his head. "Bloody buggers. They never can take the hint, can they?" He grinned. Sean felt sick. William's grin faded away. "Where's Bridget?"

"Gone." Sean forced the word out.

William looked as if someone had just struck him dead. "Not possible. She's a faerie. Furthermore, she's a Huntress of Hell. She should be here in the middle of the fray with us. I mean sure, the battle came to our doorstep sooner than we had anticipated, but we still have a good chance of prevailing."

Sean glanced toward the Church. Exhaustion ripped at his being. He raised his eyebrow when he caught sight of Ridley and Rowan fighting back to back. His people were proving themselves in this struggle. He itched to join them, but his heart ached for Bridget.

He needed to do everything in his power to rush to her aid. But he was still limited by the curse. He didn't know where Octavia's lair was located, and he had a pretty dead on feeling that Octavia would've been clever enough to base it outside of his territory.

"Blast and damn!" He began to pace restlessly. His village had been invaded, and his true love had been taken from him. He had been attacked on all fronts, and he didn't like it one bit. This time...this time Octavia would not win. He'd make sure that the bloody bitch got everything that was coming to her. He had some outstanding dues to pay back, and the sooner he meted out his retribution, the better.

"We should fight." Father Clancy prepared to jump into the fray.

Sister Mary Clarence and Sister Agnes already battled the vampires. Sean had to admire them. They had guts.

"No. Father Clancy, I need you to go back into the Church and scan over the old documents of my father's. There just might be something in there that could tip us off as to where Bridget has been taken."

"Sean, I've told you time and again. I've studied those documents so much that I've almost memorized them."

"Look over them again, Father Clancy. You might surprise us all by finding something that we've previously missed. Sometimes things are smack dab under your nose, and you don't discover them until you have need of them."

William darted his gaze between Sean and the battle.

"Keep me updated. But by the looks of it, I'm needed." William winked at him, grinned at Grace and then dashed out back into the fight.

"I should go with him," Grace murmured.

Sean grabbed her before she could leave.

Orla had already disappeared and Mary had obviously gone with her. He grunted. For once in his life, just once, couldn't the women of his village do what was best for them? It wasn't safe for them to be fighting. They could get themselves hurt. He'd already lost Bridget, and he'd be damned if he lost anyone else.

"Uncle Sean, you have to let me go. I can be William's fighting partner." Sean pursed his lips. "I don't think that William needs a fighting partner. And besides, I need you to help me in my search for Bridget."

"I don't think I can. Did you see that thing? That portal was opened by dark magic. That's way above anything I've ever done." She gasped. And then slapped her hand over her mouth. "Oops! You weren't supposed to know about that."

He narrowed his eyes. "Did you think that you could practice white magic without me realizing what you were up to?"

"I thought..."

"Save it. The women in our family have always had that annoying trick. I just never thought that you'd be the one to explore it."

"Actually, Mum has been reacquainting herself with it as well. She said that Grandmother had the gift. And that from the records your mother did as well."

The muscle in Sean's cheek bulged. "You shouldn't have gone rooting for that information."

Grace groaned. "Look, I'm not as good as the faeries or the elves, for that matter. Why don't you just get them to help us? As soon as they realize what's happened to Bridget, they'll be frantic to get her back."

"I'm already frantic. I'm at my wits end!" He raked his hand through his hair.

"We already know, Grace Sutherland."

Sean's heart dropped into his stomach. Whoever had spoken stood directly behind him. By the expression on Grace's face, he could tell that it had to be an impressive sight.

Cautiously, he twisted around.

The woman that stood before him was bathed in ethereal light. She resembled Bridget so closely that it nearly took his breath away. She wore a crown of what seemed to be sparkling stars, but what were probably only diamonds. This had to be Bridget's mother.

"Why are you here?"

"As you've already realized, I am Bridget's mother. Did you honestly think that I would not be keeping an eye on her? Who do you suppose put the thought in her head to come here in the first place?"

Sean looked around him. They were no longer standing in the village. "What is this place that you've taken us to?"

"It's a safe haven. We will not be interrupted here." She smiled.

Grace let out a sound that conveyed her wonder.

"Why did you bring me here? If you have this sort of awe-inspiring power then you should be using it to save

Bridget." He nearly shouted, and her eyes filled with love.

"I have brought you here, because it is your time to become my daughter's savior. Or rather, your niece will have the task of bringing her back to us. I can't leave my kingdom. Right now it requires my protection. I would never leave my daughter without some protection. As we speak, there is an ancient poison running through her body. This poison has the ability to kill her."

Sean swayed. He felt as if someone had just sliced him through with a claymore.

"Whether my Bridget realizes it or not, she is the key to breaking your curse. I have always known this. Now, it falls to her to discover it for herself. Time stopped when the two of you met. But Bridget is stubborn. She will deny her heart with all of the fervor in her."

"Then how will the curse be broken? If she keeps denying her heart, she will never confess her love." A bitter taste filled his mouth.

"Oh, she already has confessed her love. Inwardly, she hears her heart. It will only be a matter of time before she gives in, and tells you what you've been waiting to hear." Her eyes softened. "Grace, I must have your consent for what I am about to do."

Sean turned to Grace and stepped in front of her, shielding her. "Whatever is churning around in that mind of yours, you can just forget about it. Nothing happens to Grace."

"Sean Sutherland, I admire your courage. Your heart is true. That is why I pushed my daughter to meet you. Vampire or not, you are good."

"Uncle Sean, please. I really don't think she means me any harm. And if it means that I'll be able to free Bridget, I'll agree to anything. She saved my life!"

"Aye. She did. And it is what has bonded you to my daughter. The two of you were always aligned spiritually. But when Bridget made the choice to save you, she endowed you with some of her glamour. Whether you realize it or not, you have become a different person. You have become a lightening rod for good magic."

"I'm ready for whatever you must do." Grace stood up straighter, and threw her chest out.

"It's good to know that you are willing." From her

long white sparkling robes, Bridget's mother produced a camera and a torch.

"Bridget kept thinking I had those." Sean glared at the powerful faerie.

"Did she? Well, I needed to take them from her the very first night. Grace will need them if she is going to succeed."

"I want to go with Grace." Sean stepped forward, just as Grace accepted the camera and torch and placed them carefully into her knapsack.

"How will I know what to do with them?" Grace sounded doubtful.

"When the urgency is great, you will know." Bridget's mother gently touched Grace's cheek. Sean watched entranced as a bright white orb shot out of her fingertips, and illuminated Grace's entire body. "You are now ready. Bless you, Grace Sutherland. But there is one last thing." She snapped her fingers, and two vials appeared in her hand. One was bright violet and the other was black.

"This one will counteract the poison that is in Bridget's body. Once you give this potion to her, she will be back to her old strong self. This one," she held up the black vial, "will open the portal back to the village."

"What about Octavia?"

"Grace will be able to face her."

"Is that all? You should be telling her things to do. Why don't you give her some protective charms or crystals, or jewels? Bloody hell woman, you need to give Grace something to defend herself with."

"She has her inner light. That will be enough." The Faerie Queen turned to leave.

"Wait."

She whirled back to face him. "Yes?"

"Is that all you're going to tell us? Nothing else? I mean I'd like to know that everything is going to be fine. I don't feel like it's going to be all right. I need some proof."

"Love is all the proof you need." She waved her hand in farewell to them, and then raised her other hand to open a portal. "That will take you to Octavia, Grace. Goodbye, Sean."

He could feel himself floating away from Grace. He watched horrified, as she jumped into the portal without thinking twice. He reached out for her. He needed to go with her. She needed him to look out for her. But he had drifted too far. The next thing he knew, he was staring up into Father Clancy's bright blue eyes.

"My son, how are you?"

"Grace!" He sat up and shook his head. He was getting sick of feeling as if he had cobwebs lodged in his brain. He found himself sitting on a church pew. "Damn."

"Where did you go?" Father Clancy inclined his head.

"I went into a reality that Bridget's mother created." He grunted. His head felt as if it was about to split in half. He swallowed. His mouth felt like sandpaper. "Did you find anything?"

"I was just about to get to that. But you have to answer my questions first. Where is Grace?"

"She's gone to save Bridget."

"Oh, good Lord." Father Clancy crossed himself, and lifted his eyes to the heavens. "That wee one will be no match against Octavia."

"Bridget's mother seems to think otherwise."

"Why didn't you go with her?"

"Obviously, Octavia's lair is out of my reach." He hated feeling so helpless. He wanted to charge into battle by Grace's side. He'd always taken care of Grace, and watched over her. She was fragile. He feared for her safety. No one had ever been able to stand against Octavia's wrath. How could Bridget's mother expect Grace too? It was too much! He slammed his hand down. The resulting cacophony made Father Clancy jump. "How goes the fight?"

"I think it's pretty safe to say that our side has the advantage. And the battle will not last much longer. The sun will rise in an hour. But we have suffered casualties. The faeries and elves have arranged it so that as soon as someone falls their body is transported back to the castle, where healers await them."

"Well, we can be thankful for that." Sean felt restless. The stirring pulled at him. He had to fight it. If Octavia found a way to instigate their connection again, he'd be tempted to drive a stake through is own heart. "You mentioned that you had found something." Sean arched an eyebrow.

"Aye. I have. And, I know that it was never there before. I've read the documents so many times. It boggles the mind to think how I could've possibly missed it."

"What did you find?"

"Fortify yourself, Sean." Father Clancy spread the old papers out across the front dais.

"What are you on about? I'm perfectly fine, considering what's going on."

Father Clancy still looked doubtful. "Sean, I know that you're trying to control yourself, but this…well, let's just say this could come as quite a shock to you."

"I've been shocked before. No worries, Father Clancy. Somehow, I doubt this could top any of the other things I've had to deal with."

"Your mother, how much did you know about her?"

"Plenty. She was the daughter of an English duke, but her mother was a MacKinnon."

"Oh, is that all?"

"Well, of course I know more about her, but that's her family history in a nutshell. When she met my father she fell madly in love with him, and came here. After that, she bore him many children, and she helped him in his hunt. She also made sure that her faith never fell far from her mind. And she died with the knowledge that she could do nothing to save her cursed children."

"Oh, I wouldn't be so sure of that. I think she may have had an inkling that your suffering would one day come to an end. Of course, she must've pined for your father, because I believe that they shared the same strong love that you and Bridget share."

Tears stung Sean's eyes. He felt as if he was about to choke up.

Father Clancy opened his mouth to make his announcement, when something crashed against the Church door. The next moment it was open. A vampire came staggering through looking stunned and confused. When his eyes caught sight of the various religious icons, he tried to back up, but it was too late. With an agonized cry, he blew up into smoke. His ashes dusted the church floor.

"Well, that was definitely interesting." Sean snorted.

"He had not been invited." Father Clancy grinned.

Sean's eyes wandered to the fight outside. William seemed to be in the thick of it. And by the looks of it, he required Sean's help. Sean clapped his hand on Father Clancy's shoulder.

"My apologies, Father Clancy, but I'm afraid I'll have to listen to you later. William needs me."

"I'm coming with you." Father Clancy slung his bag of hunting supplies over his shoulder. "I may not be as spry as I used to be, but this old body still has some fight in it."

"I know," Sean grinned. "Just watch yourself. I'm not ready to bury you yet." He thumped him on the back. "Come on, let's go and smoke some vamps. If I'm really lucky, Bridget will be waiting for us when we're done." Apprehension still wound its way through his gut. He could do nothing. All that he could do was put his angry frustration to use. In his current mood, Octavia's vampires didn't stand a chance in Hell.

No pun intended.

Chapter Thirty-One

Bridget winced against the thudding pain in her head. She wetted her dry lips. Someone had placed her in a darkened room. Dust particles floated through the air, making her nose itch. She coughed, and strangely enough drew no one's attention. When she tried to move, she found that she'd been tied to a board that resembled a rack from the medieval times. She groaned.

This couldn't be a good sign. She felt horrid. Pain throbbed in every single muscle. Even biting her lip seemed to take an awful lot of energy. Her eyes scanned the room she had been placed in.

It was small. The walls were draped with red velvet. A skull sat on the far wall. She grimaced. If she'd doubted it before, she knew now that Octavia had taken her. Breathing deeply, she tried to activate her magic, and instead she was rewarded with searing misery.

She had to bite deeply into her bottom lip, to muffle her agonized scream. Heat poured through the room making her break out into a clammy sweat. She rolled her head to the side when a loud crackling noise filled the room.

"GRACE!"

Grace jumped into the room and smiled at her.

"Hello! I'm here to get you out of this nasty old place." She wrinkled her nose. "Is it just me or does it stink in here?"

"It stinks in here." Bridget coughed as another spasm of pain worked its way through her body. "If you don't get me out of here soon, I'll throw up."

"Well, then, not a problem. I'm here to help." She dashed to Bridget's side, and stared at the manacles that were around her wrist. "Huh. Those are going to be a trick and half to unlock." Grace reached to touch them, when something clicked inside of Bridget's brain.

"Don't touch them! They could be rigged."

"Who in the world would think of booby trapping shackles?"

"We're talking about a psychotic vampire sorceress here."

Grace's eyes widened in dawning clarity.

"Oh. Aye. That we are. If I can't touch them, how do I get them off you? I don't know what to do!"

Bridget gasped. Excruciating pain built up inside of her. She needed to scream, but she couldn't. Reaching deep inside of her, she tried to calm herself and stop the flow of whatever poison had been injected into her system.

"You could…" Her voice drifted off, when she caught sight of the bag that Grace wore slung over her shoulder. "What have you got in there?"

Grace's eyes lit up with excitement. "Only a camera, a torch, and oh! I almost forgot." She opened the bag, and rooted inside of it. "Aha! Here it is. You have to drink this. I'm on direct orders from your mother." She popped the stopper off it, and tilted it up to Bridget's lips. "Maybe once this gets through your system you'll be able to break through the chains with your faerie strength." Bridget managed to muster a weak smile. The cool liquid rolled across her tongue. She swallowed it all in one big gulp. Grace pulled a tissue out of her bag and wiped it across her brow. "Now, then. How do I get those things unlocked?"

"You said you brought my torch. Pull it out of the bag."

"What am I going to do with it? I can already see. I don't need something to light my way."

"Just look at it!"

Grace furrowed her brow, and glanced down at the torch. "Why, it has different settings. I didn't see those before when your mother gave it to me."

"She must have made it so that you'd be able to see what I'd cloaked. Now, pick the setting right below the red button. I believe it's a purple button."

"Are you sure? Believing and knowing are two different things. I'm not going to like, blow you up am I?"

"Not on the purple setting. Just don't touch the red or black buttons."

"I don't want to know what those do, do I?"

"Not right now. I'll tell you later if we're in need of them." Now that the effects of the poison were quickly wearing off, she could hear a loud commotion going on right outside of the room. "Grace, I don't want to pressure you or anything but you're going to have to move it! In about two minutes, I'd say that we would be having company."

"Oh, no!" She rested her finger on the purple button, closed her eyes, and mouthed a prayer. Pushing the button, she cracked one eye open and then the other.

"Oh, for goodness sake! Nothing bad is going to happen to me with you wielding that torch. But if you don't hurry it along, something bad is going to come charging through that door!"

"I'm hurrying. Uh, what do I do know?" A thin emerald green light emanated from the torch.

"Point it at the manacles, and they should unlock. Hurry!"

Grace did as Bridget instructed.

"Oh, cool!" Grace was in awe.

Bridget tried to look up at her wrist. Her arms were heavy with fatigue from being in such an awkward position for so long.

"These little gadgets you have sure do get the job done."

"You can say that again." Bridget grunted. Both of her wrists were now free. She began rubbing one wrist and then the other. "So, did my mother give you a way to get out of here? Because much as I'd like to help, I don't think I'm strong enough to conjure up a portal back to the village."

"I've got it taken care of." Grace rummaged inside of her bag again, and swore when the black vial she produced flipped out of her hand and rolled across the floor toward the door. They both scurried after it. "Oh, bloody hell!"

Bridget bent to pick it up, and had it in her hands when a dizzy spell washed over her. Stars exploded in front of her. "Oh, head rush!"

"You okay?" Grace gripped onto her, just as the door flew open and rattled back on its hinges.

"I was. But I don't feel so hot now."

They both exchanged a horrified look, and then glanced back at Octavia and Catherine.

"Grace, the torch. Press the red button!" She grabbed onto Grace's free arm, and watched as Grace pressed down on the red button. Bright light bounced off the walls, a large laser-like beam spewed forth hitting Octavia and Catherine head on.

"Come on!" Bridget threw the black vial toward the floor and when it broke it emitted a swirling multi-colored smoke. The smoke slowly transformed itself into a portal just big enough in diameter for Bridget and Grace to jump through. Pulling Grace behind her, she dove into the portal.

"Oh, man, I really don't like this feeling," Grace cried, but her voice became lost as they hurled through the void.

Bridget somersaulted to her feet. She took in her surroundings, and let out a sigh of relief.

Twilight crept across the landscape. The battle seemed to have already been won. An acrid stench filled her nostrils, and she grimaced as she recognized it for it was. She could feel Grace standing behind her.

"Thank you." She hugged Grace and then stepped back.

The village seemed to have been abandoned, and she guessed that the faeries and elves had gone back up to the castle. William stood over by the Church, surrounded by Mary, Orla, Father Clancy, and Rupert. She rushed over to them, with Grace hot on her heels.

"Where's Sean?" Bridget asked.

Mary and Orla let out surprised gasps. Orla pulled Grace to her side, and sighed.

"He's out on the cliffs. I tried talking some sense into him, but he won't be deterred. He's determined to wait out here until you come back to him."

"But the sun will be up in no time at all."

"I tried to tell that to him, but when it comes to Sean, I might as well talk to my ass." Orla snorted.

"Aye." Father Clancy nodded his head. "I know the feeling."

She dropped her arms to her side.

"Well, this behavior just will not do. Didn't you say

anything to him, William?"

"I value my sanity, thank you." He smiled.

She blew out a gust of frustrated air. "I'm going to go and knock some sense into him if the need arises." She ran away from them, and headed for the cliffs.

She could hear the waves crashing against the shoreline below them. Slowing her steps, she breathed in deeply as her eyes fell on Sean.

He looked like a wild man. His hair was blowing in the strong wind, and his feet were planted apart as if he were waiting to take on a thousand men in battle. She softened her steps, so that he would not hear her approach.

"If you intend to jump, I'd advise against it."

"Bridget!" She'd never heard him sound so thankful. He crossed the distance between them in two long strides. Before she knew it, she had been pulled to him. She clung to him, just as desperately as he clung to her. His lips found hers before she could even catch her breath. She wound her arms around his neck, as he lifted her off of the ground. "You taste like Heaven!"

"Do I?" She couldn't seem to get enough of him. Out of the corner of her eye, she glanced at the rising sun in the east. "We have got to get you out of the elements. You'll burn up if that sun touches you."

"It's only twilight. I'll be okay for a bit longer. I like the smell of the morning."

"Yeah, well, I'm not too crazy about the smell of this particular morning. I mean the stench of burnt vampire really doesn't put me into the mood for much of anything."

"Is that so? Pity. That's a crying shame. Because I actually had something planned."

She smirked.

"Oh, well. I'm rather tired. And, dirty. And hungry. Not to mention the fact that we've been invaded by a faerie force."

His face fell. "Ah, I had forgotten about that." He kissed her neck. "But you know what? I do believe that my quarters will still be quite free. And as everyone knows in these parts, my castle has thick walls."

"Why, Sean Sutherland, you never fail to surprise me." His cobalt eyes glittered. She wished that she could bottle up this moment and cherish it for the rest of time. She looked at the soot smear on his forehead, and tried to wipe it away with her finger. "You need a shower as well. You don't exactly smell like roses, I'm afraid to say."

"Strangely enough, you still do."

She laughed. "Oh, go on."

He twirled her around, and her heart froze when she saw the sun emerging from behind a canopy of clouds. Multiple colors swirled across the horizon, as dawn declared a new day.

"Sorry, but I don't think you have time to get back up to the castle on foot. Hold on."

"My pleasure." He wrapped his arms around her and whisked her off her feet.

"You didn't need to pick me up."

"You told me to hold on. Well, I'm holding on."

She rolled her eyes. "Whatever am I going to do with you?"

"I can think of a few things," he retorted. A mischievous gleam had entered his eyes.

She laughed. Then, before any more time could slip away from her she snapped her fingers. They reappeared in Sean's sitting room.

"Phew."

After putting herself through so much magical stress, she was actually thankful for the fact that Sean had decided to play the macho man. He was quite strapping. And brawny. Lord, he had everything in all of the right places right down to...her thoughts trailed off, when she noticed the wary glint in his eyes.

"What is it?"

"Nothing. I just can't seem to shake this feeling of impending doom."

"A moment ago, you were quite ready and willing to make love to me."

"I know. But now I feel like I need to hunker down somewhere and wait for the world to come crashing down around me." He carried her to the sofa, sat her down, and then settled himself beside her.

Her stomach rumbled. She grimaced. "Sorry."

"No need to apologize. I'll fix you something to eat in a minute."

"No. You don't need to go to any trouble. I'll just conjure the food."

"Are you strong enough for that?"

She pursed her lips. "I think so. That shouldn't take too much effort." She winked at him. In a bright burst, the table in front of them filled with food. "Don't worry that's food that doesn't come from my realm."

He smiled. "I don't think I'd ever have to worry about getting trapped in faeryland. I'm a vampire; remember? Which reminds me; your mother had some pretty fascinating tales to tell me."

"Did she, really?" She'd just stuffed her mouth with chicken, and she hadn't been expecting him to get all chatty all of a sudden. She pointed to his rare steak that she'd magically summoned. "Eat that. You look terrible. And when I leave the room, feel free to...well you know."

He smiled. "Actually, when you left the room I was planning on following you."

"Well, for what I have in mind, you'll definitely need your strength so eat up."

He reached for the plate and carefully balanced it on his lap. She sat for a few minutes and mulled over what he had just said. She couldn't imagine what her mother would have to say to Sean. Narrowing her eyes, she inclined her head toward him.

"What exactly did my mother tell you?"

"She told me that you came to the village because of me."

"No." She grunted. "I didn't come to kill you. She's way off base in that thinking."

"Not to kill me. She said that you came because we're meant to be. In essence, you and I are a match made in Heaven."

"So to speak." She stopped chewing, and widened her eyes. "You're serious, aren't you?"

"Cross my heart."

She squinted, and leaned in closer to scrutinize the look in his eyes and the look on his face. "Well. I wasn't expecting that. The next thing you'll tell me is that my dear mother sent me here."

"She did. Or so she claims."

"Why? Because she knew I'm the key, right?"

"Aye."

"Well, it would be really nice if someone could enlighten me about how I break your damn curse." She could feel her cheeks reddening.

"She also said that when we first met, time stopped."

She dropped the slice of bread she'd been holding.

Realization ripped through her. That would explain why her watch had stopped. New battery or not, when true love was discovered time did actually stop for her kind. She leaned forward. She was beginning to feel sick to her stomach. He rubbed the small of her back.

"If I'm overwhelming you, I'll stop."

"No." Her voice came out as the barest of whispers. "Is there anything else I should know?"

"You mother seems to approve of me."

"Well, that's something to be thankful for." She snorted.

"She also did something funny to Grace."

"What do you mean by funny?"

"She touched her finger to her, and a bright orb came out of the tip and flowed through Grace's body."

"There's nothing to worry about. Grace hasn't been hurt by it, if that's what you think. She just amplified Grace's powers in case she had need of them. In case you didn't know, Grace already has a talent. If it's nurtured, it will grow and she'll become quite the force to be reckoned with someday. When I healed her, I only activated the part of her gift that had been laying dormant for her whole life."

He slackened his jaw. "Oh."

She pressed her hand against his.

"You know, I've almost had my fill. I could go and get the water started in the shower while you do what you need to." She winced. She really didn't like to think about that part of his curse. It always made her feel icky all over.

He placed his plate aside, and in one fell swoop he had her cuddled against him. She felt a tingly sensation course through her as they touched. Being near him made her spirit soar. He had become the center of her universe. How could she leave him? She didn't even want to think about it. A pain ripped through her heart at the thought.

On one hand, she wanted to stay with him, for all eternity. On the other hand, she wanted to leave him. The prophecy had to be wrong. She still hadn't broken the curse, even though she'd come closer to Sean that any other woman ever had.

As his lips touched hers, all of her worries faded away. Her inhibitions loosened up. Soon, his kiss would start to weave a spell of enchantment over her. If only they could remain this way forever. But despite what her mother said to the contrary, a faerie and a vampire were just not meant to be. She sighed as he cradled her to his chest, and kicked open the bedroom door. But they had the present. And as far as she was concerned, the past and the future could just leave them be.

Chapter Thirty-Two

Sean sighed.

He was in pure bliss.

Rolling over, he pressed his lips to Bridget's ear. She'd revealed the faerie point just last night, and he'd become rather fond of it. Brushing the tip of her ear with his lips, he pulled back when she didn't wake up. Wrinkling his brow, he sat upright. Of course, he'd expected her to be exhausted, but the sun would set soon, and his restlessness would begin.

"Bridget," he murmured, in a singsong voice.

"Mmm..." her voice trickled out like the sweetest melody he'd ever heard.

"It's almost the end of the day." She made an inaudible noise, and then kicked her legs out. Silly goose, she'd fallen back asleep. He ran his index finger down the length of her spine, expecting to get some sort of a reaction. Instead, he was met with a muted snore. He grunted. Well, wasn't this just lovely? They'd made wild passionate love for hours, and now she had just left him high and dry. He let out a large gust of wind. Reaching up, he scrunched his pillow beneath his fingers, and stared up at his ceiling. Suddenly, he realized that his bedroom needed to be painted.

Frustrated at having such thoughts, he sat up. The temptation to poke Bridget awake had just about gotten the better of him, when a knock sounded at his door.

"Who could that be at this blasted hour?" Grumbling, he reached for his dressing gown, and pulled it shut over his naked body. Whoever had come calling had better have a really good reason.

He wrenched open the door to find Grace staring back at him.

"They're leaving," she muttered, reaching in to pull on his arm.

"Who's leaving?" He was still groggy from his hours of fitful sleep. He'd tried to get some rest but the thought of Octavia still lurking out there somewhere had spooked him to no end.

"Who do you think I'm talking about? The elves and the faeries. They're leaving. I don't have a good feeling about this, Uncle Sean."

"Fancy that." His tone turned dry, though he smiled when he caught sight of Grace's distress.

"I've asked Uncle William to stay down there and stall them, but they seem pretty adamant."

"Well, I'll just be happy to have my home back again, lass."

She stuck her tongue out at him. She folded her arms and lifted her eyebrow. He decided pretty quickly that he didn't care for this side of Grace. Normally, she seemed so carefree and easygoing. Now, she was being a right big pain in his arse.

"Just give me a sec. I have to go and put something on."

She groaned. "That will do. Now come on. I don't know what's been going on with everyone today. Father Clancy hasn't emerged from the Church at all, and everyone else seems determined to sleep the whole bloody day away!"

"Hate to break this to you, Grace, but that's what one normally does when they've been up all night battling the forces of evil."

She rolled her eyes, as she continued to drag him along behind her. He didn't know why he had agreed to accompany her. He should have just dug his heels in and told her to go jump off a cliff. Why did he care that his castle would soon be abandoned? It made no difference to him whatsoever.

Somehow they made it down to the great hall in record time. Sean blinked, and then yawned. He still felt the need to go back to bed, and he sort of resented what Grace was trying to do to him.

"Don't put me in the middle of this. I shouldn't even be dealing with them because look at me. In case it's suddenly slipped your mind, I'm a vampire. You should've just woken up Bridget. She's much better at negotiating things than I am. Besides, we don't need their help anymore anyway. We took care of the vampires last night."

"Oh, please." Grace huffed out a large gust of air. "If you think that's the end of it, then you have another thing coming. I was in Octavia's lair. She's got something much bigger than that planned. I can feel it in my bones. Something just keeps nagging at me. It's in me, and around me; it won't let me go!"

"Grace, I think you're a wee bit strung out. But nothing that a hot cup of tea, a chocolate biscuit, and a good long sleep won't mend."

"No! I'm staying here. They're supposed to be second sighted, they should be able to tell that there's something big looming on the horizon. Something bad is in the making and I want to know what it is."

"No alternative plans are being brewed for now. I don't think that even Octavia is foolish enough to strike again after such a disheartening defeat."

"Oh, really? She's a vampire. And, in case it slipped your notice last night, those vampires that we fought were all part of the same clan. What happened to the so-called dissention among the masses that we heard reported? I saw no signs of a vampire civil war, did you?"

When she put it that way, he had to stop and think. He sighed, and rubbed his temples.

"Grace, I feel a headache coming on. I don't know why the elves and faeries are leaving, but if they are, then the danger must've passed." He stopped. Something stung behind his eyes. His belly flip-flopped. Despite, his bravado, he was like Grace. There was something fishy going on.

"I mean I think we might've put Octavia and Catherine out for the count, but I can't be sure. Bridget shoved me into the portal back to the village before I could collect my wits."

"Hang on." He put his hand on her shoulder, and turned her to face him. "What are you on about?"

"When I saved Bridget, we blasted two female vampires. They looked remarkably like Octavia and Catherine."

He swallowed. He could feel his life passing by his

eyes. If they were truly gone, vanquished, then he had nothing to live in fear of. No retribution could be coming. That had to be why the forces of light were abandoning his castle. As they drew near to the great hall, he could hear William trying to catch everyone's attention with the tales of his exploits.

Rolling his eyes, he cleared his throat. He locked gazes with the warrior elf that had recognized Bridget. The elf looked at Grace, and Sean slung his arm around her shoulders. He'd seen that look before, and he didn't like it one bit, especially when it was directed at his niece.

When Grace tried to step forward, he held her back. Grinning at the elf, he darted his gaze around the room, and searched for Iris. She was the only faerie that he knew on a first name basis, and well, frankly he'd taken quite a fancy to her.

"We bid you farewell, Sean Sutherland," the warrior elf said.

He knotted his brows. "Why are you leaving? I don't think the danger has passed."

"Our intelligence tells us otherwise. Our time here has passed."

"Owen, I don't think we should be making such a hasty decision." Iris came fluttering in. "I was under the impression that we'd be staying for at least a few days."

"Circumstances have arisen that make that impossible."

Iris sighed. "What circumstances?"

Sean looked to Owen, waiting for a reply.

"Lady Iris, this is none of your concern. You are not a warrior." Owen looked a bit annoyed.

Well, jolly good for him...at least Sean wasn't in the boat all by himself.

Iris narrowed her eyes. She looked about ready to spit nails. "I have a right to be appraised of any changes. I am here on direct orders from my queen."

"Aye. As are we. Our alliance has always remained strong and true. But for now, I must take my forces and leave this village. You would be well advised to abandon this outpost as well."

Iris crossed her arms. She looked toward her faerie commander. By the way that Sean saw things; it looked as if the faerie commander had already set about mobilizing his troops.

"If you don't mind, I will wait until my princess wakes. Then, we shall set about making plans. How can you be sure that the forces of darkness will not return this night?"

Sean grunted. He wanted to know what the hell was going on between Owen and Iris. For some reason, they seemed to be locked in a silent battle of wills. Iris's eyes were glowing, as were Owen's.

****

Iris had to keep Owen and the rest of his forces here at the castle. She knew Bridget would feel the same way that she did.

She glanced toward Sean, and then continued with the telepathic argument she'd started moments before with Owen.

If your brother knew what was going on this day, he would tell you to keep your forces here until Bridget disbands you.

My brother is only the Prince Regent of my ancestral lands. My father is still the King.

With your mother missing in action, your father is going insane. Your people need a stable leader...that leader is not your father.

I won't listen to this anymore, Iris. You have no right to tell me what to do. You wouldn't know how to fight in a million years. Besides, I thought you didn't like getting your hands dirty.

She wanted to do more than just argue with Owen. He was a pompous pig...and as far as she was concerned, he didn't deserve the noble post he held in his father's kingdom. But, he did seem interested in Grace. Perhaps, she could use that to her advantage. If Owen agreed to stay, the faerie warriors would remain as well. She couldn't lose her one shot at tipping the scales in her favor.

Grace Sutherland would be glad to have your company, for a few more days. I can see the look in your eyes when you stare at her, Owen. I'm well schooled in love...you've been bitten hard.

She is mortal. I can't allow myself to get deeply

234

involved with her...if I did, it would bring disgrace to my house. I must leave, posthaste.

She hated the way he said, *mortal*. True, she'd always believed mortals to be selfish and petty, but now, after seeing the inhabitants of this village, she knew better. These good people had caused a great change in her...a change she knew was for the better. She would defend them to the end, if the need arose.

You can take your prejudices and run back to your ancestral lands, Owen. We don't want your kind here, anymore.

With that, she cut off their telepathic exchange. But, before she left his mind for good, she'd give him a few things to think about.

****

He cleared his throat. Grace whispered in his ear.

"I think they're communicating telepathically."

He glanced down at her and frowned. "Someone should tell them that's rude behavior." Narrowing his eyes, he stepped forward. Thinking on his feet, he stuck his right hand out and passed it between Iris and Owen. Neither one flinched. He tilted his head to the side. "I don't like this. I feel as if they're talking about me."

"Most likely. I mean we can at least take comfort in the knowledge that Iris is fighting on our behalf. Owen can't possibly go through with abandoning us. If we're left alone, we'll be left open and vulnerable to a counter attack. I really don't have a good feeling about tonight. I feel like my heart is up in my throat."

"Are you sure your heart isn't up in your throat because of the way Owen's looking at you?"

"I don't know what you mean." He watched as Grace pulled at the collar of her blouse. She was blushing profusely. He smiled. It made him feel good to know that he still could read the signs. He seemed to be missing all of them with Bridget. She still didn't even seem close to professing her love for him. At the rate they were going, he'd be damned for all eternity. If Grace could find luck in love, then he'd tell her to go for it. It almost seemed as if his luck with Bridget was slowly running out.

"You know; if you could find a way to distract Owen, that might just buy us a few more minutes."

Grace widened her eyes.

"Oh, no. Are you suggesting that I throw myself at him?"

"Well, I could throw you at him." He grinned.

Grace gasped, and punched him playfully. "Never you mind. Though, you have given me an idea. You're right. We do need more time. Maybe you should slip upstairs and wake up sleeping beauty. Right now, Bridget's our only hope."

"I couldn't have said it better." His heart fell.

Grace winked at him. "And I'll put on the old Sutherland charm and see if I can't bewitch Owen." She smiled and pushed up her sleeves. "It's a big job, but somebody's got to do it."

He laughed. "Then get to it, Grace," he reached a hand out and circled his fingers around her tiny wrist. "Be careful. If that..."

"Don't worry." She patted his hand. "Somehow, I really doubt that Owen would do anything to hurt me. He just doesn't have it in him."

"How do you know? People can hide a lot of their faults."

Her eyes softened. "Do you think that you've hidden things from Bridget, or that Bridget is still hiding stuff from you?"

He shuffled nervously. "I don't know what Bridget's mother did to you, but she should've kept her little gift to herself. You were a little spooky before, but now that intuition of yours is going to drive me up the wall." He sighed as her eyes flashed with pain. "I'm sorry. I let my mouth run off. I need to learn how to control myself."

Grace closed her eyes. "No. You need to learn how to stop being such a..."

"What?" He lowered his head so that they would be at eye level.

"Tell me, do you act this way with Bridget?"

"I don't know what you're getting at." He clenched his jaw.

"Do you hurt her, just when she's getting too close for comfort? I know you don't want to admit it, but you do have a nasty habit of pushing people away because you think they need to be protected from you." She lifted her arm and touched his cheek.

"I do no such thing."

"Oh, but you do." Her soft touch made a shiver pass through him. "You've done it all of your life. Or rather, for as long as I've known you. You're one lucky man though, Uncle Sean."

"And how do you figure that?"

"Because we Scots are an infernally stubborn lot. You keep trying to push us away, but we can still see that you have a good heart."

"Even though I have no soul."

Her eyes flashed with fire. "That's what I'm talking about. You just did it. You're trying to make me think that you're a bloody freak of nature. But I won't. Whether you like it or not, you're stuck with every single person in this village. We'll never abandon you. And you can't abandon us. You have to go and fight for Bridget. If you're released from your curse, we'll all be rewarded."

His heart slammed against his ribcage. For one so young, Grace seemed to have a wealth of knowledge stashed away.

Grace had hit the nail on the head. As he reflected upon his long life, he could see what she was trying to get at. He did have a nasty habit of pushing people away. He always had to keep them from seeing his inner self. His emotional anguish ran deep. If anyone knew just how tortured he was, it would rock them to their very core. He could recall countless nights where he just sat idly in front of the fire, contemplating his own demise. He knew what he was. In his cursed form he had become a creature of nightmares. And though he only admitted it when the stirring became too great for him to resist, he always felt the pull. In the days since the curse had been bestowed upon him, it had become his constant companion. When it came right down to it, he feared himself. Oh aye, he trusted every single person in his life. He knew that they would never fail him. Yet, nightmares of betraying everything that he held near and dear plagued him. And, now that Octavia had already taken control of his body, there was no telling what he might do.

He couldn't let her gain the upper hand again. If he felt her drawing upon his strength again, just in case she wasn't really dead, he'd make the ultimate sacrifice. Under no circumstance could she hurt anyone close to him. He'd vowed on the day of his father's death that he would always remember.

The Sutherlands stood against everything that Octavia represented. They knew no earthly fear. The only person he had to fear when it came right down to it was himself. Not Octavia. As long as he had breath in his body, she'd never get her true heart's desire.

"Uncle Sean?" Grace's urgent voice pulled him out of his reverie.

He looked around. The castle seemed to have been abandoned. He swore.

"How could they do this?" He turned around when he felt a familiar scent tickle his nose. Bridget stood a mere few feet from him. He took a step toward her. Her eyes filled with pain. He couldn't understand what had brought on such a sudden change in her disposition. When he'd left her, she'd been sleeping but she had been contented.

"They have left." Her eyes brimmed with tears. She started to chew on her lower lip. He closed the gap between them. "I should follow." He stepped back, as if she'd served him a physical blow.

"No." He didn't know what else to say. Rage and confusion tore through him. He glanced behind him to search for Grace.

"She left. Owen and she have some unfinished business, or so I imagine." Bridget's voice faltered.

"And Iris? Where did her little precious ladyship get to?" He flinched at the coldness that had seeped into his voice.

"She'll be down in the village waiting for me. She needed to cool off. She's terribly upset at Owen. I do think that you should try to afford her some much-deserved respect. As it's the least you owe her. She fought for you and the people of this village. Actually, their telepathic argument became so loud that it woke me from my sleep."

He couldn't seem to get any words out. He was still stuck on the thought of Bridget leaving him. He couldn't go on without her. Not when he knew that he'd come so close to being released from his living hell.

"Bridget, I..."

"I still need to get a few things off my chest."

Hope flared in his heart. If she professed her love for him everything would change for the better.

"Go on, then."

Her eyes brushed over the full length of his body before settling on his face.

"I'm not the right woman for you."

He felt a pulsing pain tear through his heart. He wanted to gasp for breath. Damn, if he wasn't careful he would give into temptation and fall to his knees.

"No." His voice came out as the barest of whispers. He grimaced. When had he suddenly become the sort of man that wouldn't fight for what he knew was already his? She loved him. He knew that with every fiber of his being. No woman could kiss him the way she did without being deeply in love with him. The tenderness in her touch conveyed her love. Why did she have to deny her feelings for him?

He swallowed. Oh, right. He was a foul, loathsome creature.

"Sean, let's not argue. You have to see in your hearts of hearts, that I'm not right for you. We bicker all the time, and..."

"No. You're wrong. We don't bicker all the time."

"Well," she raised her eyebrow as she considered his contradiction. "To be fair, fine, we don't bicker all the time. But we do get on each other's nerves quite frequently."

"I can't survive without you."

Her eyes flashed with fire. "Of course you can. Look around you. You've got your family, and your loyal friends. Sean, what more could you possibly want?"

He let out a growl, and lunged toward her. Pulling her to his chest, he tipped her face up so he could meet her gaze. She wasn't even flustered in the slightest. Cool as a cucumber. He clenched his jaw.

"I want you. I'll always want you. You are the only mate I'll ever have. We're connected. You know it. So please stop being such a bloody hypocrite and admit it!"

She pushed against his chest. "Sean Sutherland, you're acting like a brute. Either let me go, or I'll turn you..."

"What will you turn me into? I doubt that your magic could affect me in any way. I'm cursed; remember? And, in case you haven't already been briefed on the full workings of my curse, nothing can affect me. Nothing! The only way I can be transformed into anything else is when this bloody curse is finally broken. And, since you haven't done that already, I'm doomed!"

He wanted to smash his lips against hers and prove to her that what they'd shared only hours ago still filled her with undeniable passion. He slackened his grip when he finally realized how tightly he had his fingers wrapped around her arms.

Silence reverberated off the walls. The look she gave him said a thousand different things. He could see her passion boiling just below the surface. But coupled with the passion was something that remarkably resembled distaste.

He swallowed. His mind raced, while his heart beat in perfect timing. "Why do you persist in torturing me?"

"Is that what you think I'm doing? Do you honestly believe that I want to hurt you?" Her voice had risen to an unbelievable pitch. "I should've known from the very first moment that we met that nothing good could result from our pairing."

Her cruel words made him clench his eyes shut. When he opened them, he noticed one tear trickling down her cheek. She was fighting her emotions, and failing.

"You can't deny your feelings for me forever."

Her eyes dulled. "You'd be surprised at what I can and can not do." Her cheeks bloomed with redness.

He wanted to pull her against his chest. But if she didn't want to give in to her emotions then he wasn't about to force her. He'd never forced a woman to do anything. He raised his hand up, and cupped the side of her face. To his astonishment, she didn't shrink away.

"I love you. I'll never forget what we shared, and what we could've been."

"See? There you go again. We could never have amounted to anything. I'm defective. I can't break your frigging curse, and since no one will tell me what I have to do, I have to leave. I can't watch you, knowing that I failed you." She reached up to wrap her hand around his, just long enough to remove it from the side of her face.

His heart thrummed. "I need you."

"And I need to be away from you."

Stunned, he allowed her to wrestle her way out of his grip.

"Farewell, Sean Sutherland."

"Don't do this, Bridget!"

"I'm no longer needed here. I must go and spend some time with my own kind. I've been away from my ancestral lands for far too long. They call to me." She waved goodbye to him, and then disappeared.

He let out a cry that sounded remarkably like a wounded animal. He charged around the great hall. He was in a mindless rage. He pushed over a table and some chairs, and then fell to his knees. His savior had abandoned him, and now Octavia had won.

Chapter Thirty-Three

Bridget couldn't breathe. She slumped down onto the dewy grass. Hot tears blazed their way down her cheeks. She glanced back at the castle and gasped. Sean's agonized cry echoed across the landscape.

What had she done?

She clutched at the grass, and uprooted a fistful of dirt in her hands. She had to move on. She had to leave Sean, and his people. The battle had already been waged, but the war against the darkness still had not been won. She had plenty of work to do, and she couldn't do it in a remote village.

She hiccupped. She had never felt so desolated in all of her life. A sour taste filled her mouth, and she coughed. Invisible hands made her turn her head toward the village. She pressed her lips together.

The Church beckoned to her. But she could not go there. Licking her lips, she pushed herself to her feet. Why couldn't she just leave this place? The rustic atmosphere wasn't really to her liking. But then, she'd settled in as if this had always been meant to be her home.

The cool sea air whipped against her cheeks. The sting rejuvenated her and made her want to press on. A howling wind ripped across the rugged land. She had become accustomed to its song. And right now, it told her to go to the Church. Come what may, she had to at least make a visit there before she left this land for good. Once she had taken her leave, she knew that she'd never be able to return.

Opening her hand, she let the grass and dirt trickle back onto the ground. She snapped her fingers, and in an instant her hand was sparkling clean. She tugged her leather coat around her, and began the long trek down to the village. Only once did she dare to look behind her. Her heart fell, when she realized that Sean had not chosen to pursue her. It was for the best really, but a lot of what he had said rang home.

She did love him. But a love like theirs could not last. After all, he was a vampire, and she was a messenger of light.

She bit back a cry, when she tripped over a wayward twig. The next moment she was on her knees.

"Damn it all."

What was the matter with her?

She struggled to catch her breath. Then as a calming sensation flowed through her, she pushed herself to her feet. Her knees still smarted even though her jeans weren't ripped. Sutherland Castle beckoned to her. The pull had almost become inescapable. If she didn't get away soon, she'd be back up at the castle, and flinging herself into Sean's arms. She needed to leave. Once she'd found what she needed in the Church, she'd be off.

Hollowness invaded her heart. The glow of the moon skimmed over her, and she lowered her eyes to the shadow that she cast.

"Just get on with it, Bridget." She didn't know why she'd started to talk to herself. The emotional turmoil she found herself in had started to take a toll on her. Within minutes, she was jaunting through the village. Everyone seemed to be safely inside of their homes. She stared at the village square, and the First World War monument that stood in the center of it. This village had become a part of her, and when she left, she would mourn it just as she mourned anything or anyone else that was near and dear to her heart.

Sean.

Everything she looked at reminded her of him. Why couldn't she just get him out of her head? More importantly why did she have such bad heartburn?

She made her way to the grounds. Sean's mother's gravestone made her halt in her tracks. She brushed her hand over the stone, and leaned down. There were no flowers for her.

She snapped her fingers, and laid the bouquet of violets down upon it. Straightening, she squared her shoulders, and reached to open the door. Candles warmed the inside, casting a brilliant glow around the small interior. She glanced around to see if Father Clancy was up and about. Finding it empty, she sighed, and made her way to the altar. She genuflected, and murmured a fervent prayer. She reached to light a candle. Standing up, she whirled around and slipped into a pew. Pain ricocheted throughout her body. She wanted to double over with the intensity of it. She closed her eyes, and lost herself in her thoughts. She became so absorbed in thoughts of Sean, that she didn't even hear the Church door open.

A cool breeze brushed through the church.

"It's a fine night, isn't it?" She started at the voice. "Och, I'm sorry for disturbing you."

The footsteps retreated.

"Don't go." She whirled around, and smiled when her eyes rested on Mary.

"I just came to give my regards to Father Clancy. I didn't expect to see you here." Mary glanced toward the altar, and then rested her eyes back on Bridget.

"Honestly, I didn't expect to find myself here. I've just come to stay a short while, and then I'm off."

"Back up to the castle, then?" Mary slid onto the bench next to her.

"No." A catch formed in Bridget's throat and hot tears stung her eyes.

Mary frowned, and narrowed her eyes. "I think my ears just betrayed me. Would you mind clarifying that answer?"

Bridget sighed. "Mary, I'm leaving the village."

Mary pressed her hand to her heart. "Good heavens! Why would you leave us?" Fear had stolen into Mary's eyes. "Did we offend you in some way?" Mary reached out for Bridget's hand, and had it gripped tightly before Bridget could think to retract it.

"No. Everyone has been more than kind to me. But I don't belong here, Mary. I have to return to my own people."

Mary snorted. "Ah, I see. You're turning your back on us."

Bridget shook her head. "It's nothing like that. I'm leaving because it's my destiny."

Mary laughed. "Your destiny revolves around this village. What does Sean think of your decision?" Mary bored her eyes into Bridget.

She'd never seen Mary riled before. If she didn't know better, she would've thought that Mary was angry with her.

"Sean wasn't too happy when I broke the news to him."

"As well he should be. When I was a younger lass, I always wanted to be you. But alas, I am not Sean's savior." Mary's eyes clouded. "Do not misunderstand me. I'm deeply in love with Rupert, but I had an awful crush on Sean, and I wanted to be the woman that would save him. But I'm not!"

"Mary..."

"You are." Mary's eyes filled with determination, and she accentuated her meaning by squeezing Bridget's hand. "You're the one that has given new life to Sean. You invigorate him. Being around you has done wonders for his outlook on life."

Bridget could feel her eyes stinging again. "I can't be with him. It will never work."

"Oh, aye, it will. You mark my words, Bridget Sinclair, once you break the curse; it will be clear sailing for the two of you. I can see the fire that burns between Sean and you. You two literally ignite the room when you're together. Sean loves you. And frankly, I can't understand why he hasn't already told you that."

"He has." Bridget winced against Mary's intake of breath.

"Why you silly little bugger!" Mary swore, and then slapped her hand over her mouth. "Dear Lord in Heaven, please forgive me! I know not what I am saying. I should go and wash my mouth out with soap for swearing in God's house." Bridget sighed. If she weren't careful, she'd end up sobbing with abandon. "So, let me get this all straight. Sean has actually told you that he loves you?"

"Yes."

"You foolish lass. Why would you hurt him so terribly by telling him that you were leaving? And here I thought that you of all people would realize the power of pure love."

"Sean will move on. He will love another."

"Bollocks! Sean will never love another like he has loved you. You're his everything. You are his light in the darkness. Now, he is alone. You have forsaken him."

The inside of Bridget's mouth became unbearably dry.

"I have done no such thing." Pain sliced through her heart.

Mary cocked her head to the side. "In my world, Bridget, you do not run out on someone just because you're afraid of loving that person."

Tears welled in Bridget's eyes. She slammed her fist down upon the top of the pew in front of her.

"Sean is a vampire!"

"That excuse is becoming tiresome. You're his savior. You could rectify that sad fact."

"How? I haven't done anything yet, even though I've become closer to him than any other man."

"You write romance novels. What conquers everything?"

She shook her head. "Mary, you are beginning to give me a headache. Love conquers all, if that's what you're hinting at."

"Aye. And so it does. Tell me, do you love him?"

"Of course I do." She nodded her head.

"You know, Rupert has a saying. He says that one must never forget to tell his loved ones how much they mean to them. Life is precious, and it can slip away in but an instant."

"Rupert is a wise man. But his advice does nothing to help me. I still have no choice but to leave the village."

"As I see it you only have one choice. And if you don't take that path, you will regret it for the rest of your life! If I must, I will beg you to stay. If you desert Sean, he will waste away without you. I shudder to think of what he might do." Mary's voice trailed off at the sound of the church door flinging open.

"That wind tonight has a bite to it."

Bridget stared straight ahead.

William came up beside them, and rubbed his hands briskly together.

"William, you do pick the times." Mary looked up,

and Bridget sighed.

She could sense the tenseness in the air. William was trying desperately to figure out what he'd walked in on.

"Mary and I were just having a chat. But we just finished. You don't need to worry. You didn't interrupt us. Bless your heart, Mary. I'm sorry, but despite your best arguments, I can't stay."

William snorted. "Of course you can't stay. My brother will have need of you, I'm sure."

She shook her head. Why did everyone assume that she was going to stay with Sean forever?

"She's leaving Sean, William." Mary's eyes filled with sadness. "This is the saddest night that the village has ever seen."

"What's this? You can't be serious. Bridget, I don't know what's come over you, but shake it. You simply can't leave Sean. He'll be shattered."

"He already is." Bridget fell silent. She didn't know what had possessed her to say such a thing.

Mary lifted Bridget's hand, and sighed. "I'll leave you to William's care. If he can talk some sense into you, I'll give him a medal." She smiled. "Despite what you might think at the moment, Bridget, your time here in the village has affected us all. I will never forget you. No matter what, you'll always have a place in my heart." Mary pulled her into an embrace. "God keep you safe."

"And you." Bridget smiled, and brushed her tears away before William could see her.

Mary stood, and hurried out of the church.

"Well, isn't this a fine kettle of fish."

Bridget glanced at William. She closed her eyes. "William, I really must be going."

"You stay put. I have a few things to say to you, and you're not leaving until we have it all out in the open."

"I see that pomposity is a family trait."

William laughed. "Now I really know why Sean is so in love with you. You're quite a woman, Bridget."

"I don't know what to say."

"Accept the compliment. I don't hand them out like candy." He grinned. "Speaking of candy, would you like some?" He offered her what seemed to be some sort of butterscotch candy drop. She took it from him and popped it into her mouth.

"Thank you."

"The pleasure was mine. You do know that he loves you, right?"

She nodded her head. "Sean just isn't the man for me."

"Oh, he isn't?" William looked at her pointedly. "Then why do you seem so bloody miserable?"

"William, I really must go." She tried to stand up, and he pulled her back down.

"Don't run away from me. I can find you wherever you run. Unlike Sean, I'm not restricted to these lands." A hard edge crept into his voice. "I won't let you destroy Sean."

"I haven't done anything to him."

"You've bloody well ripped his heart into shreds. Sean might give off a stoic and brooding exterior, but on the inside he's got a heart of pure gold. Vampire or not, he's the best man I've ever met. He loves you. Do you know what that means?"

She sighed. "William, I don't require a lecture."

"Nonetheless, you'll be getting one. When Sean loves someone he loves that person with his heart and soul."

Bridget flinched. "Sean doesn't..."

"Don't you dare tell me that my brother doesn't have a soul! I know what he is. And I know that no matter what, his spirit still resides in his body. Octavia cursed him, but I don't believe that even she could steal his spirit."

"The threat from Octavia is over. The elves and the faeries have left. I must follow."

"You keep telling yourself that, if it makes you feel better. But you look like hell. I can tell that you care deeply for Sean."

"I can't..."

"Oh, but you can't deny your heart forever, Bridget. Why won't you just listen to what your heart says? I'd warrant it's the best guide you'll ever need."

"Why are you doing this to me? What makes you such an expert on love?"

William's eyes flashed with fire. "I've loved and lost. And I know what it feels like. Despite what Sean will say to the contrary, he has never loved anyone like you. Oh sure, he's had a fair share of relationships that have masqueraded as love. But never in his life, has he felt the way that he feels for you. And I can see what you're thinking. He doesn't love you just because you're the answer to his curse. Sean is above that."

"I'm not the answer to his curse."

"Oh, aye. You are. It's a fact."

"I haven't broken it yet."

"You will break it. I can feel it in my bones. But if you take off on him, you'll never get a chance to bring him back into the land of the living. Don't do this to Sean. Accept what your heart is already telling you. Love him. Love him with everything that you have. And if you're willing to take some more of my advice, cherish every moment that you have with him." He stood up. "I think I'll go and look at the stars."

She craned her neck to look up at him. "That's all? I thought you told me to stay put."

"Oh, I've said all that I need to. I don't think you're going anywhere."

"Oh, yes, I am."

"Oh, no, you're not. Can't you feel it?"

Bridget shook her head. Her pain clouded her senses.

"Trouble is in the air. And, if I'm not mistaken, you've got a date with destiny."

She snorted, stood, and then nearly collapsed to her knees again, as her senses reached out to touch the trouble that William had referred to.

"Get the village ready. I need to consult with Iris."

"I'm already here." Iris stood in the doorway, bathed in the moonlight.

"Iris, we aren't prepared."

"I know. How could they have made this big of a mistake?"

"What's done is done, ladies. We can't cry over spilt milk."

"William, don't you know the gravity of the situation we're in?" Bridget moved forward.

"Oh, I know. But where there's a will, there's a way."

Bridget's mouth gaped open. She was a Huntress of Hell, but even she could openly admit that the odds were stacked against them.

"Ever heard of the saying, we've got the chance of a snowball in Hell?"

"Oh, I practically coined the term. We'll just have to make sure that we create the biggest snowball this side of the Atlantic. Trust me, Bridget. It isn't over yet. You just have to believe in yourself."

She looked to where Iris stood.

William vacated the Church, and shut the door behind him.

Iris shrugged her shoulders. "You can't possibly think of leaving now."

"Iris, of course I'm not leaving. This change of events alters everything."

"Well, that's the only positive side of it. I'd have been very disappointed in you if you'd left Sean."

"Iris, I can't believe that even you believe in him."

"His heart is true. And it belongs to you."

"Iris?"

"Yes?"

"Do you think we'll be able to stand against the forces that are making their way to the village?"

"Piece of faerie cake. I hope." Iris laughed nervously.

Bridget rolled her eyes. She linked her arm through Iris's and walked out of the church just as the village siren ripped through the air.

This was it.

If they lost tonight, the entire village would be ruined. She looked to Castle Sutherland, and her breath caught in her throat.

Sean had just entered the village. People streamed out of the buildings and clustered around him. He seemed to have it all in hand. He met her gaze, and then frowned. There was anger burning in his eyes. And she could feel his animosity. He hated her, and she knew now that she was the one that had been forsaken.

Chapter Thirty-Four

Octavia would have her revenge. She stared at the ashes of Catherine and let out a strangled cry.

The Sutherlands had done it again. But this time, she would make sure that they met their doom. Catherine had fallen protecting her. When the blast of light had hit them, Catherine had thrown herself protectively in front of her.

"Curse you, Grace Sutherland." This time she would eradicate all that laid in her path. As she spoke, her vampire soldiers readied themselves. There would be no rest for the people of Durness Village this night. "Ah, ma chere. You will be avenged. I will make sure that no one is left living. And the one they trust the most will be the one to lead them to their slaughter." She looked to where her handmaiden stood in the corner. "Come to me."

"Yes, Mistress." The young vampire dragged her feet as she walked toward her.

"You will fill the place that Catherine has left empty."

"Oh, thank you, Mistress."

Octavia smiled, and grasped the girl's chin with her right hand.

"But you still must prove yourself worthy. You will be my companion during the battle tonight. You will watch me, when I am in my trancelike state."

"It will be my pleasure."

"Of course it will be. It is the highest honor that you could ever be given. Come now, we must go. I am hungry. I am hungry for death."

Chapter Thirty-Five

Each of the villagers had seemed to gain a newfound courage in the face of danger. No one screamed or began to panic. Sean felt pride surging in his heart.

These were his people. No matter what he had believed in the past, he belonged here. He looked to his side where Ridley stood.

"We should go inside the pub and strategize." He spoke in a tightly clipped voice, and tried to avert Bridget's gaze. He didn't want to even see her. The urge to run to her, and scoop her up in his arms was far too great.

"Shouldn't we ask Bridget for her suggestions?" Ridley craned his neck to look in Bridget's direction.

"I think we should do what his lordship says," Mary interjected.

Sean gave her a grateful smile, and then narrowed his eyes when he caught the glint in her green eyes. He could see that she knew what had transpired between Bridget and him.

"We'll have to reset the traps, but we should be able to get it ready in time."

"I don't want to interrupt or anything, but I think you should know that your time is running out." Bridget's voice carried over the chatter and made everyone fall silent.

Father Clancy had come up to stand behind Bridget. Father McNeil, Sister Agnes and Sister Clarence were nearby and wonders upon wonders, Father Monroe had actually remained in the village.

"I've called for some more fighters, but it seems we'll have to stick this one out ourselves." He met Father Monroe's steely gaze. "I'm not going to hold it against anyone if they wish to hightail it out of the village. If I'm not mistaken these vampires are after me."

"Oh, but you are partially mistaken."

He grunted. Why couldn't Bridget just keep her mouth shut?

"What do you mean?" He opened the pub door, and watched as his people streamed through.

"Princess Bridget is correct. Octavia is after this land." Iris nodded her head solemnly.

"And you," Bridget said, finishing where Iris had left off. "I think we should get the children to the Church as soon as possible. They'll be safe there. No matter what happens, the vampires won't be able to get to them. As for being up against insurmountable odds, we only have to hold our own against them until daylight. After that, well, they're at our mercy."

He waited for Bridget to enter the pub ahead of him. She was the last. She brushed against his body, and sent electricity rolling through him. Her eyes would get to him soon. He swallowed.

"What about your kind? Where are they when we have need of them?"

Bridget paled. "I didn't want them to leave. But they have. So we must work with what we have at hand."

"Why can't you just magically summon them?"

"I've already seen to that. They are occupied elsewhere. But we can survive this. I feel no impending doom."

Every single one of his villagers seemed raptly interested in each and every word that Bridget spoke. He hated that they were beginning to rely on her more than they did on him.

"Fine. Since we're strapped for time, I suggest that we get the children to the Church. Anyone that isn't able or that doesn't want to fight can stay there with them."

Murmurs rang through the pub.

"Everyone wishes to fight," Rupert said, voicing the thoughts of the villagers.

Sean sighed. Couldn't they understand that they had physical limitations?

"And what about you?" He turned to Iris.

She glared daggers at him. "What do you think?"

"I think you don't look capable of putting up a fight," he drawled out, delighting at the violent shade that had erupted across her milky white complexion.

"I could take you out in an instant."

"Without breaking a nail, no doubt."

Iris stepped forward, and grunted when Bridget pulled her back.

"Ignore him. He's just trying to get your goat."

"Well, he's doing a bang up job of it, I must say. When he's with you, he is more bearable, you know."

Sean closed his eyes against the clenching in his gut. He looked away from Bridget. He couldn't stand gazing into her eyes at the moment.

"Ridley, I need you to assemble all of our weapons."

"I could help in erecting a few traps that would send those vamps back to Hell. Iris and I can have them up in a blink of an eye. Literally."

He didn't want to acknowledge her.

"That would be grand, Bridget. Just grand," Father Clancy piped up. "We can definitely use all of the help we can get, isn't that right, Sean?"

Sean stared into Father Clancy's kindly blue eyes. They sparkled. Sean didn't like the fact that Father Clancy was trying to repair the rift between Bridget and he. Little did the Priest realize that it had been Bridget that had created said rift.

"Aye." He watched as the villagers settled themselves at tables. "We've been up against vampires before, and I have no reason to believe that the outcome this night will be any different from any other nights."

"I'll second that," Ridley announced, holding up his pint of beer.

"Sean, you need to know that they're getting close."

He turned and nearly bumped right into Bridget. She was so soft footed that he hadn't even heard her approach. Had he not been so furious with her, he probably would've sensed it.

"How close?" Mary asked. She looked anxious.

"Mary, it will be fine." He had to try to soothe his villagers.

Mary's eyes flickered. He hated seeing everyone he loved in such peril.

"I'd feel a lot better if Bridget's kind were still here."

Bridget sighed. "Iris tried to convince them to stay. I'm sorry that they've left us. But I'm highly skilled, and if wc pull together, we'll be able to beat them."

William coughed. "Well, then we'd best get to it, eh? We should wake the children and get them to safety. As Bridget has already pointed out, we need to keep one step ahead of them."

The chairs scraped the floor as everyone stood with nods of agreement.

Sean blinked. His vision had become cloudy for a moment. He placed his finger against his temple.

"Are you alright?"

He grimaced. He didn't want Bridget near him. Why was she inquiring about his welfare, when she'd just split his heart in two?

"I'm fine. I didn't have quite as much sustenance as I needed."

"Oh. You could always fly back up to your castle, and get some more. You'll need all the strength you can get. I can take it from here."

He fumed. That damn muscle twitched in his cheek again.

He whirled on her. "You are not the leader of this village. You have no place here."

She looked stunned. He reviled himself. She actually looked genuinely hurt. He wanted to apologize but his pride wouldn't let him.

"I know. You've made that quite clear to me."

"If you were my wife, than aye, you could give orders."

Time stalled. Her eyes actually lit up at his suggestion. Then, to his deepest chagrin, they dimmed again.

"Sean, if you were just proposing to me, I can't say it was the most romantic moment we've shared."

He slanted his mouth. "Why would I propose to you? You've made it quite clear to me that I disgust you."

She blinked. "Why would you think that? You don't disgust me. You enthrall me. But our lots in life are clearly defined. I am a Huntress of Hell. You are a vampire. We shouldn't be mixing company."

"It's a little late for that don't you think? You've shared my bed, and enjoyed every moment of it, if I might remind you."

Her cheeks burned. He liked to see that he could still fluster her.

"Keep your voice down! Do you want every single person in the village to know our personal business?"

"They already do. It's a small isolated village. We're their current form of entertainment. The cable has been out for weeks."

Now he had her livid. She stepped forward. Her breasts brushed against him. Though he knew he shouldn't think of anything but the impending battle, having her so near to him still shook him to his very core. Oh, how he loved her!

"Well, tonight they won't need television. They'll have all the excitement they can take. And once tonight is through, we'll be over!"

"Why are you so ready to throw what we have away?"

"We've been through this already. I don't have the time to rehash it all. I'm needed out there."

"As am I." He tugged on her arm, and pulled her against him. "Admit it, you care for me. You love me. I can see it in your eyes."

She sighed. "You're keeping me from..."

Before she could finish her sentence, he gave into temptation and kissed her. Their lips met, and she responded to him with the same amount of passion as he felt. Heat rolled between them. She couldn't deny it any longer. She had indisputable feelings for him. And try as she might, she couldn't run from her heart for long. In fact, he was ending it here and now. He wanted her by his side at the battle. He needed to know that they were a united front. For as long as he lived, he wanted her as his partner in everything.

When they at last came up for air, she slumped against him. He could hear her heart beating. Her breathing had become ragged.

"Damn you, Sean Sutherland."

"Are you thinking about leaving me, now?"

She looked up at him, and met his gaze. He watched as turmoil raged in her eyes. He had to hold his breath.

"No." Her honest reply made him the happiest man in the village.

He exhaled. And kissed her again. Then he picked

her up, and twirled her around.

"Thank Heaven!"

"At least not until tomorrow."

His heart sunk. He wanted to scream out in frustration. Instead, he plastered a very forced smile on his face.

"By tomorrow, you won't ever want to leave me. This village needs you. I need you. And you can't deny the love that's in your heart."

"Just watch me."

He hated her galling stubbornness. She could rival any woman that he knew when it came to her bloody determination. The pub had emptied out while they had been interacting with each other. Then, out of the clear blue, the pub door rattled back on its hinges. The bell tinkled, and lost its merry sound as Orla came rushing in, gasping for breath. He ran to her side. She was buckled over.

"She's...she's been taken."

"Who?" Bridget dashed toward them.

His heart raced. They couldn't have snatched Grace...the thought was unbearable. Bridget had her hand on Orla's back.

"Calm down, Orla. You're going to give yourself a heart attack!"

"They took..."

Sean held her steady. "Grace?"

"No," Orla stammered. "Mary. She's vanished into thin air!"

Chapter Thirty-Six

Bridget gasped. She didn't know what else to do. Acid rolled in her stomach. The thought of Mary in the clutches of Octavia's vampires made her want to cry out in frustration. She tried to steady her breathing.

At the moment, Orla and the rest of the villagers required her attention. She met Sean's gaze. The fear that shone back at her probably mirrored the expression in her eyes. "I don't know what happened to her. One minute we were talking and making our way back up here. Then, in an instant, something clouded my vision and knocked me sideways. The next thing I knew, I heard Mary scream. When I looked to the side, she was gone! Rupert is outside nearly beside himself. Sean, you have to do something. I fear for him!"

Sean sighed.

Bridget bit her lip.

"What do you have in mind?" His question startled her, especially since it had been directed at her.

"I simply don't know. I'm going to need a moment. Why would they take Mary now, when they'll be here in a less than an hour? It simply doesn't make sense."

"You were in Octavia's lair. Did you see anything that would tip you off to this sort of behavior?"

She blinked. "I didn't see her whole lair, if that's what you're thinking. I was drugged and by the time I regained my senses, all that I could tell was that I'd been tossed into a dank cell. I know nothing about her lair. By your accounts of your previous life experiences, you would know more than I."

His eyes blazed. She puffed indignant steam out of her flared nostrils. Ever so gently, she guided Orla over to a chair. "You should go out and calm Rupert down."

"The man won't need me. It doesn't take a genius to

realize that we are at the disadvantage."

She didn't like the edge in Sean's voice. "He might do something foolish."

He darted his eyes to the door. "I believe in Rupert. He always acts with a level head."

"Oh, really?" She crossed her arms. "Well, I can say from firsthand experience that when someone you love is in peril, you rush headlong into something without giving it an ounce of thought."

He stepped closer to her. "Would you have me go out there and tell Rupert that he'll never see Mary again?"

"Of course I wouldn't have you do that. You'd crush him. All that I'm suggesting is that you go out there, and make him see reason."

A sound like a firecracker exploding caught both of their attentions.

"Orla, you need to make your way to the Church. As the village doctor, you're too valuable to be out in the midst of battle. You need to stay in the Church. The wounded will be taken there if possible."

"I've already moved my medical supplies down there. Bridget, do we have a chance at winning this battle?"

Bridget hesitated and then smiled. "Of course we do. The future is what we make of it. The people of this village will not go down without one hell of a fight. And I'd wager that we have what it takes to drive the darkness into oblivion." She squeezed Orla's shoulder, and then fell into step behind Sean.

The sight that met them caused Bridget's world to sway. Rupert looked at his wits end. Someone had accidentally set off a flare gun. She caught the look of anger on Sean's face, and inconspicuously slipped her hand into his. He enclosed her fingers over hers.

"Don't do anything you'll later regret. Remember, each and every person in this village is under a lot of stress right now. Your job is to remain calm. That way, they will follow your lead."

"You have it all under control, don't you?"

"Always. This is going to be a bad night."

"As long as you stay by my side, nothing bad can happen."

Ridley jogged toward them, and saluted. Sean

groaned.

"Iris helped us to erect some rather clever traps. When they infiltrate the village they won't know what hit them."

"Good. That's just what we need."

She glanced at Sean. "You know, you could thank Iris for going to all of that extra work."

"Extra work? She's doing what she's meant to do."

"What do you mean by that?"

"Isn't she the same as you?" He seemed befuddled.

"No. Didn't anyone tell you? Iris is not a Huntress of Hell. She failed training."

"Failed?" He sounded as if he wanted to punch himself. "You're just horsing around, right?"

"No. Actually, she never took to having to go to that much physical exertion. She rather prefers the quiet life."

"And you like adventure?"

"I'm here, aren't I?"

He glanced to where Iris stood bedecked in her flimsy ethereal dress.

"She should change. That particular outfit won't do when the battle starts."

"Oh, don't fret so. Right now, you should be focusing on Rupert. Doesn't it worry you in the slightest that Mary is in danger?"

"Mary is a strong, brave woman. I've known her all of her life. She'll pull through this with flying colors."

"What if we can't get her back?"

"That will be your mission. You can leave the village, I can't." He seemed suddenly inspired.

She didn't like the almost crafty glint in his eyes.

"What are you getting at? One moment you're telling me that you need me by your side for the battle, and the next moment, you're telling me to go and rescue Mary. I don't understand you. You are the most..."

"Keep your voice down. It's the only way. Look at Rupert. He has a right to be worried. I know what happens to a person when a vampire takes them. We have precious little time to spare. You'll have to leave the village, and try to save Mary."

"Out of the question!" She couldn't leave the village. As much as she wanted to run to Mary's aid, the village required her fighting skills.

She let out a startled gasp, when Sean gripped a hold of her shoulders. The expression in his eyes made her narrow hers to thin slits.

"Sean, are you okay?" She touched the side of his cheek, and he shivered.

"Fine. I just feel a bit under the weather that's all."

"Sean?"

"Aye?"

"You're a vampire."

"I know. But as I said, I didn't drink enough..." Removing his hand from her shoulder, he reached up to wipe the sweat from his brow.

"Are you hot?"

"Only for you," he rasped.

She didn't like the way he looked. If he'd been human she would've really been worried.

"Sean, I think it would be in your best interest if you went into the pub, and ate something that will successfully restore your strength. You really look sick."

"I can't get sick. I can only become weakened."

Bridget felt like a lazy arse. Everyone around her was rushing to prepare the village against an attack except for her. She cocked her head to the side, when he became another shade of frightful white.

"Sean?" She looked around her.

William stood nearby talking in a low comforting tone to Rupert. She hated employing her telepathy when it came to human interaction, but she didn't suppose that any of the Sutherlands were completely human. Which would make what she was about to do almost okay.

William I need your assistance over here.

William moved his head to the side, when her telepathic voice entered his head. He didn't look very happy. She shrugged her shoulders. So, she'd ticked him off. In light of what she was dealing with, it didn't seem very serious.

He patted Rupert on the shoulder, and then turned toward them. In a few long strides, he'd crossed the distance between them. Sean remained silent, and Bridget's fears intensified.

"I don't know what's the matter with him. He looks

like he's on deaths doorstep!" Quirking his eyebrow at her, William turned to study Sean's face.

"I don't dispute the fact that Sean looks a little peaked."

"Peaked? He looks bloody frightful. I think you should get him into the pub."

"No." Sean's voice made her shudder.

Her heart raced. William turned to her and crossed his arms.

"As my brother said, no. I think you're overreacting Bridget. He's looked this way before, and he's pulled through."

"You don't understand!" She groaned at the uncertain gleam in William's eyes. She was genuinely frightened for Sean. What if he was beginning to lose his grip on his sanity again? What if...a jolt ran through her like a bolt of lightening, when Sean sagged against her.

"I'm right as rain," he mumbled. He looked about ready to drop, and even though he was acting as if he'd lost his footing, she knew that something else was amiss. She supported his weight, and breathed a sigh of relief when he stood up on his own power. They needed him to be with it for the fight. If he fell, then their chances of victory would be greatly diminished.

"I have to go and make more preparations. We have a man posted on the watchtower but there's no telling how they'll take us by surprise."

"They'll come using dark sorcery."

"Come again?" William knotted his brow.

She glanced at Sean. He was sending off pulsating vibes that made her want to wrap her arms around him, and kiss him senseless.

"Sorcery." Sean groaned. She knew that the mention of sorcery stirred up horrible emotions for him, but she couldn't avoid it for long. The village needed to know they were at a distinct disadvantage.

"What's this?" Father Clancy came up alongside them. "I thought I heard Bridget just refer to sorcery. Saints above, say it isn't so!"

"I'm afraid it is, Father Clancy."

"I thought we were done with that when Sean drove the force that possessed him out of his body."

William looked thoughtful. He cast her an inquiring eye. She now knew that he had placed the pieces together. Fortunately for her, he'd figured out that she'd been worried about Sean being vulnerable to another possession.

"Sean, on second thought, I think it would be best if we stepped into the pub. You need to be in top form for the fight."

She held her breath. Sean met her gaze. Then he smiled.

"Of course. When Hell freezes over. We still have to find Mary!"

"Leave that to me." Bridget looked around.

Rupert had returned to assisting Ridley, though she could feel the tension rolling off of him in rippling waves.

Sean gave her an uncertain stare. "I don't know...you seemed hesitant before."

She couldn't believe her ears. Was he actually intimidating that she'd only offered to find Mary in order to pacify him? Sean had jumped to a lot of conclusions before when it came to her actions, but this one beat all of the others.

Irritation flowed through her. "Are you saying that you don't trust me?"

He blinked. Father Clancy had wandered off, and William had gone over to wait by the pub entrance.

"I didn't say that. Stop putting words in my mouth."

"We wouldn't be having this conversation if you would just go and take care of yourself." She planted her hands firmly on her hips.

In an instant, something altered in his demeanor. "I trust you. I'll always trust you." His eyes softened, and her heart melted.

"Well, that's more like it. But we can't be making love here and now, with so much at stake."

"Aye. But there's always tomorrow." He pulled her against him, and gave her a fervent kiss that curled her toes.

"Go! For goodness sake, take care of yourself. I'm going to need you by my side, when I return with Mary."

"There's no other place that I'd rather be." She kept an eye on him while he made his way to the pub.

Something had unsettled her.

"Bridget!" Grace dashed toward her.

"I think I know where they took Mary. I just had a flash like vision. Mary was in it. But if we don't get there soon, she'll meet her death."

Bridget swallowed. Ever since she'd gotten involved with Sean her abilities to sense and predict danger had been altered.

"Where did you see her?"

"On the cliffs. She looked terribly frightened. They've got her rigged to this device that will have her crashing to her death if we don't reach her in time."

Bridget's heart fell. She knew what Octavia's plan entailed. Octavia wanted her to leave the village so her forces could descend upon them at their weakest state.

"We'd best get a move on." She looked to the sky and sent out a telepathic call to Iris. Before she knew it, Iris stood at her side.

"What's going on?"

"Grace and I have to leave the village. Do you think that you and the council can hold the fort while we're gone?"

"Where are you going?"

"Grace has located Mary."

Iris breathed a sigh of relief. "That's wonderful news. Of course, the two of you must go. I'll make sure that Sean behaves, don't you worry."

"Iris, you have to watch him closely."

"Why would she have to watch Uncle Sean?" Grace's face scrunched up with confusion. Then her muscles relaxed as realization dawned. "Uncle Sean forced Octavia out of his body. I have full faith that she'll never be able to return."

"I think when it comes to Octavia that we should expect the unexpected." She hooked her arm through Grace's. "If we go my way, we'll get there much quicker than on foot."

"Oh, I love flying." Grace beamed.

Bridget bit her lip. Even under these extraordinary circumstances Grace still managed to retain her sense of wonder. It was a gift to be sure.

She grabbed a hold of Grace, and took to the sky. The

moon glowed brightly down upon them. The night had become eerily quiet. She couldn't even hear the howling of the wind. It sent a shiver through her and made goose bumps erupt across her skin. She'd never been a great fan of the unknown. She didn't have a clue of what Octavia had in store for them. But she did know one thing. Whatever happened this eve would forever alter the course of her life. For better or for worse, every single person she knew would be different, including her.

Chapter Thirty-Seven

Sean placed his cup down on the kitchen counter top. William waited for him out in the dining area of the pub. His gut clenched and then unclenched. He clutched the china cup as if his very life depended on it. He took a long gulp of air, and then let it out in a gust. Bridget's image haunted his every thought. Focusing on the task at hand seemed almost impossible. As soon as he began to think about the fight, his thoughts were wrenched back to Bridget. He missed her already.

The stirring hadn't taken hold of him for a while, but now that Bridget had left his side, he could feel it sneaking up on him again. He reached for a napkin and carefully wiped his mouth. Then he raised his hand to his forehead and felt to see if his temperature had lowered. Clammy hot skin met his palm. Closing his eyes, he pulled his cloak closer around his body and made his way back out to meet William. His brother eyed him almost nervously.

"Feeling any better?"

"A wee bit," he admitted. He stuck his hands inside of his cloak and tried to avert William's gaze. He still worried about Mary. He knew that Bridget would rescue her. She'd never failed them before, and he didn't suppose that she would start now.

"I know this life must be hard for you, Sean. I wish I could be here to help you to carry your burden."

Sean smiled. "You needn't fret about me, William. I'm the older brother if you'll recall. I've had many battles to fight and win against myself. But somehow I've always managed to prevail against the stirring with the assistance of my friends."

"If Bridget does leave you, what will you do?" William's question caught him off guard.

He didn't really want to think about what life would

be without Bridget. He'd barely known her for a sennight, and yet she'd consumed his life in an unimaginable way.

"I will carry on as I always do." He didn't believe himself, but he figured that putting on a brave façade would be for the best.

"You do know that you can't pull the wool over my eyes, don't you?" William placed a hand on his arm.

"William, I appreciate what you're trying to do. But right now, I can't think about myself. I need to think about keeping this village safe."

"After the battle your life could change."

"Aye. As far as I'm concerned I'll be done with Octavia. I plan on getting rid of her once and for all."

William opened his mouth to speak again, when the pub door opened.

"They're coming. Iris has alerted us." Ridley stood outfitted from head to toe in battle gear. The sound of bagpipes could be heard over by the church. Rowan was playing *The Earl of Sutherlands March*.

This was it. It was about to begin. And maybe just maybe, he could finally put the demons of his past to rest.

William clapped his hand on his shoulder. "Ready?"

"I've been ready for this moment for over three hundred years."

"As have I." William sighed. "Let's just hope it all turns out the way that we plan."

They rushed out of the pub, into the night air.

Iris looked at Sean and grinned. "Think you're up to it, Sean?"

"I'm up for it if you are." He had to admit that she'd changed as well since she came to the village. Perhaps the people in his family had been right when they'd told him long ago that the Sutherland lands were filled with mystical magic. It had to be the only explanation. Whenever people came to his lands they were irrevocably changed for the better. He stifled the rioting emotions that rolled through his body, and concentrated on focusing it into physical energy for the battle ahead. With his perceptive eyesight, he could barely make out the portal that was being used to transport the masses of vampires to his village.

"I don't think I've given my thanks to you for sticking

it out with us through thick and thin."

Iris's head jolted. Her eyes widened, and a silvery laugh encompassed him right down to his core. Her eyes softened at him. He expected a sarcastic reply, but was thrown off guard when she spoke.

"You're a good man, Sean Sutherland. And the people that have given you their undying loyalty obviously see the good in you. Never doubt yourself, Sean. I fear that's what Octavia and her followers want from us this night. But we must never waver."

He couldn't agree with her more. "You must think that I am not good enough for Bridget."

"On the contrary. I can see now more than ever that the two of you were always meant to be. Don't ever lose sight of that, Sean. You are worthy of Bridget's love." Her voice trailed off, as the first round of the battle began.

Dark figures began to cloud his vision. They fell out of the sky, and landed everywhere. He clenched his jaw. His knapsack weighed heavily on his back. It was stuffed with supplies. Shouts and cries filled the air, as his people began to fight. He felt desolation pass through him. He would lose friends this night if he weren't careful. They didn't deserve to be put in this situation. He knew they were vulnerable because of what he was. He bared his fangs as pure animalistic fury overwhelmed him.

Ridley was hunkered down behind some wooden tables that they had pulled out of the shops and houses. He scanned the area for Rupert and found him fighting back to back with his cousin.

He swallowed. Bile rose in his throat. Three shadowy figures made their way toward him. He reached inside of his knapsack and pulled out a stake. He could take these three easily, but for every single vampire he killed, he knew there would be dozens more. They were outfitted for battle as well. It would seem that Octavia wanted more than to just have a feeding frenzy on her hands.

Not far from him, Iris battled like a warrior from a bygone age. As he embedded his stake in the third vampire's heart he took a moment to watch her in action. Perhaps, she wasn't as ill skilled as he'd originally believed.

Now that he thought about it, he should've made

sure that he had his claymore as a battle companion. A loud explosion tore through the village square. He turned just in time to catch a glimpse of several vampires writhing in agony before they combusted. Ashes flew everywhere.

They had triggered one of Iris's nifty traps. When they'd stepped on the trap wire, a fuse had been set off, and then a wall of fire had exploded forth in a circle around them. When they'd tried to escape they had literally toasted themselves. Out of the corner of his eye, he saw Ridley discharge his crossbow. Ridley's target moved out of the way at the last minute, and Sean found the arrow traveling right toward him.

"Oh, bugger it! Get out of the way, your lordship!"

He lunged for the ground just as the arrow whizzed by his head, missing him by a breath of an inch. Ridley ran toward him and helped him to his feet. Dazed, he shook his head to clear the cobwebs.

"Next time, make certain that you've got your target locked."

"Aye. I swear there won't be a next time. I wouldn't want to dust you, sir."

Sean grimaced. "Good to know, Ridley."

Hisses of fury rang around them. For now, it seemed as if they were holding their own. Without William and Iris, they would have had to fight a much more desperate battle.

The ethereal light that Iris gave off danced across the ground and reflected off of something that was made of steel. He fought his way through several vampires to reach it. He couldn't quite believe his eyes.

It was his claymore. He reached for it, and smiled as the warm wood grip molded to his hand. Now, he would be ready to meet Octavia. He let out a terrifying war whoop, and jumped back into the fray of battle.

Chapter Thirty-Eight

Octavia stood on the hilltop and perused the scene of battle that she had created.

"Mistress, what will happen now?"

"Ah, never fear ma chere. The tide of the battle will soon swing in our favor. Sean, will not be suspecting what I have in store for him." She glanced at her handmaiden and tried to recall her name. Yvette. Yes, that was it.

"But I do not understand, Mistress. What could they not suspect?"

"I have distracted them all. At this very moment, Bridget is on a fool's errand. Little will she know that if she'd sacrificed the one they call Mary, she could've saved her precious, Sean."

Yvette stared at her and furrowed her brow. "You intend to kill, Sean, Mistress?"

"No. Worse. I intend to break him. As soon as I think the moment is ripe for the picking, we shall go down there and I shall have my revenge. Ah, ma chere, do not look so troubled. All will be well."

"I know it will be. As long as you are in charge, nothing can go wrong for us."

Octavia smiled. She had chosen correctly. Yvette was still young for a vampire, but soon she would grow into an even better companion than Catherine had been. At the thought of Catherine, Octavia narrowed her eyes. Soon, she would have her vengeance fulfilled. With a little help from her, Sean would betray all that he held dear. By doing so, he would turn into the monster that he had always been meant to be.

Chapter Thirty-Nine

Bridget freed Mary from her bonds, and caught her in her arms, before the contraption Mary had been tied to could give away. As she flew them to a safe distance, the contraption lost its precarious footing and fell to the rocks below. The sound of the water crashing against the shoreline made her heart pitter-patter. For some unknown reason, she felt as if she had to get back to Sean.

Placing Mary on her feet, she doubled over as a cramp lodged itself in her stomach.

"Are you ill?" Grace was at her side in mere seconds.

"I think not. Just a stitch," she muttered. She slowed her breathing and knotted her brow. Salty air, tickled her nose. A strong wind blew up toward them. Wild weather stood ready to descend upon them all. The storm that waited in the wings would be severe indeed.

Mary wrapped her arms around her, and gave her a gentle hug. "Thank you for coming for me."

"It was the least I could do for a friend in need." She tried to smile, but more pain ripped through her.

Sean.

Her thoughts could not be swayed from him. Something had made her worry. Whatever had happened, or was happening could not bode well for them. Mary gripped one arm, while Grace took her other arm.

"Do you need help to walk?" Grace peered intently into her eyes. "You look really bad. We should get you to the Church. Maybe Orla could help you."

"No. Whatever it is isn't to be explained. For some reason, I've got this gnawing feeling that Sean is in danger."

"Of course he is. He's fighting a battle against Octavia's vampire clan," Mary remarked. She tossed her head. "I was frightened near to death when they abducted

271

me. I thought they were going to turn me, but then this young female vampire intervened and said it was not the wishes of their Mistress."

Bridget's mind raced. So, Octavia did have something up her sleeve as suspected. She winced and bit her lip. Why had she not stuck close to Sean? The answer was simple. Mary had needed her. Grace wouldn't have been able to free Mary on her own.

Strength surged through her body. She couldn't face losing Sean. Thinking of him, in grave peril made her want to hurl. She had to reach him in time. She took Grace and Mary's hands.

"I'm going to blink us there. Hang on tight; the sensations might spook you a bit."

"From my experience this night, nothing can affect me." Mary grinned.

Moonlight dappled across the ground. The wind howled again. The banshee was coming.

Hurry my daughter.

She gasped at the sound of her mother's voice in her head. Instead of comforting her, her mother's voice only served to intensify her feelings of dread. Coupled with fear, it nearly paralyzed her. Sean had become her everything. She loved him more than life itself, and even though she couldn't figure out how to break the curse, it didn't matter. Nothing mattered, except that they share the rest of their lives together. Gripping Mary and Grace's hands tightly, she shut her eyes, and activated her faerie magic.

In a heartbeat, they were back in the village. She had placed Mary in the church for safekeeping. After Mary's most recent ordeal, she decided that the woman deserved it. Grace stood at her side. Releasing her hand, Bridget looked around for Sean. She breathed a sigh of relief when she saw him taking down another vampire by severing his head from his body.

She grinned. Her heart surged. She was about to dart toward him, when an icy sensation coursed through her. She whirled about, and locked gazes with Octavia. She stood not a hair's breath from her.

"So, we finally meet in person."

Octavia's striking appearance caused Bridget's heart

to race. The woman looked positively diabolical. She'd met a lot of vampires in her time as a Huntress of Hell, but this woman had to be one of the oldest and most powerful of her kind. And, since she now had many vampire clans under her power, her strength would only continue to increase.

"Octavia, I presume."

"Your brilliance astounds me." Octavia raised one perfectly manicured hand, and with a flash of her dark magic several of her own followers blew up in smoke. Stunned, Bridget looked back at her. "You may wonder at my course of actions, but with time, all will become crystal clear to you." Her faint French accent made Bridget's stomach roll for the hundredth time.

"Do you realize who I am?"

"Of course." Octavia smiled. "That's why I'm here. To witness your heartbreak."

"Fight me."

"I would. But the night is not right for our meeting in battle."

Bridget summoned her elvin blade, and lunged toward Octavia. She swore, when her blade plunged through thin air. Mist swirled around her. Octavia had been using her dark magic to make her think she was seeing her in person. She shook her head. In a blaze of faerie light, Bridget transformed herself into her huntress persona. She was done with playing games. Octavia had angered her for the last time.

She took to the air, and widened her eyes when she saw a dark mist swirling around Sean. For the most part he seemed completely unaware of it. Until, his hand jerked back. She watched in horror, as he turned and raised his claymore to strike down Grace.

"No!" She zoomed in toward them, and used her magic to knock his claymore from his grip. It went arcing through the air, and clattered against the ground.

"Bridget?" His voice had become hoarse.

She shoved Grace aside. Iris's traps and Octavia's own betrayal had taken out most of the vampires.

Grace hit the ground. She stood in front of Grace. Come what may, Octavia wasn't about to hurt the one person that Sean's life revolved around.

"Fight me, Octavia!" she screamed.

Another battle of wills was waging inside of Sean's mind. Sweat glistened across his brow.

"Get away from me." He batted at the air. Obviously, he had become aware of Octavia's presence.

Bridget backed away, and reached for Grace. Extending her hand, Grace reached for it, as Bridget pulled her up. Father Clancy walked toward them.

"Sean, fight it!" She could sense his inner turmoil. "Sean. Listen to me! You have to get a grip and force Octavia out of your head. It's the only way!"

Seeing the trouble, Father Clancy let out a shout, which caught the attention of William. She pushed Grace away from her.

"Get away from here, Grace. You can't be open to an attack!"

Grace stumbled toward Father Clancy, who caught and held her.

"You can't defeat me."

Bridget shuddered when Octavia's voice spewed out of Sean's mouth. For the time being, Sean seemed to be out of commission. She had to cling to the hope that he would be able to regain control over his body. She didn't know what to do. Raising her hand, she tried to throw Sean off of his feet. But Octavia blocked her blow.

"What the..." Her voice trailed off, as she was rooted to the spot. She couldn't hurt Sean. If he'd been any other vampire, she would've already plunged her blade through his heart. She summoned her faerie fire, and let it rip at him, praying that it would only force Octavia out of his body.

Multi-colored flames enveloped Sean. No cries of agony could be heard. Her flames died away, and revealed Sean unscathed. Her breath hitched in her throat.

"Impossible!"

"I've centuries on you, you little brat. You are no match for a sorceress with my talents."

She swallowed thickly. So, maybe this wasn't her finest hour. Out of the corner of her eye, Iris descended from the sky. Iris shot a lightening bolt at Sean from behind.

Bridget's eyes widened, as the lightening bolt

suddenly switched directions. Instead of hitting Sean, it swerved back and struck Iris. Iris let out an agonized scream, and fell lifelessly to the ground.

Bridget cried out. Iris couldn't be dead. Faeries couldn't die. But then, everything else Octavia had done this night had caught her unaware. She could only pray that this time wouldn't be the same.

Lightening flashed across the sky. It arced downwards and hit a vampire that had been about to gain the upper hand against Ridley. Thunder rumbled the ground and nearly rocked Bridget off her feet. In her moment of confusion, Sean got the better of her. He wrapped his arms around her in an ironclad grip. Right at that moment, Heaven opened up and water poured forth.

Raindrops spattered against his face. She hoped that it would knock some sense into him. But his eyes were still glazed over. Her heart raced.

She fought against him, but Octavia's strength seemed to be boosting his own strength. Her heart sank as he bared his fangs, and leaned in to bite her.

"No!" Her voice was lost on the wind as he sunk his teeth into her, and drank from her life essence. The last thing she heard was his voice.

"And the first taste is the sweetest taste of all."

Bridget fell to her knees, as horrified gasps echoed around her. She felt woozy. She glanced up in time to see the blood dribbling from Sean's mouth.

Her blood.

Her stomach heaved. This couldn't be happening! A loud scream ripped through the landscape. A vision of Octavia's lifeless body filled her mind's eye. William stood over it, claymore in hand. While she'd been out of it, he must've taken Sean's claymore, and found Octavia's physical body. In her trancelike state, he had struck her down. She was out of their life forever. The hold she had on Sean broke.

His features cleared, as the spell was broken. He fell to the ground. His vampire fangs disappeared, as gradually, he regained control of his body.

"Sean!" She crawled toward him. Reaching out for him, she pulled him against her. If only he hadn't drank from her blood. Octavia had known what she'd been doing. "Sean, stay with me!"

A painful spasm wracked through his body. He was dying. She brushed his wet hair off of his forehead, and leaned down to wipe the blood from his mouth. As suddenly as it had started, the rain stopped.

She looked up. Twilight had begun to creep across the landscape.

It was finally over.

"Bridget?" He coughed.

She shook her head. Hot tears streamed down her face.

"I'm here. Don't you dare leave me!"

"I'm sorry. I didn't mean to..."

She shook her head. "You didn't hurt me. I feel fine. Octavia did this. She made you bite me. But even I don't believe she knew what would happen."

"What is happening to me?"

She didn't want to tell him. How could she tell him that he would die now because he had tasted faerie blood?

Vampires could not feed from a faerie. They were blessed creatures and as soon as a vampire tried to feed off their blood, it meant instant death. She didn't know why Sean still lingered.

"You're dying." She forced the words out. She could hear Grace crying.

Father Clancy had her clutched against him. The rest of the villagers milled around them, and those that had sought sanctuary in the Church emerged.

A smile formed at the corner of his lips.

"At long last." His eyes lit with love as she cupped his face with one of her hands.

"I can't let you go."

"You must. It is my time. You made me whole again, Bridget."

Her tears clouded her vision. Didn't he know how much she loved him?

"I love you, Bridget." His eyelids fluttered close.

Pain tore through her. She had to do something, and yet she'd never felt so helpless in all of her life. She remembered what he'd said to her. He'd told her to listen to her heart.

"I love you, Sean Sutherland," she blurted out.

Gasps rang around her. She met his warm lips with her own. Their kiss was short. He broke it first and looked over her toward the rising sun.

Lavender swirls colored the landscape.

"A kiss at twilight is one to cherish forever." His voice was hoarse and yet, she'd remember the sound of it for the rest of her immortal life.

She shook her head. Sobs consumed her. She tightened her hold on him. She wouldn't, couldn't let him go. She'd given her all for him, and yet it still had not been enough.

She had failed.

Sean Sutherland had died. For love, honor and family. She ran her fingers over his cloak. It was the only thing that she had left of him. His body had disappeared. Time stopped for her.

She hung her head low, and let out a wail. She would never be the same. Without Sean, her future looked bleak.

"I love you, Sean." But her words were of little consolation. She'd never see him again. And, she'd never be whole again.

Chapter Forty

Bridget sat alone in the Church. She couldn't seem to stop crying. Pulling Sean's cloak around her, she looked up toward the Madonna. It had been three days since Sean's death. The village had gone into mourning. No one knew what to do. Even Father Clancy seemed unable to get over Sean's passing. He had lived a hero's life, and he had died a hero's death. She blinked through her tears.

Iris had lived through the lightening bolt attack. There had been many wounded, but through a stroke of good fortune no villager had lost their life.

But they had lost their heart.

Sean.

Grief battled its way through her. No matter what people tried to say, she still felt responsible. She had killed Sean. There was no two ways about it. She put her hand up to her Celtic cross and smiled, as an image of Sean struck her. The way he had looked that first night, when he had inquired about her cross. She swallowed, and licked her parched lips. She couldn't dwell on the past.

Sean was gone.

She had to face it.

Sighing, she pushed herself to her feet. Then, before she left the church, she went to the altar and genuflected. She would remain in the village. Now that Sean was dead, they needed a protector.

She shivered. The Church door swung open and rattled back on its hinges. A gust of sea wind tore through the church blowing out the lit candles. She turned around to leave, and halted in her tracks.

She gaped. Blinking her eyes, she then decided to rub them.

Her eyes had to be betraying her.

"Sean?" She couldn't move.

He looked almost carefree. He exuded love. She had to be looking at an apparition. Maybe he had made it to Heaven after all. She tried to move again, and gasped when he crossed the threshold.

Sunlight spilled in. Questions rioted through her brain.

"Hello, Bridget."

She backed away. She had to be going nuts. Unless...

"Sean? How can you be here? Were you sent to give me a message?"

"Oh, aye. You could say that."

"Tell me." She didn't want to get to close to him. If she touched him, and then had to face losing him again, well, it would destroy her.

"I'm here to tell you that you broke the curse."

Time froze. More tears streamed down her face.

"But you're dead."

"No. I'm quite alive." He bounded toward her, and gathered her in his arms. Before he could kiss her, she pulled back.

"I don't understand!"

"It would seem that my mother had a little secret, which she failed to share with the whole family." Sean paused. "Your kind was able to bring me back, because my mother was of the fey. When you broke the curse in the nick of time, I only needed to be healed."

Relief washed through her at his words. She laughed. And then she cried. She sighed and began kissing his entire face.

Father Clancy wandered into the church, and stopped. "Sean?"

Sean put her down, and slung his arm across her shoulders pulling her close.

"Aye."

Father Clancy let out a triumphant hoot. "I knew it. It's a miracle to be sure." He ran out and began shouting for the attention of everyone in the village.

A soft breeze rippled through and Bridget looked to the open Church door. The gentle wind brushed the hair away from Sean's face.

Smiling, she reached to touch the tip of one of his beautiful ears. "I seem to recall you admiring my faerie ears. Now, I can admire your elvin ears. They are a sight to behold, my love. I'd say you made a great trade in when the curse was broken."

"What do you mean?" He laughed, at the teasing in her voice.

"You traded vampire fangs for elf ears."

****

Sean drank in every single inch of Bridget. He had been given a second chance at life. Because of Bridget, he had been pulled out of the darkness.

She was his savior. She was his one true love. She was his soul mate.

No longer would he have to live in misery, and fear the stirring.

He pulled Bridget to him, and let out a husky growl. "If you agree to become my wife, I'll be the happiest man alive."

Her eyes lit up with newfound joy. "I still can't believe that you're back with me."

"I'll never leave your side again."

"Is that a promise?"

"You can hold me to it." He smiled. For the first time that he could remember, he actually felt at peace. He had not feared dying, but he had feared losing Bridget.

"Sean?"

"Aye?" He molded her body to his. He couldn't wait to get her back up to the castle. They had a lot of planning to do.

"Kiss me."

"With pleasure." And as his lips molded to her eagerly waiting ones, he knew that he certainly was the luckiest man in all of the realms, magical or otherwise.

About the author...

Marly Mathews resides in Ontario, Canada with her family and their two Yorkshire Terriers, Shylah and Brynna.

Marly writes romances, with Alpha kick ass heroes, and Alpha kick ass heroines. Her romances have drama, comedy and adventure all mixed into one. Marly writes historical, paranormal, fantasy, futuristic and contemporary romance.

Visit Marly's website at www.marlymathews.com.

4062622

Made in the USA
Lexington, KY
17 December 2009